THE BROTHERS THANATOS

BY
JOSHUA GAMON

A NOVEL

FIRST PRINTING, January 2023.
Harry Markos, Director.

Paperback: ISBN 978-1-915387-17-2
eBook: ISBN 978-1-915387-18-9

Book design by: Ian Sharman
Front cover art by: Sam Healy
Back cover art by: Renae De Liz

www.markosia.com

First Edition

Contents

For my mother, who never once stopped believing in me.

BOOK I
-
OF MONSTERS & HEROES & MEN

CHAPTER ONE: BOMBAY, 1909

Max hoisted himself onto the metal railing of the P&O Line's *Dewan*, and watched as the frigate's hull below split the ocean in two. He leaned forward into the night, allowing the fullness of the cool sea spray to wash over him. With a flick of his finger, he dismissed the wind-shear barrier he had created to keep him from toppling into the ocean, and dangled himself fearlessly over the black abyss. The *Dewan* had finally discovered the faint lights of the Port of Bombay after being delayed at sea. They sparkled like a thousand glittering stars in the distance. Max couldn't tell where the ocean ended and where the night sky began.

He grinned as he removed his top hat from his rapidly balding head, and playfully extended it outwards until the strong winds tore it from his hand. Three weeks at sea he had spent, and the *Dewan* was days behind schedule. But India was finally before him. He wouldn't have missed his brother's wedding for the world. "Charlie," he bellowed, for all of India to hear, "I made it!"

***

Max stepped out onto the plank. The Port of Bombay looked as if it someone had kicked an anthill. Workers bustled, soldiers marched, vendors hocked. The trains left the station, ships were docking. Nothing ever stopped moving.

"Hello there," he heard someone shout from the crowd. There emerged a middle-aged Indian man dressed in a white suit of silk. "I presume you are Mister Maximilian Thanatos."

The magus walked down the plank to the dock. "Call me Max. Not Maximilian. Not Mister Thanatos," he insisted. "They are names I associate with my father."

"Well, it's a wonderful pleasure to finally meet you, *Max*," he said as he took the westerner's hand into his. "You certainly match the description given to me by my employer. I work for your brother. My name is Mahesh," he added with a nod. "His assistant. I am here to collect you."

"Why isn't Charlie here to meet me?" His disappointment was plain.

"Ah, yes. He told me you would say that, and instructed me to be frank. The port is hardly a place for my employer at this time of night. The Swadeshi Movement has found its way to Bombay."

Max shrugged indifferently. "I don't know what that means."

"To put it simply: it complicates everything, especially for someone of your skin colour."

That, Max understood. As a man born in the American South, he knew prejudice intimately.

"Please, I have a carriage and an escort waiting for us," the Indian said, beckoning urgently with an arm. "Where is your luggage?"

Max simply patted his left breast pocket, "Close."

Mahesh didn't understand, but nodded anyway. "Come. It'd be best to have this place at our backs as quickly as possible."

They hustled behind a spice-and-fish bazaar, careful to avoid the crowd, if that was even possible. The combined stench of curry powders and seafood was overwhelming, and Max didn't hesitate to pull a handkerchief over his nose to mask the smell. The locals took notice. Shouting reverberated throughout the marketplace. He ignored it until he realized the people were screaming at him. Max spoke over a dozen languages, but Hindi was not one of them. However, the content was clear: he was not welcomed.

"Hurry, before the matter escalates," Mahesh warned.

Max was relieved when they finally reached the carriage. He was met with a curious sight: four mountainous Sikhs flanked the carriage on bicycles. Rifles were slung over their backs. Sheathed sabres dangled on their hips. Mahesh wasted no time in ushering Max inside, as rocks and vegetables pelted the sides of the carriage.

"Still, friendlier than Five Points," Max admitted, as he watched the Sikhs disperse the mob with warning shots into the air.

The port faded away in the distance, along with the drama. From his cushioned seat, Max watched as children, dressed as brightly-coloured demons, danced in the streets, exploding firecrackers at each other's feet. He leaned towards Mahesh, "What's the occasion?" He parted the window's curtain further for a better view.

"The children are dressed as Ravana, the demon king," he said. "It is past midnight, so that makes it the first day of Diwali: a celebration of the victory of light over darkness."

"So this 'Ravana' of yours loses the fight?"

Mahesh chuckled at the broad claim. "You speak as though it's like a game of cricket, with winners and losers. Good versus evil isn't a contest, it's a struggle. When I was a young soldier, I visited Istanbul with my brother. There, we watched Ottoman soldiers partake in a strange sport called oil wrestling. These two men, matched evenly in size and strength and covered in olive oil, fought to a stalemate again and again. They could not secure a grip. They crashed into each other; one soldier would be forced to take a step back, while the other stepped forward, but neither would fall."

Max rubbed the stubble on his chin. "Sounds like a tedious thing to watch."

Mahesh smiled. "That is the struggle between good and evil, my friend: victory in small measures, not dominance. Are you a religious man, Mister Thanatos? Ah… Max," he quickly corrected.

Max shook his head. "Faith is a man stepping off a cliff expecting to fly." His voice softened as they rolled past a mob burning a straw effigy of Queen Victoria at a stake. The brightness of the fire stung his sensitive eyes. "After I watched my mother pass away, I stopped believing in God."

They travelled north along the Mahim Bay, which glistened like precious stones in the moonlight. It was quiet and serene, a stark contrast to the civil unrest behind them. Reclaimed from the sea, Bandra was the wealthiest district in an already prosperous city. Charlie called it home. His bungalow was a sprawling estate overlooking the bay, and it was nearly as large as their father's plantation. Perhaps even larger.

Max beamed at the sight. How proud he was of his brother. Every foot of the grounds was immaculately manicured. Palm trees swayed in the breeze. Monkeys roamed freely. The grass was emerald. The scene was pristine; regal. Charlie even had Sikhs posted around the bungalow, and he wondered if the troubles had even reached all the way to Bandra.

A dozen servants stood like sentinels along the path to the entrance. Everyone, seemingly, had come out to meet him, except for his brother. The agitation of that clawed at him. A lanky man, taller than Max, broke away from the line, and tried to assist the magus out of the carriage, but Max ignored him, only caring about one thing. "Tell me my brother's on his way."

"No, sir, the master retired for the evening, some hours ago."

"Then wake him up, or I will. I had spent weeks at sea just to see him. The least he could do is meet me at the door."

Mahesh exited the carriage behind Max. "Mister Thanatos—"

"Max," the magus bit.

"I was referring to Mister Charles Thanatos," he politely corrected. "He will be away on important business at dawn, and requires his rest," he implored, obviously trying his best to soothe his guest. "But he cordially invited you to join him for brunch tomorrow in the conservatory."

"How kind of him," Max sneered, shaking his head in dismay, surprised his brother even had the time to fit him into his schedule at all. But he had waited weeks to see Charlie. A few more hours wouldn't hurt.

***

The morning sun was relentless. There was no escape from the blasting Indian heat. The windows were open, but there never came a breeze. Max had spent most of the night watching the insects bombard the netting hung over his bed like a tent. He peeled himself from his sheets. His tongue felt like cork. On the dresser, a servant had placed a kettle of coffee while he slept. The rising steam from the spout was enough to twist his stomach into knots. He already hated India.

He removed a snuffbox of wood and ivory from the jacket he had left draped over a chair. He opened the lid and, with a simple command, caused an entire wardrobe of clothing to emerge and settle in the corner, with his blown-away hat on top.

The last thing he needed was to 'layer up' in that furnace of a country, but he wanted to make a good impression on his brother. They hadn't seen each other in a long time. Much had changed. He felt menial being in Charlie's house. He stood before the dressing mirror, and saw an exhausted, aging man, whose fledgling beard was growing out in patches. But he smiled anyway. A nice, crisp suit always lifted his spirits.

The conservatory was on a terrace facing east. Max couldn't help but sigh. There was no safe quarter from the morning sun. His brow was already beaded with sweat.

Charlie was seated at the wrought iron table in a white wicker chair, his face buried in a newspaper. "You're late, Max. I was about to begin without you," he said. "May my servants get you anything? Tea, coffee?"

"Water," he practically begged.

"I wouldn't," Charlie warned. "The water here would turn you inside out," He motioned for the waiter. "Raj, we'll start with coffee. Black."

"Very good, sir."

"You could have at least shaved this morning. You look like a vagrant." Charlie had folded the newspaper and placed it atop the table, revealing a bruise under his right eye. Despite being six years younger than Max, he nearly looked identical to his brother, except that Max had inherited their father's long, pointed nose. And Charlie had the well-groomed beard. "Charlie, your face."

"What? This?" he dismissed, touching the bruise with his left hand. "It's nothing. Just a disagreement. It'll fade in time for the wedding."

Max knew he was lying. Charlie had the easiest 'tells'. But he didn't pry. "I was hoping to meet your fiancée this morning," Max said. "You've told me nothing about her. Not even her name."

"Her father is very traditional. Even I won't see her again until the ceremony."

"About that," Max said, reaching inside his jacket pocket. "I brought you a gift." He removed a four-leaf clover encased in a glass slide, and slid it across the table.

Charlie didn't even look. "What do you expect me to do with that?"

"Nothing, Charlie. It's just for luck," he said, taken aback.

The two men paused as the waiter served the coffee.

"More of your superstition? I have everything I need. Nothing more, nothing less."

"A little luck won't kill you." Max shooed the pot of coffee away. "Water," he commanded.

Charlie just shook his head, as he turned again to the waiter, "Give my brother whatever he wants. As for the first course, we'll have the pesarattu." He looked at his brother, "my chef makes an incredible pesarattu."

"I don't even know what that is."

Charlie wasn't surprised. "Of course, you don't." He motioned to run his right hand through his thick, black hair, but winced as he tried to raise his arm. Instead, he used the left to smooth back his hair. "Didn't that beloved 'master' of yours teach you anything about culture, besides pulling rabbits from hats?"

The waiter carried a pitcher of water to the table, and filled Max's glass with a liquid that was hardly crystal clear. But Max had spent years wading through the wilds of the Congo, and learned how to adapt. When the waiter left them alone, Max dipped the tip of his index finger into the water, transforming it into something pure, cold, and delicious.

"Don't belittle him, Charlie. Ammon was always kind to you. He brought us to London when we had nothing, gave us a home, took care of us."

"I already had a father. I didn't need another."

"And is *father* here for your wedding?"

Charlie hesitated to answer. "He… never replied to my invitation."

"Did Ammon?"

"He wasn't invited," Charlie returned.

Max just shook his head. "Who do you think got you into Oxford?" He saw his brother sneer at the suggestion.

"I did," he shot back. "While you were off playing make-believe with your friends at the Golden Dawn, I studied like a fiend for a better life. Now, I am an American serving British interests at the Port of Bombay in India. More precisely, I *am* the Port of Bombay. Every ship, every train, every crate—nothing enters or leaves without my permission. That's who I've become," he said, sliding the clover back over to Max. "And I accomplished all that without *luck*. What have *you* accomplished?" He finished, pounding his fist on the table, rattling the silverware and plates. He winced again, but far more noticeably than before.

"Is everything all right, Mister Thanatos?" the waiter asked.

"Yes," the two brothers bit out in unison.

The waiter served Max an omelette that was green and looked practically spoiled. His stomach twisted again, but he didn't know if it was from the food, the heat, or the hospitality. He sat and studied his brother. Charlie was temperamental, at best. A kind soul to others, but always emotionally distant to Max. He understood his brother's tantrums, lived with them. This was something different.

"Charlie, what's really going on with you?"

"Nothing," he quickly dismissed.

"Enough games. Did you think I wouldn't have noticed? The way you've been shifting your weight onto your left side, how you've only been using your left arm, despite being proficient with your right. The way you wince at the slightest erratic movement. How you didn't even bother to stand to greet me when I joined you?"

"What are you going on about?" his brother asked, pushing his plate away. The meal was hardly touched.

"You were never one for a fight, Charlie. You're a pacifist to a fault, like mother," his voice was heavy with concern. "I see no wounds on your knuckles. Did you even try to fight back?"

His face flushed with anger. "What utter nonsense," Charlie balked. "I think we're done here," he said, trying to stand, but the pain was too much. As he sat back down, the shame was too great. He couldn't face Max.

"If you can't talk to your own damn brother, Charlie," the mage flustered, throwing his arms up.

Charlie exhaled slowly, laboriously, eventually resigning to the nuisance sitting at his table. With a dismissive wave, he ushered for the waiter to leave the conservatory. Once he was gone, he spoke. "If you must know, last night, I was given an ultimatum."

Max leaned forward. Finally, he thought.

"I will tell you no more about it, but I tried to reason— you can't just reason with those men." He motioned towards the bruise. "From there, they said they were doing me a favour, for the wedding, you see. They... brutalized me everywhere below the neck, to hide the severity of the injuries from Nisha. That's her name. My fiancée." But there was a soft regret to his voice. He was disjointed. Visibly shaken.

"Who did this to you?" Max demanded to know. "Tell me, and I will burn their world to the ground."

"No, Max. This isn't your fight," Charlie almost begged.

"Like hell it isn't."

"You purify water with a finger, and now you think you can fight an army? This is well beyond your tricks. The Cult of the Ten Heads controls most of the port these days, and they're everywhere," his voice lowered, as he motioned for Max to look out into the garden. Both men watched as a Sikh sentry passed by the window. "Even here," he said. "India is on the cusp of a revolution against Britain, and the leader of Ten Heads is a profiteer playing both sides. He is twisted and foul, a subspecies of man. And he knows how to get to a person. Not just physically, Max. They know things about me: things I'd be ashamed to tell even you."

"Try me."

Charlie didn't answer. He was too afraid.

Max wiped his brow. "Then come back with me to London. Let them have this place. It's too damn hot for any sane man to live."

"I can't," Charlie said. "If I leave now, it'd be a death sentence for my love."

"Take Nisha with you. You'll marry in England."

Charlie shook his head, despairingly. "No. Nisha is not my love."

Max cocked his head. "Then take the other woman. Take them both. I don't care."

"Max," he said, his eyes dropped to the table. "I'm not talking about a woman."

The magus wasn't following.

"My lover, you met him last night. He's… my assistant."

"Mahesh?" The answer came before the realization. Then Max just rubbed his temple. He really hated India. "Christ, Charlie," he said, softly. "It's a good thing mother isn't with us anymore. She was old country. This would have killed her. And father," he said, shaking the terrible thought away. "So that's what this is all about? This gang—this Ten Heads, is extorting you for favours at the port, or they'll expose you as a Nance?"

Charlie didn't like that word, but nodded. "I'm not ashamed of who I am," he assured Max. "But my employers; they would ruin me. The police would arrest me. Hell, if word ever reached the port that I lay with another man, I would be destroyed, in every sense of the word. India is far from tolerant."

"You've been away from the civilized world for too long, Charlie. It'd be like that for you no matter where you go. And you're doing this to protect your… lover?" The word felt awkward on his tongue.

Charlie nodded again.

"Does Nisha know?"

"No. Not at all. It would break her heart," he said, ashamed. "It pains me to deceive her, to use that poor girl. But to be an unwed man at my age? This marriage was just to keep up appearances. I tell everyone I'm a widow, but people were beginning to suspect otherwise."

"Then how do we fix this problem?"

"You don't," he stressed. "I will fight them on my terms: politically. I am not without allies. I have support from various groups. I am to meet with the Heads' leader, Kraal Mali, tomorrow tonight, and I will show him he's not the only one with leverage."

Max crossed his arms across his chest. "The night before your wedding, you're going to counter-extort a gang leader? That's a ridiculous plan."

"Bombay is a ridiculous place. It's the only way to ensure my freedom. I will match their violence with non-violence."

"Then I'm coming with you."

"Most certainly not."

"Charlie, you have never won an argument against your own brother, what chance will you have with this Mali figure?"

"Then so be it," he sighed. "Tomorrow night. Just before midnight. Meet me at Pier 13." Charlie mustered up through the pain to get back to his feet. "Now, if you would excuse me, I still have a port to oversee, while I still have one." Before he left, he motioned towards Max's chin. "About what I said earlier. I was wrong. I think you should grow it out."

***

Max was a guest at Charlie's home, but he might as well have been a prisoner. He wasn't permitted to leave, under the pretext of his safety. Everywhere he went on the estate, the Sikhs clung to him like shadows. He felt eyes upon him as he walked across the grounds, past the peacocks and around the pond towards the garden behind the house. At the centre, amongst the sunflowers and the yellow daffodils and bamboo, there was a hedge maze twice as tall as a man and as thick. If he had to break away, he noted the hedge maze would have been ideal.

Night came too soon. It was the first day of Diwali, and Max could hear the festivities from all across the city. And somewhere, amidst the chaos of celebration was Charlie, shuffling papers at his office, trying to make everything right.

The gentle fool, Max cursed. He knew Charlie was going to fail. His brother was a good man, and good people do not understand malice or greed. But it was a language Max understood. He had dealt with savages before. He promised Charlie he would be by his side, but that was a lie. Charlie would have been a distraction, a liability. The last thing he needed was a pacifist brokering for peace during a fight. Instead, Max planned to destroy the men who threatened his family before that meeting took place. Whatever their deal was with Charlie, Max would propose a counter-offer that evening of fire and blood.

In London, he had powerful friends. But Max had no allies in Bombay, even his own brother begged him not to fight. Yet he suspected there was still one other man who cared about his brother. Charlie had kept Mahesh at the house for his own good that day, far removed from the dangers of the Port of Bombay, but not far enough from the Cult of the Ten Heads.

Contacting the man in secret was simple enough, despite them both being kept under heavy watch. Talking to him directly would have drawn too much suspicion, so he used an antiquated technique from the Napoleonic Wars called projected writing. He kept the note plain, signed it *Istanbul*, and transferred his handwriting to a piece of paper in Mahesh's room. It was a reckless gamble. For one thing, the trick only worked one way, so Max couldn't receive the man's reply. He didn't even know if Mahesh was aware of Charlie's extortion. And, more importantly, if he did, would Mahesh place himself in danger to aid him?

It was hardly seasoned espionage. He used his room's dressing mirror to cast an illusion of his reflection for anyone who peeked inside, making it appear he was writing at his desk. Simple distractions were enough to sneak past the men stationed out at the doors, and the torrential rainstorm that evening provided the rest.

He crept his way inside the winding corridors of the hedge maze, his stated meeting place, and waited. Minutes went by in the rain, but it felt like hours. He heard the rustling of sentries continue their rounds beyond the hedge. The storm hardly deterred them. Lantern lights flirted with the greenery, but no one ventured within until he finally heard a voice from the darkness.

"Max, if you wished for us to speak, you could have simply invited me to join you for dinner," a drenched Mahesh said, stepping out from the corner of the maze.

"I didn't even hear you approach."

"I'm an old solider. The training never goes away."

"We need to talk."

Mahesh nodded. "That is quite apparent, given our meeting place. But don't worry, I wasn't seen, in case you were wondering. After all, I'm the one who arranges their schedules," he said curtly. His voice became urgent. "I only came because I assume this is about Charlie"

"Then you knew he was in trouble?"

"There are no secrets between us, my friend. As, I am sure you are now aware, he is more than just my employer."

Max nodded.

"It's a poorly kept secret within the house," Mahesh admitted. "He's a good man, but hardly discreet, which is why I fear for him."

"And not for yourself?"

The Indian shook his head, wiping the rain from his eyes. "I'm not as courageous as your brother. War has made me a coward, but I made my peace with that long ago."

The wind howled through the hedge. "I need you to tell me everything you know, Mahesh, about the Cult of the Ten Heads, about Kraal Mali."

He flinched at the mention of Mali's name. The rain continued to pour, drenching both men in the maelstrom. "They are cannibals, despots, worshippers of Ravana. They are obsessed with the darkness. And they are after Charlie."

"Then help me save him."

There came a long pause. "I cannot."

"What do you mean?" Max shot back, incredulously.

"I promised him I would not get involved, as much as it pains me. While I'm here, that lovely man is at the port right now, with the Ten Heads, trying to save us both, but he's fighting a war he cannot win."

Max stepped forward, and gripped the man's collar with fists clenched white. "He told me that meeting was tomorrow!" Max growled, as lightning streaked across the sky.

"He told you that?" he exhaled. "I'm so sorry."

Max let the man's collar slip out of his hands. His legs were failing him. He could hardly hold himself upright. He braced himself up against the hedge. "You had no right to keep that from me. They'll kill him." The words were bile in his mouth. Max didn't even realize he had struck the man's jaw until after his fist throbbed from the blow.

Mahesh was driven down to a knee, but couldn't bring himself to face Max's fury as the tall man lurched over him, fist cocked for a second strike. "I promised him," Mahesh returned, ashamed. "I never break my word."

"You will tonight," Max cursed. "That man is my only family, and I'm not ready to lose him, not tonight, not ever. So, if you truly care for Charlie, you will take me to the Ten Heads right now, or I will go down there myself and sink this entire godforsaken country into the sea."

***

They stuck to the shadows, blending in with the foliage as lightning cascaded over the grounds in brilliant flashes. The stables were locked, but that was a simple matter for Max to undo. Time was against them. Charlie had taken his best carriage to the port, leaving only one behind for the servants. But hitching horses to the transport would not do. They had to ride, but the storm put the animals on edge. Mahesh protested for another way, but Max assured him the horses would be calmed with a word. The men were experienced riders, and saddled their beasts with a proficient speed. Shouts called out over the thunder. Wild gunshots nearly found their mark. The sentries were finally privy to their escape, but, by then, it was too late. As the Sikhs nearly fell upon them, the horses, with a command, exploded from the stables, and both men made for the road.

Their destination was clear: south to the port following the same route down along the bay. The horses were strong, bred to pull the weight of a carriage, but the rain made the ground soft, slowing their approach. Max cursed the steed under his breath. He was certain the Sikhs were in pursuit, but their bicycles could not have fared any better in the mud. Onward they rode. They pushed the animals past their limits. It was still miles to the port.

"We should begin at Charlie's office," Mahesh said. "If we're lucky, the meeting will take place there."

"And if we're not?" Max asked.

"Then Charlie could be anywhere, or already dead," he shouted back, over the storm.

Max didn't like that answer. The wealthy estates gave way to workers' slums, as they drew closer to the port. The storm had eased up in the southern tip of the city, leaving remnants of a drizzle and an unkind humidity in its wake. "Diwali is our New Year's Eve. Thousands will be out celebrating tonight. Finding one person in this crowd would be like finding a raindrop in the Arabian Sea."

"No matter what it takes," Max vowed.

Mahesh was right. When they had reached the port, they were met with walls of people in the fish markets and curry stands. Decorated elephants were led through the marketplace. Children rode atop them, tossing handfuls of purple flower pedals into the air. They had no choice but to abandon the horses and continue ahead on foot. The two men dived into the crowd of hundreds. People were dressed as demons, and danced in the streets, blowing fire, eating, twirling swords in the air. It was madness.

Their only reprieve came when a theatrical funeral procession cut through the thick of it. It was an acting troupe; men dressed as horned beasts paraded a glass coffin through the crowd, twirling it around and around for the masses. People mocked it, slapping and shaking the coffin as they went. They were spellbound by the sight, and sang, and swayed with the music of the band that followed behind.

Mahesh pointed towards a red-bricked building arched over the Victoria Terminus. "There," he said. "That's his office on the second floor."

The man wasted no time racing up the staircase. But the sight was dire. The door had been kicked in, shattered off of its hinges. Inside, the office had been turned over in a struggle. An office chair had been broken, a desk flipped over. And on its corner's edge was wet blood. "The fool," he bit out under his breath. He turned to the Indian, "This cult, what would they do to Charlie? Is there still time to save him?"

The man just stood at the doorway and stared in disbelief.

"Mahesh!" Max called out, snapping the man out of his shock.

The Indian turned to Max, but struggled for an answer. "They wouldn't kill him outright. No," he thought, aloud. "He would be sacrificed. What they want—what they truly want, is for darkness to finally vanquish the light by corrupting the hearts of men. So they would make it a spectacle for all to see."

Max dabbed his finger on the spot of blood on the desk, and pressed it against his tongue.

"What are you doing?" Mahesh cried out.

He ignored the Indian. He rummaged inside his jacket pocket, and removed a small brass compass from within. He would need a better way to sort his trinkets, he noted, as he opened the device on his palm. "I'm going to find my brother." The compass pointed east. "Come, before the spell wears off."

"Spell?" he gasped. "Just what are you?"

Max paused at the doorway. "It's reassuring to know Charlie hasn't told you everything," he replied, proud to know his brother had kept his secret. Max stormed out of the office, no longer concerned if the man followed behind, and he headed east through the chaos.

The crowd was heavy; immovable. Max struggled to make any progress. He heard the shouts of an already inflamed mob of people. The speakers controlled the crowd. They cheered and rallied and spat nonsense in what he regarded as their filthy language. All he could do was shove his way through, now south-east, the direction had altered its course and remained fixed. Whomever he was chasing had finally stopped. Hopefully, it was Charlie. Or perhaps it was one of his assailants. But the person was close.

The mob wailed again, as something ahead had whipped it into a frenzy. The crowd chanted in unison.

His gut wrenched. Their words were foreign, lost upon his ears. But the violence on their tongues was clear. Max had heard the sound before: the sound of bloodlust. And just when the magus believed the noise had reached its apex, a single scream of a man above the rest nearly stopped Max's heart. It was a scream left incomplete. A shriek from a man who was cut down before his agony had fully been realized. It was one he recognized as only family could. It was Charlie.

The celebration continued, but not for Max. Whatever bloodlust occurred beyond his vision had not sated the crowd. It only fuelled them. But the magus was no longer concerned with the safety of those around him. They were objects in his way. Nothing more. He had to find his brother, he had to know nothing was wrong, that Charlie was unscathed by the barbarians. So, with a word, an invisible force shoved the droves of people aside, allowing Max to walk freely. If he exposed himself as a mage, so be it.

But what Max saw was far more sinister than mere violence. The men from the funeral procession dangled Charlie before the crowd like a puppet. His brother was naked, lifeless; his face frozen in a death scream. His body was crimsoned, sleek: blood caked his entire body, which glistened in the gaslight. The man's chest had been ripped open, his ribcage shattered to pieces. The group of men, dressed as demons, held his brother's heart in their hands and bit into the organ, tearing at it with their teeth. There, before Max's eyes, they consumed the man's power and his soul for their own.

Their leader held up the murder weapon for the crowd. In one hand, a thin sword cane blade coated in

Charlie's blood. Its pommel was a wolf's head carved from ivory. In the other he held the cane.

Max was too late. His brother was dead. He had passed by the procession completely unaware his brother was trapped inside the glass coffin. If only he had looked! Now, Charlie hung mutilated before a crowd of hundreds frenzied with blood-lust. But Max did not scream. He did not cry. He hardly faltered as he approached the cultists from the crowd. All reason had left him. The magus reverted into something primal, something animalistic. He was beyond madness, beyond rage, and fury. He had become death, itself.

His brutality was swift. The cult leader didn't have enough time to react before Max placed the palm of his hand over his mask, and obliterated him into a thousand moist pieces of flesh with a simple word. The other men fared no better, as Max gripped the sword and sliced off their heads with the blade sharpened by his magic. Five, six, seven men: one after another fell to the weapon, as he twirled in a *danse macabre*. No one was spared as he turned Charlie's instrument of death against them all.

Max finally came to a stop. There were no more cultists to kill. Blood was everywhere beneath his feet, it seeped into the cracks of the port, it had stained the grass a dark hue of crimson. And that pool continued to expand as more left the bodies of men. His every step was met with it. He sheathed the stained sword back into its case, and approached the corpse of his brother. His faculties had returned. That was when the agony wrenched his body. Despair seized him, brought him to his knees. He collapsed onto Charlie, and took the body up against his own. He ignored the milling crowd, and he ignored the cries of Mahesh, who had finally reunited with his lover. Max simply knelt in the blood, and cradled the body onto his own, and wept.

At that moment, right then, as the hundreds around him euphorically screamed for more, he realized the Cult of the Ten Heads had won. The darkness had him. It claimed them all. The Indian was wrong, he understood. It wasn't a victory in small measures. It was absolute. There was no salvation for him; there was no coming back. He placed the palm of his hand down onto the ground and into the pool of blood, which rippled to his touch, and closed his eyes. What he did then was not an act of vengeance, it was love. Without his heart, Charlie's soul would be damned to Hell. He had to be saved, by any means. The heathens, around him, did not.

"Burn."

CHAPTER TWO:
DAUGHTERS OF NEW YORK, 1929

The *Ulysses* docked at the mooring station at the top of the Rockefeller Tower in Lower Manhattan. Thomas Edison had repurposed the warship, originally the grandest Zeppelin in the Great War, as the country's most luxurious airliner. The Captain's Suite, alone, was practically the entire portside, and cost nearly as much as the ship. But the magus knew it was worth the price. The ship's proprietor owned most of the patents in America, along with half of the United States Congress, so the *Ulysses* was granted the wonderful reprieve of serving liquor during prohibition. How could he resist?

But Max hardly touched a drop. He spent most of the trip locked away in his suite, glaring at the top hat resting atop the sitting room table. Every so often, he'd see it quiver, and move an inch on its own. It would have seemed childish to be so frightened of a thing like a hat to anyone not knowing that deep within the recesses was a creature of unspeakable malice. It was Max's latest acquisition, and he was smuggling it back home to be held under lock and key for safekeeping.

Did we really have to take the slowest way? Charlie moaned, just happy to be back in New York. *We could have taken the train up the Atlantic coast. It's a beautiful route, especially this time of year. And we would have been home days ago. You know how much I hate to fly. It's unnatural.*

Max sat back deeply in his chair of thick red velvet upholstery, waiting for the official announcement to disembark. He smiled for his brother's benefit, but didn't take his eyes off of the hat. "Your feet don't even touch the ground, Charlie," he mused. "Aren't you always flying?"

Gliding, really, Charlie corrected, a bit insulted his brother couldn't tell the difference. *And that's not the point. You were thinking again with your liver, and put your life at risk by staying in this powder keg. One spark,* he insinuated.

Max wished to speak, but he found the rantings of his little brother too amusing to interrupt. It reminded him of when they were young, and how Charlie famously pounded his feet during his tantrums.

And to make matters worse, our accommodation is in the hull of the ship. Alongside the flammable gas.

"So?"

So, Charlie accused in the same snarky tone, crossing his incorporeal arms over his chest, *last night you were reading by candlelight. How many light spells do you know? Seven?*

Max just dismissed the remark with a wave of his hand. "I really just know five," he confessed, smiling. "But Ammon always told me, 'Never waste perfectly good magic on the mundane,'" he said, mimicking his old master's baritone voice. "Besides, Tesla's electric lighting burns my eyes. And some people fear *magic*? Honestly, this world of industrial marvels has left me behind. I will always prefer the candle," he said. "And that book I picked up in New Orleans might just be the key to solving your case, so be thankful I spent any time on it at all."

The magician knew the ghost of his dead brother Charlie was just anxious to be home. So was he. The announcement was taking its sweet time, so Max peeled himself away from the hat to walk over to the cabin's porthole. New York looked tiny from over a hundred stories above the city. People looked like insects frantically scurrying along in tidy little lines. It made him feel like a god atop Mount Olympus, ready to smite anyone with a conjured bolt of lightning. He knew a spell or two, but the airship was full of flammable gas, and his aim wasn't what it used to be. He then imagined the entirety of the ship crashing downtown in a fiery blaze. The grim thought made him laugh a little, simply because the flight home had been such a bore.

There was a gentle knock on the door. When Max answered, a meek little man in a steward's red uniform suit held forth a small silver platter with a bill on top, and greeted him with a curt nod. "Mister Thanatos," he said, with a stern, professional edge to his voice, "I regret to inform you that your line of credit has been declined by the bank. Your bill has gone unpaid, and all passengers cannot disembark until every account has been settled."

Max sighed. He had expected as much, given that the life of a part-time detective hardly paid for his own expenses, let alone covered the cost of a luxury suite. But he reached into his wallet, and flashed the man with a thick stack of cash in the sleeve. It was a simple con. The cash was jinxed to return to his wallet at dawn. "How terrible," Max pandered to him. "I hope cash will suffice."

"I'm terribly sorry, Mister Thanatos," the steward returned, "but we are not a bank, and do not handle cash."

The magus was annoyed by the persistence. Growing up poor had made Max overly-adaptive when it came to getting by. He motioned for the man to stay put as he returned with a small velvet sack. "Then what about gold?" he asked, emptying the pouch. Several golden coins glinted as they rained down upon the steward's silver tray, dinging with each impact. "Alone, each one could pay for this room for a week. But take them all," he said, "as a token of my good standing with Edison Airways."

The steward didn't know what to say, as he appraised the wealth before him. He simply nodded. "Consider this account paid in full. We value your patronage, Mister Thanatos. If there's anything—"

Max just smiled, and closed the door on the man before he could finish. The sooner he left the ship, the better. He had simply enchanted the coins with an illusion spell, tricking the man into believing they were something more than the loose change he had collected down south. It wouldn't last for long, but it was a last resort that had yet to fail him.

The ship moaned as it was finally winched into place. New York waited for no one. It simply kept pushing into the future. Max had been gone for much longer than planned. He only travelled to Robespierre to capture a minor demon. Now he was back in New York, along with the monster he had magically imprisoned. He was glad to be home. The city changed with every blink of an eye. Any time away might as well have been an eon. His dead brother was even more isolated from the world around him. He was a mere spectator trapped at Max's side. Eating, drinking, even the most rudimentary tasks in life were just memories. A ghost was, after all, just an echo of another life.

The announcement to disembark came at last. He was happy to finally rid himself of that giant balloon, and to have New York under his boots once more. Even heavily spruced with cologne, he couldn't wash the stench of Louisiana out of his clothes. He was paranoid the other people around him would have taken notice of the Deep South aroma, as the elevator brought him to the main lobby. He thrust his way through the stampede of a hundred inward and outward passengers hurriedly exiting and entering the building all at once. New York, he thought, always in motion. Stand still at your own peril.

The air was tinged with the crispness of winter. He breathed in as much as his damaged lungs would allow. The air smelled of industry and horse shit. There was no other smell like it in the world.

34th Street was alive and in motion like a flash flood. As he walked, women averted their eyes at the sight of the magician. At least some things never changed. Max wore his extraordinarily long, greying beard wrapped around his neck like a scarf. It was his most distinguishable feature, but it made things incredibly itchy in the summertime. His enchanted spectacles were tinted raven black. His resting face was locked perpetually in a scowl, whether he was angry or not. Though, by his own admission, it did help with avoiding unwanted conversation. Max looked over to his brother. Charlie floated by his side in silence.

Max felt the hat shift on his head.

The creature was always in his head, and it never ceased to remind him of how it diseased the children, how it maimed men, or how the girl it possessed pleaded during her final moments to God for salvation. Even then, standing on the street corner waiting to cross, he felt the demon wailing on the walls of its enchanted jail cell, desperately searching for a weakness. Night and day, it screamed his name, laughed, and often taunted him in the voice of the girl once named Marie.

The malevolence seeped from the creature little by little, and it was slowly driving the magician mad. But it was a madness he hid very well from Charlie. The abomination was relentless with its torture. It never ceased. It was a battle of attrition. Some days were better than others. But, to Max, it felt like spiders were burrowing into his skull, and the sensation grew stronger with each passing moment. He flashed a deceiving smile at his brother. Even if his brother knew the truth, there was nothing he could do.

It was irresponsible of him to bring it back to the city. That he knew, but the magician also knew it was wisest to keep it close, at the risk of his sanity. It was, after all, in the safest place possible: atop his head. The monster within was the key to saving Charlie, so he had to endure his personal nightmare for a little while longer.

He looked at his pocket watch with a frown. Disembarkment had taken longer than expected, and he knew traffic was a nightmare that time of day.

***

Manhattan was like a hornet's nest after being beaten with a stick. It was alive and buzzing, angry and always in motion. It was exciting and dangerous. If you got caught by the spectacle, it would poison you with its sting. But the city was nothing but spectacle. Erected monuments of capital flirted with the skyline. Every city street, every avenue, neighbourhood and borough were lit up like the Fourth of July with its prismatic intoxication. Zeppelins, mostly (like *Ulysses*) repurposed after the war, patrolled the city from above, sweeping the streets with crepuscular beams of light. It was Tesla's utopia of progress fashioned from glass, concrete, and steel. It was a tomorrow city built without an off-switch, and it wasn't slowing down.

Max Thanatos watched the city slip away behind him from the aerial Harding Tramway as it crawled uptown above the madness of Times Square. The number 29 carriage was overcrowded with sullen men. All wore despair like a mask. Black Tuesday still lingered on their lips. It was impossible to escape, very like the stench of their cheap pipe-tobacco in such close quarters.

As the tram progressed the lights of the city reflected off the glass, accentuating the sickening haze of industry. The world was changing too fast. Max thought the rising popularity of the automobile would just be a fleeting fancy. He considered them a death-trap on four balloon tires, and Max certainly didn't trust the subway system. The only time a man should be underground was when he was dead and buried.

Max gripped the polished mahogany rail tightly as the tram carriage bobbed past a junction tower, showering the street below with a spray of electrical sparks. It was never a comfortable ride, but Max knew, from the memory of many previous ones, that he had finally crossed W. 95th Street. He was nearly home.

He was the only one to exit at Dorenia Station. It was a particularly unpopular stop, even for locals. Alafair was a tough neighbourhood. Romani, displaced by the war, made it their home, and brought with them old-world superstitions. As he walked, the wind blew south, carrying with it scents of cloves and incense and boiled cabbage. The neighbourhood was a patchwork of fortune tellers and thieves, charlatans and soothsayers. They preyed on the desperate, and made small fortunes doing so. Most of the divination to be found there was mere theatricality, designed to separate fools from their money. But some people had the gift and some, fewer still, practised certain things far worse. They were Max's people, but even they made him feel like an outsider.

On his street, dark-skinned boys were shattering milk bottles in an alleyway. They saw Max and whispered amongst themselves. Max didn't have to hear to know what they were saying. It was the same said by everyone in Alafair: "Max, Max the eater of sin. He'll steal your soul with a toothy grin." Naturally, he smiled, inciting the children into nearly toppling over each other as they fled screaming down the alley, with their souls intact.

You couldn't resist, said Charlie.

"It's the small things," Max replied, as he neared the bakery. *Look, another has been added to the others.*

Fading photographs of young girls were plastered on the store front window; girls that had disappeared from all across the city. Before he left, there had only been a few reported missing; now, mournful parents have covered the baker's shop with images of their children believed lost to New York.

The baker's only daughter, Mirela, was the first who vanished. Her photograph, placed months ago, was now almost entirely bleached by the sun. Only her smile remained. None had been found. His shop had become a beacon of hope for some, a memorial for others.

As someone exited, Max saw the broken father through the shop door, hunched over the counter. The magus used to leave white candles outside the bakery. It was an old tradition he learned from his mother: he hoped its light would guide the lost girl back to her father, but time was a curse for lost children. After the second week, Max knew the girl would never come home again.

You could help them.

It was the same conversation as always. "The city is no place for a child," Max replied, coolly. "I understand that fact better than most. Besides, I'm already working a case, Charlie: yours." He caught his own reflection in the store front glass and paused for an instant to regard it. His long nose came to a point. In his left hand, he gripped his walking cane, its handle a wolf's head carved from Indian ivory. He wore a silver locket around his neck with fading pictures of his mother and brother. Compulsively, he twirled the thumb ring on his right hand with his index finger. It had an onyx stone which would burn in the presence of evil.

His name was Maximilian Thanatos. In better times, he had been an agent of the Hermetic Order of the Golden Dawn, a secret society devoted to the learning and protection of ancient mysticisms. Now, he was a semi-retired detective of the arcane. Work was, understandably, infrequent.

The stoop outside his brownstone reeked again of cat piss. Max walked into the building, careful to avoid his boorish landlord. The broken elevator in the lobby had become a permanent part of the building's décor, so that day, like the years before it, he marched his way up four flights of stairs, wheezing as he went. A decade ago in

Ypres, chlorine gas had burned his lungs, so he had to be careful. His youth was well behind him.

He paused on the landing, and removed his flask. With a flick the cap was opened, and Max suckled down the elixir: a tonic to help him breathe. He turned the corner and drudged across the frayed red carpet covering the floor. The walls were thin, and did little to drown out the barking of a neighbour's dog. It was Friday, and the stench of fried fish lingered heavily in the hall. Max stood outside his door. The doorknob was cool to the touch, but it had no keyhole. The door had a very special kind of lock, and Max rat-tatted the wolf's head three times against the scuffed wood, dispelling the magic. A moment later, the door opened itself. Sanctuary existed just beyond the threshold. He was finally home.

But the satisfaction was short-lived. The door had only opened a crack when Max felt the vice-like grip of an invisible hand drag him inside by his neck. The door crashed shut behind him, and a blast of crackling energy slammed the magus back against it. Waves of pain pulsated through his body, like tiny shocks of electricity, and it brought him to his knees.

His apartment was washed in a blinding light. Even his spectacles did little to protect him. It was a struggle to see. All he could make out was the outline of a tall man approaching him from across the room. "Who—" Max tried to speak, but his words were silenced. He saw a single feathered wing extend fully from the figure, reaching nearly the length of the room. Max recognized then what had been powerful enough to breach his sanctum: a Fallen; an angel banished to Earth, but still devoted enough to do God's Will. They were fanatics.

The feathered wing wrapped around the figure's naked body like a toga, smothering the light emanating from his chest. As the room slowly returned to normal, Max felt the pain ease away until it was gone completely. He was freed, but the danger was far from over. As Max's eyesight adjusted once again to the soft glow of his apartment, an icy pang of fear washed over him. He knew the creature before him. "Uriel," he coughed. "I hope you're not still angry about last time."

"I'm not here to smite you, Max. Not today, anyway," the angel said. His voice sounded like rumbling thunder.

"Well, thank God for that," the detective half-joked, unbuttoning his peacoat, and hanging it on a coat rack in the foyer. With a word, his top hat blinked into a sealed vault in his apartment, alongside other collected dangers. It was best Uriel didn't know.

"Although, I should, actually. You've kept me waiting in this hovel of a home."

Max didn't make a habit of consorting with the creature, but for reasons unknown to him, Uriel kept coming back. And it wasn't exactly an honour to be chosen. Their single wing exiled them from returning to Heaven, cursing Fallen to walk alongside Man for eternity for their hubris, and that made Uriel particularly cranky. "You're as old as Creation. I'm sure you weren't waiting that long in the scheme of things. How did you even know I was back in town?"

"I always sense you," he said. But no explanation came.

"That's not at all unsettling," the magician said.

Try not to provoke the fallen angel, Max. The incorporeal spirit of Charlie Thanatos glided into the apartment through the neighbouring wall. He was a reflection of Max frozen in time, practically his spitting image, except for the full head of black hair and a finely groomed beard. It was nearly twenty years to the day since Charlie had been murdered by cultists in Bombay when the savages sought to obtain power by eating his still-beating heart, for it was a sacred organ that contained the human soul. Without it, Charlie had been doomed to suffer in Hell forever, but, in the ultimate sacrifice of love, Max had spared his brother damnation by tethering their souls together. The magician had thought it was a good idea at the time, but that was only the beginning of their troubles.

"*Still* playing detective with your dead brother," Uriel sneered. "That no-thing continues to wander this realm? How disappointing. Perhaps I should finally grant you both a mercy." The discontent was clear.

Max white-knuckled his wolf's-head cane. Uriel was the most powerful thing Max had ever encountered in his long life; nevertheless, Charlie was under his protection and he loved him dearly. "Don't make the mistake of threatening my brother again," he warned the Fallen, without even thinking. His body shook. He didn't know if it was from fear or adrenaline, but he expected to explode into a thousand tiny bits for his insolence. But Uriel just smiled.

Max observed the angel, studied his posture, his face. He looked for anything that would betray his true intentions, but he was always unpredictable and impossible to read. He was tall and frail with silly-looking locks of curly blonde hair, which made his persona deceptively less-imposing. But Max knew from experience there was a dragon underneath that olive skin.

Max, it's all right, Charlie said. *I think I'll go pester the neighbour's dog some more.*

"Don't stray too far," Max warned. Once Charlie left them alone, he continued through gritted teeth. "Well, you're here for something, Uriel. Shall we get down to brass tacks?" He walked over to the area that was once his bar. He picked up a crystal jar half-full of water, and poured himself a glass. The real treasures were hidden all throughout the apartment. The water was for guests, and Max would never waste the good stuff on a guest. But having an angel, even a Fallen, for company did have one benefit. "Would you mind?" Max raised the glass before Uriel and nodded. With just a touch, Uriel transformed the glass of water into red wine.

"You are to find a missing girl for me," Uriel said.

"Are you asking me or telling me?" he returned, "because, right now, I'm rather booked." He took a sip of the wine, and was unimpressed. Uriel was like a schoolyard bully, one you could only appease through playing to his vanity or with blind obedience. Anything else would have led to obliteration, but the last thing he wanted to do was take on whatever case the Fallen had in mind. "No more children," he said. "In fact, as of tonight, I think I'm officially retired. Besides, why me, given what happened last time we worked together? Our ideologies didn't exactly… mesh well," he understated. "Also, with all your power, I can't imagine you'd have trouble finding anyone."

"This one eludes even me." the Fallen admitted.

Max thought he just saw a shade of regret on the angel's face, but that wasn't what piqued his interest. If there was a way to remain hidden from angels, especially from that one, Max wanted to know. "What makes this girl so special?"

Uriel stood there for a long moment, and said, eventually, "She is my daughter."

"A Nephilim?" Max downed the rest of the cheap red wine in a single gulp. He couldn't believe such an admission. His every instinct told him not to. An offspring between an angel and human was a mythical creature, even within the world of the Fantastic. Max was hardly credulous: even the Golden Dawn balked at the idea, but still… He sat down hard on his worn, leather couch and sank deep within the confines of its comfort, lost in thought. Finally, he asked simply, "Does the girl know?"

"No," Uriel replied, with a firm rumble in his voice. "Nor will she ever learn the truth. You are the only other thing in Creation that knows my secret."

That terrified Max. "Even the mother doesn't know. Why tell me? Why not enlist the aid of your brethren?"

"A Nephilim is… an abomination," Uriel said. "If my kind were to discover the truth of her existence, she would be annihilated, and so would her mother. My *brethren* would wipe her entire bloodline from time, itself. Then, they would finally come for me. I did what any father would do: I shrouded her from Heaven and Hell. Even I can't find her. But now she is gone, taken from her own bed. Her mother prayed to me the night my daughter disappeared." Uriel's body crackled with energy, fuelled by frustration. "She is the only other thing in Creation I love other than God, and I am powerless to save her."

Max sat there for a moment or for an hour. He couldn't tell. He let the revelation sink in. He was a powerful magus, educated and experienced. Even so, he thought this case was beyond him, but it wasn't the challenge that gave him pause from refusing, it was the look on

Uriel's face. He had seen it before with the baker: it was a parent's anguish. Even a Fallen was capable of such compassion? He shook his head. Max didn't particularly like Uriel, but he respected his sacrifice. It was something he understood far too well.

He felt the hairs on his forearms stand on end, partially from the power emanating from the Fallen before him, but more significantly because the mage, for the first time in a long while, felt like his old self again; the version of himself before Charlie's death, the one who had climbed through the ranks of the Golden Dawn, and travelled the world looking for glory and adventure. He thought the Great War had killed what was left of his humanity, but the spark buried deep inside was still there. For months, he had seen the 'missing' posters accumulate in the baker's window. Charlie was right. He could have helped them. All of them. Max realized that he had grown too cynical, too self-absorbed to invest in anyone else's life. But it wasn't too late to save this one, Nephilim or not. She was out there, somewhere, and Max was going to find her.

"All right, Uriel," he said. "I will take the case."

"You never had a choice," the angel warned, implanting the image of his daughter inside the magician's mind.

Max ignored the remark. He wasn't going to let the Fallen ruin his moment or divert his common-sense. "I'll find your daughter, but not for free. There is something I want in return." He knew he was pressing his luck, but the detective also knew he finally had something that never existed until then: leverage. Uriel trusted him, needed him, and Max was going to bend that to its breaking point. "Two things, really," he corrected.

"Go on, you petty little thing."

"First things first: I want your word, that when this is over, you will spare my life. That's most important." Max knew angels were incapable of lying, and could never break their word. But making one commit to a promise was a nigh impossible feat. Harbouring a secret so dire made him expendable, and Max still had much work to do in life. Death would have only been an inconvenience.

Uriel thought about it, for a bit too long. "You already know too much."

Max found the confession to be a relief. It meant he had a chance to survive the case after all, though he would not have had one before. "Your mountain of a secret is safe with me. Let's call it client confidentiality," Max concluded, with a cheeky little smile. He gave his thumb ring another twirl.

Uriel reluctantly nodded.

"I would like to hear the words, if you don't mind."

"I will not kill you, Max Thanatos," the angel said, eventually.

"Good. Lastly, when this is all over," Max began, looking down his long nose at the angel, "I want you to introduce me to the Devil."

CHAPTER THREE:
OLD FRIENDS, NEW ENEMIES

Well, that was intense, Charlie said, finally working up the courage to poke his head inside the apartment, thankful his brother was still alive. *We should have him over again.*

Max circumnavigated the abode repeatedly, ejecting dusty books from their shelves. "Where is it?" he cursed. A thick tome caught his eye on the top shelf of the tallest bookcase, and he dragged a wooden chair across the room for a boost. "Charlie, this is the big one. The answer to all of our problems."

The book? he asked.

Max shook his head. "No, not the book. The case." The detective blew an inch of dust off the ancient text. The cloud swirled away into nothing in the dying light of the dusk. He ran his finger across the damaged, coarse leather binding. This book had been bound and rebound over time; its title worn away centuries ago; but Max could have identified it in his sleep. It was a prized possession from the Golden Dawn's private library, and was never meant to leave its halls. Max considered it a severance package. "We are on the hunt."

Charlie drifted past his brother. *A hunt for what? You're being annoyingly vague.*

"Not a what. We are looking for a missing girl," and Max flashed a finger warningly in the air to silence his brother before he could retort. "And that is all you will know, for both our sakes." Max saw his brother cross his arms in defiance, but the mage's hands were tied. He was burdened with the king of secrets, and he couldn't even tell his dead brother. "You will just have to trust me."

I've heard that before.

Max placed the hefty tome upon his dining room table, and quickly skimmed its pages, growing increasingly sour with each flip. "No," he bit. Charlie watched his brother vanish into an adjacent room, and return with bundles of rolled up parchments toppling over in his arms. He unfurled them all across the table, and rejected them as quickly onto the floor. "No," he repeated again. "No, no, no!" He swiped them all onto the floor. "I don't have it."

Should I even ask?

"Charlie, not now," Max snapped. "I can't cast my spell without it." He plucked his pocket watch out from his vest and plopped it onto his hand, souring again at the late hour. "Bah."

Max—

"I had a map of the city, one I sold a long time ago to someone I'd rather not deal with directly."

Charlie looked at, at least, a dozen maps of Manhattan at Max's feet.

"I need it for a locator spell," he added, before Charlie could ask.

I take it you're not getting paid by the hour. Shouldn't we, at least, talk with the child's parents?

If Charlie only knew, Max thought, as he shook his head. "Things are a bit…" he struggled for the right word, "delicate. But it's nothing I can't handle."

Did Uriel hire us? Was that why he was here?

Max ignored the question. His brother was angling for information, and he couldn't risk letting the truth slip out. "The client doesn't matter. Just the result."

He readjusted his suspenders, which had been loosened during his encounter with the angel, for a snugger fit. His clothes smelled of the city and of musk, but changing wouldn't do him any good when he was about to trek through the muddied wastelands of New York's social society. But he did change his shoes into his old army-issue boots. He wouldn't dare besmirch their fine Italian leather with that filth. He straightened his black neck tie, and smoothed out his black vest. Then he cuffed the sleeves of his well-tailored white dress shirt up to his elbows. It made him look working class, but that would make it easier for him to weave his magic. Max didn't know what to expect, so he planned for the worst. The last bit of the ensemble was his top hat, which he tapped into place with a bump of his cane. It didn't serve any purpose. Max just liked the way it looked.

It looks like you're going to the theatre? Charlie teased.

"Worse," he said. "A speakeasy, but one mustn't sacrifice style when faced with adversity, my dear brother." Upon his person were a dozen trinkets to protect him from other-worldly things. He was educated in the arcane and mystic arts of civilizations long extinct. His words were power. His mind was a weapon. "Come, Charlie, we're off to see an *old friend* about my map."

Like I have a choice.

***

Max was in SoHo; a refuge for the pretentious, the pseudo-academics drunk on literature and the sound of their own voices. The Dada movement had rooted itself deeply into this part of town, and gave the youth another language to proclaim how much better they were than the world around them. In another life, Max might have been one amongst their nihilistic rank and file; for he also enjoyed the sound of his own voice. But that generation was too young for conscription. They had spent the war criticizing it from classrooms, inheriting a world that many had died trying to protect. They got off easy, and Max despised them for that.

He headed towards the Hudson, lost in thought, and was nearly hit by a yellow cab as it sped through an intersection. Ten years ago, the streets were filled with carriages and reeked of horse shit. Now, only the smell remained.

The Nightshade was close. The detective never cared much for speakeasies. He found them loud and their clientele obnoxious. Max didn't like competing with the noise of the crowd, for he hardly ever raised his monotone voice above a whisper. The real appeal of those dens of debauchery was the booze, which was often watered down and overpriced. It wasn't the liquor people paid for, it was the risk. Speakeasies rarely existed for more than a month or two. They were like weeds. When one was raided, two more would pop up on the other side of town. And Max did well to avoid the police. On his person, that evening alone, were enough trinkets to send him straight to a padded cell. And that was just the trivial things. He kept the darker items sown into the lining of his clothing, including the skull of his neighbour's cat with Celtic runes carved into the bone.

The Nightshade was the one exception. It was the oldest speakeasy in the city. The law kept its distance, whether out of respect or fear of its proprietor, Sexton Graves, Max didn't know. He did understand Sexton had a way with people, and Max doubted it was because of some charming personality trait.

Max had heard stories of the man, impossible tales, things seemingly born from urban legends and slivers of actual truth. And locating his speakeasy under a funeral home only helped to serve those ghastly stories. He guessed having it at a cemetery would have been a little too on the nose. But, the truth was, Max was excited at the thought of meeting another proper mage. Magic was very old world. America was too young for such ancient traditions. While speckles of magicians did pop up few and far between, the community was dying off. Houdini and his brother, Theo, turned it into a travelling show. They preferred to hide in plain sight. Max still preferred his modest apartment uptown.

He stood in an alleyway across the street from Graves' funeral parlour and observed. A couple exited from a side entrance of the building, fancily-dressed, happy and tipsy. The building before him was discreet, with its bland façade, plain colours, and uninspired sign above the door that read *We're Here for You*. It was the perfect front, for it excelled in inconspicuousness.

This friend of yours, is it "friend" in the Max sense, or like how the rest of the world understands the definition?

Max shrugged, to him, there was no difference. "Sexton Graves is more like the enemy of my enemy," he alluded.

Ah. And what makes you so sure he'll meet with you in person?

"Mutual curiosity," Max replied. "We were both expelled from the Golden Dawn."

You're still sour about that? The Golden Dawn was nearly twenty years ago, he mused.

"Getting expelled from the Order wasn't exactly a high point in my life."

What did you expect? You slept with Crowley's wife.

Max raised a finger in objection. "It was *after* his divorce," he corrected.

Well, you got off light. He had the poor girl committed.

Max nodded in agreement, though he was never proud of how things ended with Rose. "I did get off lightly," he said. "But, from what I've heard, Sexton's exit wasn't nearly as diplomatic."

The detective waited for a green, double-decker motor bus to pass before crossing Fillmore Ave. The mammoth machine spurted out a black cloud of exhaust in its wake, sour air for his already damaged lungs. Max traced the last couple's steps, and entered through the side entrance of the building. The air inside was warm; stale. The mage plucked a chalky, peppermint candy from a dusty glass bowl at the front desk, and popped it into his mouth. It was the only thing he had eaten since the airship.

Max continued into the next room. It was a carpeted sitting room for wakes, and the floorboards underneath groaned beneath the weight of each step. The walls were draped in tacky red velvet. "Do you sense anything?"

Charlie shrugged. *Terrible décor?* he replied, half-joking. But he knew Max would not be in the mood for his jokes and avoided his brother's predictable glare. Instead, he continued, *but there is something strange in the air, little prickles of energy everywhere around us like dust disturbed by the wind. It feels like we're standing at the threshold of something powerful.*

"The entire building could be warded."

Maybe, Charlie replied. Max's own apartment was a bubbling cauldron of energy.

"It could also be the proprietor, himself."

Charlie balked at the idea. *No mage could radiate this much power. It's everywhere around us.*

"Sexton Graves is no lightweight." Max saw that his brother still wasn't convinced. "I would even dare say he could be more powerful than your favourite brother," he admitted, begrudgingly.

That got Charlie's attention.

There were two kinds of mages in the world: those are born with powerful gifts and those who had to nurture them. Max's mentor at the Golden Dawn, an Egyptian mystic named Ammon Safar, could comprehend tomes in any language simply by touching their covers. It had been said Ammon mastered every known language while having his lunch. Max, on the other hand, spent two long years in their dusty library mastering Sumerian. Max wasn't an academic. He learned by application. He preferred to get his hands dirty, and because of that, he had excelled in magic and risen through the ranks in the Golden Dawn by taking any and every job that no one else would take.

While his peers practiced from their plush offices in London, Max was wallowing waist-high in the filth of Calcutta, partaking in tribal blood rituals in the Congo, or tracking hellish beasts in the Yucatan. But Sexton was more akin to Ammon than to Max. The detective never learned what Sexton could do, but he heard his powers made even Aleister Crowley nervous. "We'd best tread with caution," was all Max could say.

He walked over to the far wall to the room's observation area. It was an obvious guess, for he easily found a door behind the velvet drapes. With a turn of the bronze door handle, Max walked through and down a musty stairwell into the building's boiler room. The air was balmy, and the raging fire within the furnace tossed dancing shadows on the concrete walls like tormented souls. His thumb ring felt warm, but he sensed nothing out of the ordinary. He crossed the room, and found another door, this one of heavy iron riveted with reinforced plates. It looked brand new.

Charlie also took notice. *Do you think it's to keep people out, or to keep something trapped within?*

Max didn't have an answer. And why iron? Max wondered. The modern age was all about concrete and steel. Iron, much like silver, was the bane of most magical creatures. Max shook his head. He was probably looking for things that weren't there. He gripped the handle, and strained to push the heavy door open. "I guess we'll find out." Max was greeted by another stairwell leading down deeper under the basement. The sound of brass and strings rose from the darkness. A young black couple erupted from the stairwell, laughing and sweaty, and greeted the detective with mischievous smiles as they went.

At the bottom, Max was greeted by a buffalo of a man, and the darkest he had ever seen. He stood a head above Max, who himself was taller than most. The man exhaled a stench of tobacco into the detective's face when he asked for his coat. His yellow eyes were vacant, and his pinstriped suit barely contained his bulk. Max's ring flared with a burst of heat at the man's presence, but, despite his ogre-like appearance, the man seemed childlike in demeanour and stature.

Max, can't you tell? Charlie asked. *This man is dead.*

A reanimation, Max thought. He exchanged worried glances with his brother. "Thank you, kind sir," Max said to the figure. "But I'd prefer to hold onto my coat tonight. Keeps me warm," he finished, with a wink. He didn't know what hell awaited him beyond the door. The man's face was expressionless as he ushered the detective through the entrance to Sexton Grave's speakeasy.

The doors opened up, unleashing a torrent of stimuli upon the mage. First was the smell of body odour heavily masked with a hundred brands of floral perfumes. It blended with the thick haze of tobacco smoke lingering above the crowd. Cigarettes were all the rage that year, and the foul things sucked the air out of his lungs. One foot through the door, and he already found himself struggling to breathe.

Max's sensitive eyes strained against the brilliance of the establishment's lights, which flared hypnotically with the sound of the seven-man band of black musicians sweating through their burgundy dress shirts. As he walked into the Nightshade, it was hard to focus on any one thing. He found it all very disorientating. The whole room was in motion. A hundred couples swirled on the dance floor, gyrating themselves in dazzling displays of vertical sex. There was no courting to be found there. It was simple animalistic needs; and urges towards even simpler, primitive desires. Flapper nonsense, Max thought. He was thankful his mother from the old world never lived to witness the new age. It would have killed her.

"Be my eyes, Charlie. Tell me what you see."

To the spirit, the room around him bled with energy. *Malevolence*, he replied, simply. *Max, I wish for us to leave. Something is very wrong here. I don't like this place.*

"Neither do I. Remember why we came, dear brother. This is not a social visit."

The Nightshade was built into an old Vanderbilt theatre, one that was most likely forgotten as Manhattan entered Tesla's new age of vertical expansion. New York was built on top of the ruins of a forgotten city in favour of something new and shiny. Max pondered if Sexton had built his speakeasy in a cemetery after all. But the black market must have been flourishing. As a contrast to allowing the funeral home to fall into a state of disrepair, the Nightshade was immaculate. Crystal chandeliers the size of yellow cabs hung from the ceiling, every table was lined with an inch of black velvet, every fixture was lined with gold trim, and the Speakeasy had a curious display of elephant skeletons. Not just pachyderm, but as Max drew in closer to that particular area, there were human skeletons, too. Hideously deformed skeletons of three children displayed in glass, all holding hands in a circle. One had a terribly misshapen skull with no eye sockets.

*Just what kind of monster is Sexton Graves? And here I thought **your** collection was morbid.*

"My collection of oddities is used to save lives. This is grotesque."

"'Grotesque,' Mister Thanatos?" came a small voice from behind the detective. "I thought you might have been one of the few who would have understood its true beauty."

Max turned around to see a well-dressed boy, probably no older than twelve, staring into the glass display. His head was completely bald and had a patchwork of visible stitching scars criss-crossing along his scalp. Much like the man at the door, his face was expressionless, his eyes were vacant. Max felt there was something 'off' about him, and it made his skin crawl. His thumb ring flared again with a burning heat at the boy's presence. "What is the old adage about beauty? It is in the eye of the beholder," Max said, cautiously.

The boy nodded, but kept his focus on the display of bones. "I knew them, once, while travelling in Haiti. I became friendly with the girl. She was especially kind," he said, pointing at the skeleton shorter than the others. "They were siblings, stoned to death in Port-au-Prince. Their corpses were mutilated and buried face-down together in a shallow grave. The Haitians believed they were children of Marinette-Bwa-Chech, the mother of monsters." The boy shook his head. "Savages and their superstitions," he said nonchalantly. "Stoning is a slow execution. They suffered immensely, simply because of their deformities. If they had been born in London, they might have shared the stage with Joseph Merrick."

"And this display?" Max asked.

"The world had lost three innocent creatures that day. This is a monument to that loss. I reunited the siblings here so they could dance eternally in my playground. It was the least I could do. Most people who gaze upon this for the first time see only death. I see life," the boy said, finally turning to address the magician.

"Sexton Graves?"

The boy gave a curt nod to the duo. "In the flesh."

CHAPTER FOUR: A MAN NAMED SEXTON

"Forgive this appearance," Sexton said. "I felt like wearing something a little different tonight. It's one of the benefits of owning a funeral parlour: the bodies never stop coming. This child died of an acute epileptic seizure only a few days ago. It's just another way for me to honour the dead."

By parading the body like a pinstripe suit? Charlie flared. He expected the candid remark to be in confidence with his brother, but was taken aback when the boy turned to look directly at the spirit.

"So, the rumours *are* true," the boy said, in earnest fascination. "You tethered your souls together. How remarkable. I consider myself often peerless, but I'm actually quite impressed. This," he said, pinching the boy's flesh, "is mere possession."

Max felt a chill run down his spine. Possession was incredibly dark magic.

"But the soul is the most divine treasure we have," the boy continued. "To manipulate it, even in the least, would be like a slight against God. Come," he urged with a motion of his arm, "I want you both to join me at my personal table. I want the honour of hosting the Brothers Thanatos tonight."

"I speak for us both when I say we'd be honoured to join you," Max began, throwing his brother a look of warning to not rile the man further, "but I'm afraid tonight is not a social visit."

They walked together towards a sectioned-off area, removed from the crowd.

"Business is my favourite topic of conversation," Sexton said. "Why have you come: goods or services?"

"I've come to buy back my Hellion Map," Max replied. The magi sat down across from each other at a round cocktail table with a single black candle at the centre. With a wave of the boy's hand, the candle caught flame. A fair-skinned waitress immediately served them a bottle of dark liquor and one small glass for Max. "I hear you and I share an affinity for spiced rum. This is from my personal collection." The boy poured Max a modest serving. "It comes from a plantation in Jamaica. They only make ten bottles a year. It's made with the blood of the family: a symbolic gesture of their livelihood."

Max brought the glass to his nose. It smelled like shoe polish. "I was hoping to meet the real you." He downed the glass in one gulp and immediately regretted it. The taste matched the smell.

"I'm afraid that's out of the question. You see, a lifetime of magic has consumed most of my real body from the inside out. I'm more husk than man these days, which is why I prefer to 'parade around in my pinstripe suits,'" the boy said, coolly, in his small voice. He saw Charlie set his jaw in frustration, but turned his attention back to Max. "I can no longer enjoy the finer things in life, much like the rum you believe smells like 'shoe polish,' but that is the cost one pays for power."

"Possession, reanimating the dead, and reading one's thoughts," Max said, tapping the side of his head, "now I understand why the Golden Dawn feared you."

"One or two of them had some clout, but the others were too in love with their little Egyptian pageantries, like Crowley and Lynn Lin. I was destined for greater things. It's a shame we haven't met until tonight. Even back then, I heard you were one of the better ones." The child shook his head. "Aleister and his juvenile pharaoh costumes," the boy said. "But if you find this body distasteful, the funeral parlour has others. Perhaps a leggy blond?"

Max politely declined with a raised hand. "Sexton, I need the map. Do you still have it?"

The boy nodded. "I do. I couldn't move it, even in the blood magic circles. Your association with the relic has tainted its value to practically nothing."

"Then I'll buy it back," Max said, removing his top hat, and extending his arm deep within the article, nearly up to the elbow. A moment later, he removed a plump sack of coins from its magical recesses. "Thirty pieces of silver. The same your agent gave me years ago." He flopped the sack down on the table.

"Yes, I remember. You were hoping to bribe the Devil for a favour," Sexton said, looking at Charlie. "Now I understand why." The necromancer tossed the sack of coins back at Max. "But that was a long time ago, and things depreciate over time. First, tell me why you want it?"

"For a case."

"Oh, that much is certain. In fact, I already know why you're here," Sexton replied, tapping the side of his flesh suit's head.

The detective shifted uneasily in his chair. It began as a burning sensation. A throbbing pulse of heat so slight it felt as if a candleflame had jumped from the wick and was burrowing through the inside of his skull. "Wha-

-" he tried to speak, but then he remembered who sat before him.

The bastard was reading his mind.

It was a magic so rare, he barely bothered to study it.

"You're… reciting, what? William Blake?" Sexton balked, almost insulted.

Max flooded his mind with endless chatter; it was all he could do. Memories of his childhood, Blake's *The Tyger*. Reliving mundane tasks again and again. He knew of no spells to block him, he had no trinkets to stop the intrusion. But his defence, as weak as it was, wouldn't be enough to hold him back for much longer. How much did he take from his thoughts?

"Not much," Sexton admitted, answering Max's unspoken question. "The mind, it never ceases. That voice, in your head, may be reciting poetry, but that is just one raindrop in a torrential storm. The true mastery of telepathy-- the art, it's not plucking the superficial thoughts from the surface, but the seizing of what's below. I could, very easily, take everything, but I won't. Not tonight. Call it a professional courtesy."

It was hardly a courtesy, Max came to realize. Sexton wanted to prove his power was on a completely different level, and it unnerved him to no end.

Sexton continued, "I also wanted to know if you came to kill me— force of habit. In my line of work, caution is the valour of discretion. As for *why* you're here: You're searching… for a girl."

"Yes," Max said, "and I have reason to believe she's in incredible danger. I need the map to find her."

"Danger? How exciting. But the urgency changes much, Maxi-boy," the child said. He leaned in closer in his chair. His face was expressionless, like a doll's, impossible to read. "I will part with the Hellion map, but for a modest sum."

"The Judas coins are not enough? You just said it was worthless."

"It's all a function of how much you need it," said the boy. "What is it worth to you? If you want it, the price is the soul-tethering spell you used on your brother."

"No," Max declined, sharply.

"What if I told you I know how to find the Devil," he stated. "You wanted to bribe Him-- I take it, to barter your brother's way out of damnation? Even without my... gift, I can put two and two together-- *I* can sense your great shame. What's the spell worth to you now, after the fact?"

"It's not the spell, it's the dark cost of casting it. I won't have that on my conscience," Max shot back.

"You've been searching for Him for all those years, and you're no closer today than you were when you began, am I right?"

The magician soured. "My answer is still the same. It will always be the same," Max spat, exploding from his seat. "Sexton, we're done here," he said, turning to leave.

"Don't you dare turn your back on me."

"You're not the only resourceful magus in Manhattan. I'll find another way," Max returned, leaving the necromancer behind, but a murmur was enough to give him pause.

"A...Nephilim," Sexton exhaled.

Max stopped in his tracks. The bastard knew.

"You almost did so well, hiding that secret from me tonight. But your last thought betrayed you."

What is he talking about Max? Charlie asked.

"Oh, didn't your brother tell you, Charlie?"

The ghost turned to Max, expecting an answer from him.

But Sexton answered instead, "The girl you've been searching for is the most mythical of all creatures, something so monstrous--"

"Stop," Max warned.

"--so reviled, even Heaven and Hell would offer any price to keep them secret." The necromancer took great delight watching Max squirm. "Oh, don't worry. I won't tell," he said, playfully placing an index finger over his thin lips. "After all, I wouldn't be much of a magic profiteer if I gave away everyone's secret for free."

"You have no idea what you're playing at," he said, realizing he had just undone his pact with Uriel.

Sexton shrugged. "You want to save your brother, I want to save myself." He waved his hand, and a rolled-up map materialized out of thin air above them. "Let us both use the map to find the girl, together, as brethren. The easiest path would be to offer up the abomination. The Devil wouldn't be able to refuse such a request, Maxi-boy, not for a prize like her," the necromancer swooned. "Give me the spell, and the map is yours. We could finally obtain our hearts' desires."

For the briefest of moments, Max listened.

He had searched for the Devil like a madman, exhausted contacts and leads, studied demonology— all to find his ultimate prize— but with no luck and only to waste years watching his brother's spirit wither and weaken. However, then he remembered the disdain in Uriel's voice when he mentioned his own brethren. It was enough to break through the haze of Sexton's alluring compromise. The Fallen had placed his trust in him back at his apartment. He would never betray the angel, or sacrifice his daughter for personal gain. "I'll find her, without the map," Max answered.

"Now that's disappointing."

A sudden hush fell between the magi, one that resonated throughout the speakeasy. The band finished their song, and the couples ceased their stampeding across the dance floor. There were no afterglow murmurs of couples talking amongst themselves. The Nightshade was quiet; like a cemetery. It was too abrupt, too queer. Max turned for a better view of the room. Every man and woman stood frozen in place, hunched over from the waist. No one stirred, not even the band.

Max.

The detective turned to his brother, bewildered. The stark urgency in his brother's voice made his blood run cold.

Everyone's dead. Everyone. This placed was so saturated with power; I couldn't even see it until now, Charlie balked.

Max felt a familiar burning sensation linger at the back of his head, and he turned back around to see boy's once expressionless face scowling at him in absolute abhorrent resentment.

"Then so be it, Max Thanatos. If you won't give me the spell, I'll have to take it." The boy rocketed out of his chair. With a wave of his hand, the small cocktail table was flung into a wall by an invisible hand and shattered into oblivion. Max stumbled backwards, nearly tripping over his wolf's head cane. "I felt your presence the moment you stepped onto my street. I wanted the spell then, but you had it locked away so deep within your psyche, so I'll have to pluck it from your mind one memory at a time, alive or dead."

"Please, Sexton, I don't want to fight you. There are so few of us left," Max pleaded.

"This isn't going to be a fight, Max. It's going to be a slaughter. You had your chance." Sexton's hand crackled and popped with white snakes of electricity coiling around his arm. "Now show me how you fare as a mage." The boy stretched his arm outright towards the detective, but the streams of power fizzled away into harmless sparks around the detective's body.

Max smoothed out his black vest in a moment of pride. "This puppet show is over. I've come to retrieve the map." He gripped his cane tightly in his hand. He was thankful he had brought the cat's skull with him that night. Sexton aimed to kill him with that spell, but the enchanted trinket gave Max seven chances to survive. But it was fickle. Nothing was guaranteed. And he had no idea how many chances were left.

Sexton just shook his head. "Trinkets?" he bit, heavy with disappointment. "You are no better than the fools I've left behind in London. You are a child with toys, Mister Thanatos. But you are too late. I know about the girl. I will find her, and I will broker my own deal. You may think me a monster, but sacrifices must be made."

"We took an oath to protect magic. Not exploit it." Max shouted, wondering how a former member of the Golden Dawn could have fallen so far. "What is this all for?" he asked, deflecting another bolt of white energy, but this time into the velvet drapes closest to the stage. They quickly caught flame, and a blaze soon burned its way throughout the speakeasy, consuming everything it touched.

"Life," Sexton spat. "I already told you I'm dying. There's no stopping it, and, quite frankly, my time is almost up. I'd spent the better part of a decade casting a unique spell, one that would have sent me back to my childhood. I planned to transfer my consciousness into my younger self, to give me a second chance at life. One hundred and twenty years of knowledge in a child's mind. Imagine what I could have accomplished with another century of learning. But the spell didn't work. But now that I'm aware of the girl, I can accomplish in one evening what originally took ten years to try. And I have you to thank for that."

"I'm sorry, Sexton, but that will never happen," Max said, striking the boy's body with the head of his cane. The vassal of Sexton Graves exploded into tiny red bits and splattered all over the wall. "This cane? I call it Smite," Max said, with regret. "The greater the sinner, the greater the impact."

The detective saw every hunched-over body in the speakeasy spring back to life like an army of clockwork soldiers fully wound. But they had been flesh and blood people who, just a short while ago, had been dancing, laughing and mimicking what it was to be alive. Now, in unison, they turned towards the detective and lurched forward with a step. He thought about the couple who had passed him in the stairwell, those who ran out into the street. How far did Sexton's power reach? Everything within his demonic confines was just a charade. Max knew the Nightshade had to be razed to the ground. "We must save the map." But a clubbing blow struck Max between his shoulder blades. The impact knocked Max hard to his knees, dazing him. The room spun violently like a top. All he heard was a baritone voice taunting him from behind.

"A heroic showing back there, but futile, as I can transfer my will to any corpse nearby, and you are utterly surrounded. You may have your trinkets to ward you from my magic, but I believe you are still a frail man who can be beaten and broken. You can't hope to stop them all."

"And I bet what's left of your living corpse isn't too far away from us, Sexton. You could either knock me around some more, or you can try and stop this fire from finishing what's left of your body." With a Roman incantation, the fire was intensified into a singeing white heat, and doubled its rate of destruction. "You won't have time to do both."

"What have you done?" Sexton screamed, turning to see the world around him burn. "You've ruined everything, you... you... faaarrghh!" The giant of a man became nothing more than dead weight as it was discarded like a cheap suit.

Max watched the corpse drop to the ground, abandoned by the necromancer. His choice was made. He snatched the map from the ground, and tucked it way inside the magical confines of his top hat. Parts of the ceiling came down like fiery rain, chandeliers rattled loose, and gravity did the rest. Bodies caught underneath were smashed in the carnage. The heat shattered glasses and champagne bottles into tiny shards. The black smoke made it impossible to see or breathe.

He waded through the inferno to find the exit. His lungs felt ready to burst, his skin felt like it was on fire. But moments later, he made his way up to the funeral parlour, and back onto the city street. He turned to watch the smouldering building collapse, sealing the fate of anything left behind.

Max saw his brother turn his head despairingly; he knew what question was coming next. "I was going to tell you... one day." He saw Charlie melodramatically turn his head to the other side. "Honest."

You wanted to talk with the Devil? Was that what this was all about?

Max shrugged. He wasn't particularly proud to admit it. He just gave his thumb ring another twirl, and tried his best to avoid Charlie's glare. "It's a long story, dear brother. I'll tell you all about it on the way home."

CHAPTER FIVE: CHINATOWN

His apartment was exactly as he had left it: in a state of organized chaos. Max smelled of smoke, the edges of his clothes were singed, and the tip of his extraordinary long beard was burnt, but nothing kept him from his task. He wasn't proud to have left Sexton Graves to die in the blaze, if a necromancer could ever truly die, but it was advantageous — indeed, vital — for the secret of the girl to have died along with him, for his own sake. Still, he wondered.

Charlie watched as his brother disappeared into the kitchen and reappeared with a brass bowl full of water, which he left on the table. He had questions, so many questions, about the girl, about the Devil, but he respectfully let his brother work. He knew Max became obsessive when it came to a case, maybe even possessed. He'd forego sleep, food, anything that would slow him down. Max vanished into another section of his sanctum, followed by the clanking of glass bottles being roughly shifted on their shelves. He returned with a glass vial he held out before him for appraisal, turning it in his hand. The tiny nail within clinked around.

"No more questions. I need to focus," Max said to Charlie, only to realize his brother wasn't saying a word. "You're just... thinking too loud," he added. "This is a particularly sensitive spell, even for me. One mistake, and the entire city could drown."

Lovely.

He placed the vial back down, and tenderly opened the tome he had left on the table. Its worn pages moaned in protest, revealing a dead language within. "And there's no guarantee this will even work. The Hellion map has been out of my care for years. Its magic could have been tainted or corrupted."

He removed his top hat, and retrieved the map from within, unfurling it across the table, revealing an intricate drawing of Manhattan in blood. Max once again gripped the vial in his hand, but now held it over the bowl. The lights of the apartment flickered as Max echoed an incantation from another era. The mage crushed the glass vial in his hand, allowing the nail and droplets of blood to spill into the water below. The crimson fluid swirled within the clear liquid of the bowl, and it hummed and rippled with a growing power. Max finished his words, and removed a single curly blonde hair given to him by Uriel, and added it to the mixture. Then he stood in place, waiting for anything, something to happen. After a long moment, there was nothing.

Is that it? Charlie asked doubtfully.

Max frowned. "I hope not, that was the only nail I had from Noah's Ark." The mage placed his hands upon the table and waited. The spell was simple enough to cast, but it didn't mean it wasn't complex. But Max had his answer when he heard a soft rumble of thunder sound in the distance. "Success."

Max, you lost me.

The mage just pointed to the sky. "I just conjured us up a rainstorm." Max turned to look out his window, one warded from view. To anyone outside the apartment, it would have just appeared to be a brick wall. "A very special rainstorm." The rain quickly intensified from a gentle patter against the window glass to a torrential storm in just a matter of moments. "If the rain touches our missing girl, even a trace of her, the location will appear on my map."

That is, even if she's still in the city.

It was a gamble Max had to take. He poured the bloodied water across the map of Manhattan, which was magically absorbed into the bone-dry parchment.

And this is Manhattan, Max. No one's ever outside during a rainstorm. Charlie pointed out the obvious. He saw his brother shrug.

"This spell is quite resilient by design. Most of its residual effects elude even me, but if she steps into a puddle, or drinks any of the rainwater from the reservoir, it will still detect her. It's an intrusive spell. Water seeps its way into everything, my dear brother. One must have a little faith. This isn't science."

Max studied the map intently, hoping the solution would present itself much sooner than later. Then a water ring appeared, like condensation left by a minuscule glass, and manifested itself around Chinatown. Max frowned, for he immediately understood its meaning.

What's wrong? Charlie asked, peering over his brother's shoulder. *Did it work?*

"The girl," Max said, pointing to a fixed location on the map, "she's in Chinatown."

Great, then let's go get her.

Max shook his head. "It's not that simple. I believe she was taken by a society of derelicts and outcasts living underneath Chinatown: a volatile and dangerous guild of unwanted children with nothing left to lose." He looked down at the calloused palm of his right hand, and balled it into a fist. "I know exactly where she is," he said, "because, for a time, it was once my home."

Charlie gave Max a look, as if his brother was really going to just leave it at that. He lost count of all of the questions he had that night.

"Remember, Charlie, my childhood came before yours. That's the privilege of being an older brother."

Max left his apartment and hurried across Davis Blvd. "Below New York, hundreds of undesirables work for men applying draconian rules in unimaginably horrid conditions. When the victims die, more children are taken from their beds to restock their numbers, and the vicious cycle continues. They are considered property, tools. Nothing more. Boys are trained as pickpockets. The girls…" he lingered, "*become* subservient, at best. But everyone's right palm is branded with a cursed mark: a silhouette of a crow inside a gear. I bore the same symbol. It marked us all as thieves within the Murder Society."

Max noticed his brother's disappointment. If Charlie only knew the worst of it.

"It was all I could do after mother passed away," Max confessed. "New York is unforgiving to the destitute. I used what little magic I knew at the time to steal. But we never starved, did we?"

Charlie sombrely shook his head, absorbing it all. *I had no idea.*

"I kept it all from you," he assured. "When things took a violent turn, I fled, but they weren't the kind of people who took rejection well. If Ammon hadn't rescued us when he did…" Max shook the awful memories away. He looked down at the palm of his right hand. It had taken quite a bit of magic and time to remove the curse, to heal the brand, but he knew it was still there. Just another scar from his past.

***

Chinatown was an orphan of New York. It was ignored and mostly forgotten, and, more importantly, largely avoided by all who knew better. It was old New York, a ghost of Manhattan's past, one where Tesla's grand vision for the future died mercilessly within a few city blocks. There, the soft glow of gaslights accented the red paper lanterns that criss-crossed over the narrow, filthy streets like a spider's web. Below, Chinatown was alive with pulsating shadows, darker than Max had ever thought natural, which bled from every crack of every decrepit building he passed. He had dispelled his rainstorm at his apartment, but it did little to wash away the grime.

His every step was met with obvious hatred of the Round Eye, as the Chinese called his kind. He knew he was not welcomed, but Max soldiered on. Labourers and mobsters walked openly and freely, and were often one and the same. A person had to tread carefully, and not play loose with one's tongue. Any disrespect could have been an instant death sentence. The Murder Society taught Max how to navigate the game of shadows at a very young age, but he had been away from Chinatown for a long, long time.

Max turned the corner onto the "Bloody Angle," the epithet given to the heart of Chinatown, and one it justly deserved. It was exactly how Max remembered it as a boy: septic, a place of isolation and deception. The police wouldn't have dared venture there. It was governed and protected by its own. Chinatown was the perfect haven for those who had to disappear never wanting to be seen again. It was the deepest and darkest of pits, and the Murder Society had made it their home.

But beneath the street, littered with garbage and ankle deep puddles of foul smelling water, was the Inverted Church, the place where they all converged. He once considered his childhood plantation in Louisiana to be his first real education in the savagery of man, but the world below New York was not so different. People were still property, exploited for another man's gain. Yet, if Louisiana was his first schooling in the evil of man, his former Dark Masters in the Murder Society made Max into something of an academic.

He was one of the fortunates who had escaped that hellish place. He thought about the girl. Max didn't have the heart to tell his gentle brother the truth about what she'd endure. Enslavement, mutilation, the Murder Society was a godless place. He had fought like a madman to be free from it, yet here he was again. This time, of his own accord, for a case. The notion twisted his stomach, but Max had to wonder why it also excited him. Was it the thought of saving her? Was it Uriel's promise to finally meet the Devil? Or deep within his vanity, did he expect to liberate the children from their pens, throw open their cages, and lead them all back into the light?

Max just shook his head. He was no hero. He was responsible for only one person, and that was Charlie. Again, he shook his head. When did this case become so complicated?

Max, I sense something.

The magus nodded, for he felt it, too. There was a sinister manifestation lurking close by, somewhere around them, fuelled by the hostility of his presence. His onyx ring warmed against his skin. Danger was near and almost certain.

But it wasn't the ring he found unsettling. The entirety of the Bloody Angle was evacuating the street, as if they were aware of the danger Max had yet to discover. All hastily retreated inside the nearest buildings, closing the doors and shutters behind them with bangs.

What's happening? Charlie asked, also watching the curious sight unfold. *I understand their discontent is almost palpable, but this behaviour is a bit rude. Even for Chinatown.*

But Max didn't have an answer. Instead, his focus turned to the rooftops. Beady little eyes glinted in the moonlight, dozens of crows perched themselves along the edges of the buildings. Silent sentries, all seemingly with the mage in their sights, and more gathered by the moment.

Max looked at the palm of his right hand, branded by the rogues many decades ago. He gripped his wrist as the old wound began to throb once again, like a phantom pain. "Do you see them, Charlie? The hundreds of crows above us."

What crows? Charlie asked.

"Look again," Max demanded. His spectacles, designed to reveal hidden magic, couldn't even distinguish if the birds were real or part of some malicious spell. He only had his instincts and Charlie to rely on. And right now, his instincts screamed danger.

Besides the vermin, you are the only living thing on this street.

Max flailed in pain as he grabbed his right wrist again, as if someone just hammered a railroad spike through his palm. It was an agony he hadn't felt in a lifetime. "No," he screamed. His eyes went wide in fright as he watched the marking of the Murder Society slowly sear itself onto his soft flesh once more.

He heard the cries of Charlie, but it was no use. He swore he had rid himself of the monstrous mark long ago, but he was only a fledging magician then. Perhaps his magic wasn't strong enough to break it entirely. Returning to Chinatown must have aggravated the long dormant mark back to life, he realized too late. He blamed himself for his lack of foresight. The residual curse was always there, even after the wound was long gone.

"I made a grave error coming here, Charlie," he confessed, through gritted teeth. He revealed the branding to his brother. "The curse has returned. The crows—they're aberrations, which only a curse-bearer can see."

What can we do? Frustration battered Charlie. He had to take his brother at his word. He saw nothing, sensed only ambiguous magic. He only saw the terror expressed on Max's face, and Charlie knew the man feared little.

"I'm a deserter," he said. "The punishment is always the same." The implication was clear. "I have to get indoors," he whispered, careful not to further disturb the crows above. Each creature turned their head in unison as the magician slowly made his way to the nearest door. He tried the handle, but it was predictably locked. He heard the protests from the other side, but he'd rather taken his chances indoors than on the street. "Unlock," Max casted under his breath.

But the people inside offered him no safe-quarter. He was met with knives and cleavers and a volley of angry fists from angry men. They manhandled the magician, tossing him hard back onto the street. The man was marked. They had seen it before. Max was met with the same hostility next door, and at the building across the narrow street. No one would help. Chinatown had abandoned the man to his grim fate. And to aid him would have condemned them to the same fate.

Max didn't even have to look up to know the birds were in motion. He heard the caws of an unsettling choir as the nightmares left their perches and trapped the magician inside the eye of their feathered hurricane. "Dispel," Max commanded, but the birds were not an illusion. He felt talons tear at his shirt and pull at this beard. They were real enough to draw blood. Max tried his best to shield his face with his arms, but there were too many. He summoned a gale of wind to blast them away. Dragon kites were torn from their tethers, garbage and debris smashed against buildings. But the birds were unaffected, and continued to peck and tear at the magician with their talons.

Charlie watched as the wounds on his brother manifested out of nowhere. It was clear Max was under attack he couldn't see.

Curses were brutal magic, intimate, nearly unique to each inflicted. Even when properly prepared against, a defence was never guaranteed to work, and he was completely caught off-guard like an amateur. Max was blinded by their black fury, and stumbled up the street into one of many puddles of filthy water. He knew of a spell, a very unreliable spell, which would turn any small body of water into a portal. He had learned it from a gentleman thief in London who stole jewels while entertaining women, and who used glasses of wine to send his ill-gotten gains to his apartment. But the spell was designed to work with two fixed locations, and certainly not for a person. Blindly jumping one way into the portal could send him to any other body of water in the world, including the bottom of the Atlantic, or worse, it might simply drown him within its magical confines.

But Max had no defence against the curse. He had no other choice: it was either flee and possibly die, or simply die where he stood. With a few Roman incantations, the puddle of water rippled before him. As he readied to flee, the horror of drowning almost overwhelmed him. But he had no time to hesitate. He had to face the fear and do it anyway. Max clasped his wolf's head cane to his belt and jumped right in feet first, praying the birds wouldn't be quick to find him again.

CHAPTER SIX: THE ELECTRIC CIRCUS

Max felt himself sink deeper and deeper into the black oblivion. Downwards he went, twisting his body in an attempt to slow his momentum, but it was of no use. An unseen force tugged at his body, dragging him further down into the abyss. The air in his lungs screamed for release, and the horror of drowning alone in that nothingness bombarded his mind. He flailed violently, struggling to retain some resemblance of control. But there was none to be had. He was like a rock thrown into an ocean.

A strong torrent of warm water painfully thrust at his body, jerking him into the opposite direction. He no longer sank, he was rising with great momentum. He felt like an arrow released from a bow. Upward he shot as his body spiralled towards a light that grew brighter and more intense the faster he went. Had he found his exit; was this to be his end? He just knew his tortured lungs begged for fresh air, and he was unable to deny them anymore. As the light nearly claimed him, the magical, watery world that contained him grew hotter.

A moment later, Max saw a flash of thick, dark-skinned legs as he was ejected into a steaming hot bath already occupied by another. Max erupted from the water, gasping in as much air as his lungs would allow.

Warm, sudsy water exploded everywhere in the small bathroom, as if the club-foot tub had been hit by a mortar shell.

Max gripped the porcelain rims and hoisted himself up, trying to gain his bearings. His extraordinary long beard just slopped around like a wet towel beneath him. He found himself staring into the terrified eyes of a portly, black man beneath him, as naked at the day he was born. The man's jaw fluttered he tried to scream, but his voice failed him. As quickly as Max had arrived, the black man escaped the bathroom and thundered down the hallway, screaming as if he had just seen a ghost.

That was… different, Charlie said, reappearing by his brother's side.

"And he had the right idea," Max returned, exiting the bath. "Time to go before he returns with an angry mob."

Charlie laughed. *Return? He's halfway to Staten Island by now.*

His brother was probably right.

Max peeped outside the bathroom door. He saw a homely hallway with a red, diamond print carpet and several numbered doors, and surmised he was most likely in an apartment building. He could tell by the décor he was not in a wealthy part of town. But the coast was clear. He scurried two rooms down, leaving a trail of wet boot prints in his wake, and quickly rapped on the door with the top of his wolf's head cane, listened, and after a quiet moment, decided no one was inside. With a quick spell the lock gave way, and he was inside a single, sparsely decorated room no larger than the bathroom he had just left behind.

It had one solitary window facing another brick wall, a dresser and a bed. A pair of soiled work boots and crumpled pants were discarded in the corner, and several sweat stained, linen dress shirts hung in the closet. It was undoubtedly the room of a labourer, and the place reeked heavily of a terrible cologne.

The occupant must have just left for a night on the town.

"Is the scent strong enough for the dead?"

No, but the way you're wrinkling your nose tells me you disapprove.

Atop the unmade bed, Max found the man's post, and he quickly surveyed it for an address. "A bit of luck has found us, Charlie. We are still in New York, and luckier still, only a few blocks from Chinatown."

And what good does that do you? If you've been cursed, wouldn't the same thing happen again?

Charlie made an excellent point. The bravado of approaching Chinatown directly had nearly killed him. He had no trinkets on his person that could ward off a curse, and his complex magic was rusty, at best. The price of being an artificer. Max knew he would have to adopt a different tactic, one he wasn't so keen to do with little preparation, but he was out of ideas. He locked the apartment door, and used his index finger to trace a hexagon across the wood, magically sealing it. Time, he had; but he also needed privacy.

He began riffling through the occupant's dresser drawers, shifting aside knotted socks and scrap books, until he found a straight edge razor. "The curse's magic works a bit like the spell that connects us together. If children stray too far from the Inverted Church, the curse would eventually kill them," he said, peeling off his drenched pants and shirt, revealing a hundred self-inflicted scars.

The Inverted Church? Charlie asked. *Then how did you survive?*

"I asked myself that very same question, for years. Lynn Lin of the Golden Dawn is a master of curses. She theorized our mother's Romani bloodline somehow nulled some of its dark power. I kept my distance, from Chinatown, hoping that would serve to keep the curse dormant. But, fifty years, Charlie," he said, shaking his head, "magic, it... can decay over time-- weaken, sometimes it can dispel itself, like the bursting of a bubble. But the moment I returned to the source, the curse... it--"

He looked down at his palm, wondering if lobbing off his hand would have been within reason.

Surely, you have something-- some trinket of yours, that could help.

"There's no time to go back across town. I'll have to break the curse right here."

How? Charlie dismayed, then he eyed the razor. *Max, not a blood ritual.*

The magician simply nodded. He sat down in the centre of the room, and folded open the blade. The clean metal caught a glint of the ceiling light. "It was reckless to return to Chinatown unprepared. I won't make that mistake again. This is my only defence against the curse."

But it's barbaric.

"Duly noted," he agreed. "Just be thankful you weren't around when I first learned this in the Congo. But, from here on, do not speak, Charlie. Not matter what happens. This is nothing like the locator spell back at the apartment. If I lose my concentration here, I will die."

He closed his eyes and turned his focus inwards. His heart still pounded from the attack in Chinatown, but without potions to slow it down, he had to rely on basic breathing techniques of meditation to control the blood flow. But placing himself into a wakeful slumber was a feat nearly impossible to do when he also had to mutilate himself with surgical precision. His mental fortitude had to be like steel.

Max never spoke of the Congo. He learned brutality through the Murder Society, the evil of men from the Great War in Europe. But Africa was its own animal. For a time, he lost his humanity so far removed from mankind. He had hunted wild beasts and man alike with spears and knives, drunk their blood, tasted flesh.

He had lived amongst the Mahari tribe, learned from them. They were brutal and violent, most of all, cultivated. In the darkest wilds, as tribal enemies were sacrificed to spirits far from Christianity, bodies were pulled apart, drained of every drop of their being. The more violent the killing, the more powerful the blood. The heart was the richest of all, and used only for the darkest of magics.

He had practised with so much blood in his lifetime, Max saw it the way other artists saw oils or clay: to be canvassed or shaped.

It was a forbidden art, not unlike necromancy, and his relationship with the Golden Dawn changed significantly after they discovered the truth.

It took considerable will to break from the Congo, to return back to the civilized world. The one he had left behind was lustful and liberating. No laws bound him; it was merely surviving through power and fear and respect. But then there came a point when there was nothing left for him to learn. The killings, the mutilations had become too much. In the darkest depths of the darkest jungles, Max nearly lost his self. He had to come home.

He had returned to civilization as a master of blood magic, deciding to rarely use it. There was always a price to pay. He had witnessed too much pain and suffering, and chose instead to hone the craft further through harming himself, instead of others. Out of that came a magical hybrid of both worlds, his spells and their rites, one that left his humanity intact. There was still pain and mutilation, and blood-- so much blood, but now it was only his risk to take. And, if it killed him, he could live with that.

Max felt the cool metal slit open the soft flesh of his left breast. The warmth of the blood felt like bath water as it flowed down his chest. The blood against his skin triggered a past memory of being impaled in Paris, and it nearly broke him out of his trance. But he swallowed the panic down deep, and just focused on his body. He told himself he was in control, not the fear. Fear would sour his blood, taint it. Instead of breaking the curse, he could amplify its power, or even kill himself.

He smeared the blood all over his chest with his right hand. The blood was cool and slippery to the touch. His torso swayed in a rhythmic circle, as if to an unheard beat, and he rotated faster and faster. His head gyrated with the movement, his eyes shot open and rolled into the back of his head. With his left hand, he cut himself again, this time with a serpentine incision from his throat to his navel. His body, once pale, now shone in the room's soft light in a crimson hue.

Max began his chanting in a Yaka dialect, but every word brought him immense pain. Something was wrong.

His body convulsed and twitched, his eyes throbbed, his breathing grew laboured. He had lost too much blood.

A vision of the girl with blonde, curly hair flashed in his mind, one left by Uriel. He then found himself back at the Nightshade, as it burned down around him. His mind frayed. His thoughts came like lightning. To break the magic right then would have been equally hazardous, but he was losing control.

Fear had him. He could feel it rotting his blood to bile.

He hastily scribbled an image of a great lion with his fingertip on the floor, a Mahari ward for bravery, in a pathetic and desperate plea to still himself; hoping, praying, it would grant him a few more precious seconds.

There would be no turning back. The spell remained incomplete— he hadn't even finished the sealing incantation, but if he didn't cast it at that moment, he was going to die.

He lifted his bloodied palm off of his chest, and slammed it hard onto the floor before him with a splat. He steadied his hand as the blood began to boil and froth on the wood, thickening with each passing second. Every drop quivered to life, and joined into a singular pool of blood that rose from the wooden floorboards, and twisted itself into the perfect form of a serpent. The thing slithered its way over to Max, and then climbed over his lap, eventually coiling itself up his chest until it found his mouth; absorbing back every drop of blood it touched as it went. The blood snake stretched the magician's lips as wide as the serpent, and it forced its way down his throat, foot by foot, until it was completely gone from sight.

Max snapped out of his trance, coughing and gagging, resisting the urge to vomit it all back up, for that would have surely killed him. The conjuring felt heavy in his stomach, but he was already digesting the spell. Every spatter of blood the snake did not consume burned away into red steam, leaving not a single trace in the room or on his body. His self-inflicted mutilations on his breast and torso were already healing, leaving behind new scars. The danger had past. It was officially over.

He appraised his right hand. The scar tissue had faded considerably, and his hand's pigment, previously pale, deepened into a crimson hue. He now had a red right hand. The blood ritual was only a partial success. He had managed to sate the mark's power, but it would only be a temporary measure. The spell would not last, but he was still alive to try again. He looked over to Charlie, who hovered around to face him, wearing a mask of absolute disgust.

"What?" Max asked, as he wiped the beads of sweat from his brow.

That was one of the foulest things I have ever seen.

Max staggered back to his feet, still woozy from the ritual. "That was one of the tamer spells," he tried to front his shame with humour, but Charlie was not amused. The magus took a moment to catch his breath before dressing. With a word, his clothes were magically dried and all remnants of the crow attack repaired. He retrieved his cane, and unsealed the lock on the man's apartment door. Leaving no evidence of his stay, he fled out of the window to the fire escape, sighing when he realized he was twelve stories up.

***

A Friday evening in New York felt like controlled chaos. A thousand perfumed 'dollies' and 'regal men' fled their abodes in search of vice and adventure, nearly toppling over one another in an attempt to be seen in the speakeasies with a risked cocktail and the promise of something more. It was the weekly night of desperation and disparity, one of seduction and deception. And Max was not one of them.

While he could have been home with a bottle of his beloved spiced rum, he, instead, hid across the street, and kept upwind from the Electric Circus: Manhattan's derogatory name for the largest vagabond camp on the island. Beneath the glowing, blue haze of a Tesla Industries billboard, beggars and shell-shocked veterans, failed men of industry, perverts, and the disturbed hung up their hats in the shadow of the Manhattan Bridge in a patchwork of shanties and coloured tents. Some begged for 'tricks', others for work.

Why are we here? Charlie asked his brother.

"There are over a hundred miles of tunnels underneath this city. It is how the thieves have operated for so long unnoticed, but with Tesla's electric subway expanding and burrowing its way through New York, the Murder Society is probably running out of places to remain invisible." Max pointed to the tunnel's gaping mouth on the opposite side of the camp. In my time, this was the back entrance to the Inverted Church, and that'll be my way in, taking me directly below Chinatown."

And avoiding it? Charlie insinuated.

Max simply nodded. "I can't risk another attack, not when I'm still recovering."

It was fair enough. *But how do you know this entrance is still being used? How long has it been?*

"Too long," he replied. But he pointed to a graffiti on the left side of the tunnel's entrance. "There," he said, motioning towards a painting of a caged crow. "They mark the way for the children. And, no doubt, they have eyes on that tunnel. Sentries, mixed in with the tramps."

Meaning you'll have to sneak your way inside.

Max shrugged. "I just have to make it to the entrance. Once inside, I could use the legends of this place to my advantage."

Legends? Charlie asked, but quickly caught himself. *Wait, I know this area,* he said, struggling for the memory. *I remember hearing about a terrible gas main explosion when Tesla Transit workers ruptured a pipe during demolition. It made the front page for a week. The entire city block collapsed into the tunnel... including—*

"The Church of Saint Germaine," Max finished. "Yes, the one our mother once belonged to."

That's the Inverted Church? Charlie gasped, making the sign of the cross on his chest.

Max nodded. "Even when it was above ground, no one would have dared step near that Romani church. Especially in this neighbourhood. Nearly everything that collapsed was laid to ruin, except for that building. It remained perfectly intact after it fell. The Irish workers called it an omen, and left it where it dropped. Even the Chinese refused to the repair those tunnels, thinking them cursed."

And everything was rebuilt on top of it; they buried a church? Charlie's tones were hushed.

"And not all of the bodies were recovered. Over the decades, the stories of that place twisted into things of lore, each tale more outlandish than the last. Some say the dead still walk those tunnels. Others swear some people survived the fall, and chose to remain, feeding on those foolish enough to enter."

And that's the idea, isn't it: 'omens' and 'curses' to keep people away?

"Except for thieves who have made it their home. Tell a story enough times, people start to believe, and those stories keep people away, including the tramps."

Charlie agreed it was clever enough to work. It was a secret so well kept, it was the first he had ever heard of the Murder Society below the city, or of the Inverted Church. *Even if you make it through the tunnels, then what?* he asked. *Passing through the crowd is one thing, Max, but to infiltrate a city of thieves? You're not exactly a child anymore, unless you have a spell to turn back time.*

"I'll offer them a trade for the girl," he said. He reached into his pants pocket, and removed a watch and a pair of cufflinks he had nicked from the apartment from before, but then he saw his brother's predictable look of disapproval. "What?" he asked. "I *was* a thief."

Charlie gave the goods a closer inspection. *The watch doesn't even work. You present that to trade, and those thieves will probably do something far worse than brand you.*

"You're right," Max said, and begun muttering an eighth-century Persian incantation from Jābir ibn Hayyān. Charlie watched as the tarnished metal of the pocket watch and cufflinks transmuted into what looked like gold. "Before you ask, no, it's not real. Just an illusion. Alchemy is absolute and utter malarkey. All magi know that."

But someone within the Murder Society knew how to cast a curse. Someone inside knows magic.

"A curse's power can exist for centuries, and the witch who cursed me was already in the winter of her life. I doubt she would be alive today." But of that, Max was uncertain. His mentor was alive well before Christ.

Sexton lived for a century. He knew magic can extend one's life, but at great sacrifices.

What about the girl? She's a magical creature. What if she is used to somehow prove you're a fraud?

That was an unsettling thought. He hadn't even considered her and, in any case, there was much for him to do before he found her. "One problem at a time, Charlie," he said.

In his day, the guild possessed a hundred thieves among their ranks. Older boys commanded them as lieutenants, but they were nothing more than brute force to keep the children in line. Knaves ruled over them all, and were the oldest of the guild, normally children who survived acts of violence and cunning long enough to grow up. They would certainly stand in his way from finding the girl. "But I do know this: the Murder Society speaks only one language, and that is of greed. If I have to 'turn' the whole damned Inverted Church to gold to win their trust, so be it. The stakes of this case are far too high."

So, you're going to con a guild of thieves into thinking you're an alchemist? What could possibly go wrong?

That made Max smile.

The blood serpent twisted uncomfortably in his stomach. As long as the summoning was still being digested, the curse burned onto his hand would remain inert. But since the ritual was rushed to save his life, time was now against him, and he had spent enough of it scouting the Electric Circus that evening.

But howling caught the magician's attention. An old crone, draped heavily underneath a tattered shawl, flaunted a deck of tarot cards to a young Chinese couple who were either brave or foolish enough to have stumbled down that particular block. "Come back, come back," she pleaded, in a heavy Slavic accent. The couple hastened their step, but it only incited a fury among the tramps as they passed. One took up a tin washing bucket, and beat it relentlessly in a poor percussive performance, hoping his misguided attempt at music would win him a coin.

But the drummer might as well have been sounding an alarm. The clanging of the metal thundered throughout the camp. A dozen destitute sprang from their shanties, ravenous for charity. Max watched as the black-haired man tried poorly to shield his lover from the brutes, but he was no match against their numbers. He was thrown to the ground and viciously trampled and mugged. The woman screamed as they tore her rings from her fingers, her necklace, and her purse.

Max, you must do something!

"If I interfere, they'll kill me," the magician said, clenching his jaw.

The frail woman struggled to help her lover back to his feet. Some of their assailants no longer cared about their prey, and broke off back to camp. Those desperate men were desperate no more, for they had their prize and pummelled each other for whatever treasures lay within the purse and wallet. But the men who remained behind eyed the woman like a rare jewel. They wanted a prize of a different nature.

Charlie saw it, too. *Max,* he screamed, nearly begged.

Max saw the frustration of helplessness on his brother's face. As a ghost, Charlie could rarely interfere with the world of the living. He was a moral man, naïve, but earnest. Charlie believed everyone was inherently good, even after being butchered by cultists in Bombay.

Even after years of Max inadvertently drawing Charlie deeper into his savage world, the magus knew his younger brother never lost hope that one day the magician would follow his example.

But after fighting in the Great War, Max knew there was no hope for mankind. He did not share in his brother's optimism. As he watched the vagabonds brace to tear the woman asunder, he was certain they were all irredeemable. And that made things much easier for the magus.

Max was tired of watching horrible people do horrid things. He was tired of holding himself back. It felt like he was living in a world made of paper. Any misuse of power would have torn everything around him into pieces. His trinkets were singular by design. Each one served a specific task, and were often useless once the magic had been spent. But spells, he could cast all day.

In the days before Tesla made electricity accessible to everyone, lightning was one of the most difficult spells to master, even if the conditions were right. A mage would tear it from the clouds, channel the power through his body and blast it from his hand or wand. But the world shifted into an expanding era of technology. Electricity pulsated through nearly every city, every building, and every room. It was merely there for the taking, so Max reached out towards the Tesla Industries billboard and beckoned its power to his will.

The entire structure rattled. The surge burst every glass bulb into glinting shards. And then it came: streams of white hot electricity ruptured from the sign, and found the fingertips of Max's left hand. With his right, the magician held forth his wolf's head cane at the assailants like a pistol, and its tip unleashed the torrent of lightning. His entire body prickled like needles as he guided the electricity internally, being careful not to stop his own heart.

Faster than the eye could follow, streamers unleashed chaos around the Electric Circus, which namesake then became quite literal. It reminded Max of the Fourth of July over the Hudson River, for white sparks erupted like fireworks from within the camp. The men recoiled on the ground as they were burnt from the inside out.

The woman grabbed her husband, and fled the nightmare crackling behind them. They were safe, at least, but Max could not say the same for the rest.

He was lost in concentration, but risked a smile when he saw the same bastards who had robbed the couple nearly fall over each other in a pitiful attempt to flee from the hell unleashed upon them. But what was good for the goose, he thought, as he shifted his cane towards the entirety of the camp. The lightning decimated everything it touched in a volley of flashes. The spell charred flesh, but anyone caught in its blast had a chance to survive, he knew, for the lightning lost most of its strength as it left Max's cane. It was the nature of the spell. Yet the power felt intoxicating as it rippled through his body. It was something he hadn't felt in a long time. The entire city block was thrown into darkness, as the last of the electricity was siphoned from the billboard. But Max wasn't finished.

He reached down and scooped up a handful of dirt in his hand, held it out before him, and blew it into a puff. The tiny cloud fell to the ground and rotated faster and faster until it spun itself into a funnel. It doubled in sized, tripled, and before it even reached the middle of the street, it had intensified into a twister reaching up as high as the roof of the Manhattan Bridge.

The wind howled like a banshee. The tornado shredded through the camp like a buzz-saw, not a thing nor person escaped its grasp, and Max grinned as he trailed behind it every step of the way towards the tunnel entrance, protected from his own incantation. He felt powerful, he felt like a god, and the Electric Circus was his Sodom and Gomorrah.

What are you doing? Charlie screamed, his voice nearly drowned out by the maelstrom.

"You wanted me to help that couple?" Max shot back. "I'll make sure these people will never harm anyone ever again."

Not like this!

The magician turned and saw the look of horror on Charlie's face. It was then Max knew he had gone too far. All around him, he saw, not just men, but women fleeing in terror, the infirm, and the elderly. Families. He had condemned them all for the actions of a few. They were bloodied and burned. Whatever little they owned, Max had just destroyed in one moment of hubris. He had just made their terrible lives even worse.

Max remembered why he relied so heavily on his trinkets. Being singular as they were, they helped to keep him in check. Magic, real magic, was the ultimate seduction, one easily abused like any other drug. His only vice was liquor. Max would never be an addict. It was a promise he made to his mother long ago, one now broken. He snapped his fingers, dispersing the tornado into a harmless gust of wind. But it was too late. The damage had already been done. The Electric Circus was no more.

Max heard strained, weary voices scream for help from the darkness, the shrill of children crying for their mothers. It was too much. A memory of Bombay flashed in his head, recalling his worst day and his darkest secret. But Max heard everything as he stood at the threshold of the tunnel, with his back towards the remnants of the camp. He refused to turn around. He refused to face the reality of the destruction he had wrought upon those people. He knew the right thing—the only thing—to do was to turn back and help, but he was too ashamed to face them. Any of them. Even Charlie.

Instead, he stared into the blackness of the tunnel before him, and heard nothing. Just silence. Silence was welcomed. A piece of charred debris fluttered into the folds of his shirt. Max plucked it from his person. It was a card from a Tarot deck, one of a slain man on his stomach impaled by ten swords. Max knew it very well. The card foretold terrible misfortune.

And so he walked into the darkness, letting the card slip through his fingers. He was no saint. He was no hero. Max Thanatos knew he was a monster.

CHAPTER SEVEN: THE LONG WAY DOWN

New York's underbelly was an ugly reflection of the world above. It was one of darkness and damp, stale air. His every step was met with sucking filth, and its grip held tight. Small Edison bulbs lit the way as the tunnel narrowed. Things in the shadows scurried around and above him. And everything smelled like rot. The confining quarters reminded him of the trenches in Ypres. The war never left him, and it was the one ghost he could never truly exorcise. It was like a splinter wedged deep within his mind. He learned to live with the pain. The booze helped a little.

A nearby rolling sound of a subway car triggered an old memory from the war. Max volunteered to fight for the British army long before his country joined the fray. The truth was, long before Charlie's spirit first revealed itself to him in his New York apartment, Max was still mourning over his brother's death, and he wanted to die. He just never had the courage to do it himself. But, no matter what Max did, bullets never found their mark. Max did whatever he could to place himself in harm's way. It earned him a soured reputation amongst the Tommies.

One day, he had charged over the trenches with the Union Jack waved high in the air. He wanted to be seen.

He wanted to be found. But what Max saw was a field of mangled corpses of hundreds of young men dead at his feet. He fought so hard to die, while others fought to survive. Crushing shame twisted his stomach, and he remembered how he ran. Max had experienced loss before, but he had never experienced death. Not like that.

The high-pitched squeal of subway car brakes echoed through the tunnel, and Max was lost again in Ypres. He couldn't ignore the vivid recall of the whistling mortar shell fired from the British side. He fled far behind enemy lines before his sanity had returned, and the blast knocked him hard into a German foxhole. When Max came to, he felt a frail grip around his neck. A German soldier, no older than a teen, was on top of him. Little fists pounded his face. Max saw tears in the boy's eyes. Not hatred. The kid fought to survive, and he reminded him of Charlie.

Max realized then he wasn't living for himself; he was living for the soul he harboured inside. The flurry of punches came no more. Max didn't know when it happened, but he had pierced the kid's neck with a trench knife. He remembered the weight of his body, the warmth of his blood as it spurted from the wound. The kid was the only person he had killed in the war. The British bombardment lasted throughout the night. The next day, the Germans retreated, but not before their chlorine gas burned his lungs. Weeks later, he was sent back home to America. The war was over for him, but it never truly came to an end.

The detective heard the urgency of his brother's voice through the nightmarish haze of his past, just in time to avoid an oncoming subway train racing down the tracks.

Max hugged the tunnel wall, and watched the machine speed violently by only inches from his face. As the last car rolled away, the gust left in its wake knocked his top hat from his head, and sent it toppling into the darkness, never to be seen again. Max was thankful that was all he had lost. The rumbling disappeared into the distance like a retreating storm, and the underworld returned, once again, to deafening silence.

He turned around to see his brother's incorporeal image floating before him. He expected another one of Charlie's tedious lectures, but, to his disappointment, none came. In a split second, they exchanged all they had to say without words. They knew each other far too well.

Shame about the hat, Charlie finally said. It was the first thing he had said to Max since the Electric Circus.

"I know," Max mourned. "It was a gift from Houdini."

***

Charlie heard the regret in his voice, which he knew was far beyond petty sentimentality. His brother lived a life of burden, and bore the weight of the world on his narrow shoulders that weighed him down like Jacob Marley from his favourite Dickens story. Despite always being by his side in death, Charlie knew Max still mourned. But what had happened outside the tunnel was a side of his brother he hadn't seen before. Max had always been selfless in his quest to save his soul, but it was a journey that had taken its toll. The search for the Devil had turned him a shade darker.

Charlie shook his head. No, he thought, it began long before. The death of their mother made Max bitter, his own murder soured his brother's love for life into cynicism, and the Great War turned him cynical towards the world. Max had killed, thieved, and lied, all for the sake of protecting him. How could he condemn his brother? Should he?

But Charlie had his own troubles to bear. He was a ghost trapped in the realm of the living. Hell wanted him, and Heaven wouldn't take him. That made him special for all the wrong reasons. He was a glowing beacon for other damned souls who had lost their way. While many were harmless, some sought only to wage havoc on the spirit for dark favours from dark things. There was a bounty on Charlie that some fought to collect, and that had brought his brother many troublesome days.

He often wondered if Max regretted ever saving him. Charlie had nothing but time to wonder. The ghost remembered very little about his murder. And the memories of his living self were also fading over time. Charlie didn't know what would happen to him if he lost what little humanity he had left. He probably would become one of those dark things as well. It wasn't a pleasant thought. Charlie tried to focus on the task at hand. He had drifted into his past, and it wasn't the time. Charlie frowned. He just then knew how Max felt during his own episodes. They were both haunted.

***

Max travelled deeper below New York, drawing ever closer to the girl. It felt like he was descending into Tartarus, itself. His every step brought him further away from the world above. The air was thick, and stank of moisture and natural earth. Smells he found oddly comforting. As he went further into the darkness, he could see old roots that had twisted their way through the cracks in the stone and trickled down from the ceiling. To Max, it felt more like he was traversing through a cave than anything man-made. Nature tussled with the modernity of New York.

Max never had reason to sneak into his former guild before, and the path ahead was hardly advantageous. Debris was left where it fell after the collapse, presenting Max with another challenge. The magus knew their alarm methods well: tripwires, bells, and false floors, so progress was slow as he waded through the clutter. A troublesome thing was the tunnel was straight and poorly lit. There were no maintenance shafts, nor divergences for cover. Even if he expected and prepared for an ambush, Max had nowhere to run; nowhere to hide.

He had no idea what made a man good. Integrity, intent, actions, words? Charlie was the closest thing to a good man he had ever known, and Max had lived for a long time. As he and his brother continued in silence through the tunnel, Charlie made sure to keep his distance ahead. But Max would catch him sneaking a glance back. That great man looked upon Max with utter disappointment. No, it wasn't that, it was something far worse. It was fear. If a great man like Charlie was afraid of his own brother, what did that make the magician?

I'll go further ahead and look around, Charlie said, and floated out of sight.

Max nodded. After his actions with the Electric Circus, he wondered if his brother would even be inclined to warn him of danger. No, he thought, shaking away the ridiculous thought. If there was one thing Max excelled in, it was burying such horrid feelings deep down within the recesses of his memory. It was an act of self-preservation that had kept him functioning. It was his one trick that didn't involve magic.

He had allowed himself the brief luxury of reflection, but it was a risky distraction being so far underground. Unlike the tunnel behind him, this area had been maintained. There were signs of stone masonry work. Load-bearing support beams reinforced what the Tesla Transit had abandoned long ago. Names of people were written all over the walls, hundreds of them, but as he passed under a dimly light Edison bulb, Max noticed the names of women were crossed out.

The lost or the fallen? he wondered.

As he continued, the ground softened beneath his feet, and muddied into brown puddles of standing water. Max saw no pipes lining the walls, and the Inverted Church was nowhere near either river. But a persistent, unnatural chill filled the air, and his thumb ring began to burn. "Charlie?" His brother vanished as the cold around Max formed his exhalation into a mist.

The main misconception about Hell was that it was a damnation of fire and brimstone. That wasn't true, it was a plane of unyielding cold. Hell was the absolute absence of God's love, so all unnatural things had its essence. The more powerful the creature, the colder it was. Charlie felt like an icicle. The tunnel felt like a Glaswegian winter. Some*thing* was near.

Ten minutes had passed since Charlie left to investigate the area, but Max was more concerned about the distance. His body was already beginning to feel the effects of their separation anxiety. It always began as a mild soreness, as if he had strained every muscle in his back. Soon, it would grow into a crippling agony, and eventually death. But Max had other concerns. There was a peculiar *clicking* noise saturating the air that Max couldn't quite define. And the coldness around him had become impossible to ignore. Frost coated the walls. He heard the crunch of his footsteps as they shattered thin sheets of ice forming on the wet ground. Then the Edison bulbs dimmed one by one until there was nothing but darkness.

Max blindly followed the sound, weary of summoning a light to guide his way. It wasn't mechanical, but it was a noise he had heard before, once in New Orleans, when a malicious spirit broke through the veil. It had created a friction in the air, the very same *clicking* resonating right then. He had to take the risk. He whispered an incantation to summon an orb of light, but it did not obey. He removed a silver lighter from a pants pocket, but the fire did not catch. The mage was thrown into an unnatural darkness. He was fighting blind.

"My Master knows you," a voice croaked. It sounded like a thousand whispers ushering at once. "Max," it teased, with a gargling sound resembling something of a laugh. "I know you, too."

"I just have that kind of face. Shame I can't see yours," Max replied. He focused on his thumb ring. He couldn't see the creature who taunted him, but the ring could detect it. As he rotated himself in place, the ring felt warmest facing what instinct told him was the north. Max remembered a pile of masonry stones in that direction. He then heard a sloshing noise as something slid across the room. The ring now burned facing the south. It was toying with him. He caught a whiff of the thing as it passed. It smelled heavily like the East River at low tide.

"What are you? Who is your Master?" Max asked, hoping to play to all evil's sense of vanity.

"All men know Him," it retorted with another phlegm-like laugh.

His body shivered uncontrollably in the cold. "Did the Devil send you?" Max tried again, but no reply came from the darkness. He decided to try a different approach. "If you know who I am, then I'm sure you know what I can do. Dispel this darkness, and I promise you mercy." Max heard it shuffle in the dark. "But if you persist with this tiresome game, I will show you why most creatures know my name."

"I fear no human. Not even you."

Max felt something thick like a fire hose bludgeon him hard in the chest. The impact knocked him back, but he managed to keep his footing. He fought to fill his lungs again with air, which was thick with the stench of low tide. The creature was close. A second blow whipped him in the ribs. The pain was excruciating. Max dropped to one knee. It hurt to breathe. Did the blow break a rib? No, he thought. It was something else. He had been separated from his brother for too long, the pain tore through his body. He was close to dying. "Not now," he begged, under his breath. But the creature must have heard him. More of its cackling taunted the air.

Max calmed himself as best as he could. He had to think. Clarity was a mage's best defence. The station was dark and cluttered; he knew nothing about his assailant, except for its insipid laughter and foul scent.

It was quick, he knew, and he surmised it kept close to the ground. He knew a few spells to slow it down, but he had to see the creature to bind it. Frustration mounted again. It was hard to concentrate through the pain, but he, instead, focused on the thing's attacks. He had been hit by something tangible. Max smiled. That showed promise. He knew the creature stalking him had flesh. If it had flesh, it could be wounded, hopefully even killed, and that was the edge he needed. Max reached into one of his many hidden pockets sown into his black vest, and removed a splinter of wood from Yggdrasil, and none too soon. His thumb ring singed his flesh. The sloshing noise thundered throughout the tunnel. The creature was done toying with its prey. It was now drawing in for the killing blow.

But the creature was too slow. Max slammed the trinket onto the ground, shouting an ancient blessing of Charlemagne. The splinter swiftly expanded into a twisting nightmare of branches encircling and engulfing every corner of the tunnel like an explosion of wood. Anything and everyone would have been decimated by the spell, which is why Max only used it as a last resort. As the sound of branches stopped creaking in growth, the mage heard a slight whimpering sound close by, like a wounded animal breathing its last breath. The spell had found its mark. Max called upon the orb of light once more, and this time it obeyed. The darkness gave way to the light, and it revealed a tangled growth that had impaled everything it touched: machines, walls, and a creature Max had never seen before. It had a soft body with translucent, grey skin. It was a large fleshy mass, and didn't appear to have any bones. The creature hung limply from the branches like a coat on a rack, and it was bilaterally symmetrical with six tentacles. To Max, it resembled an octopus, but its face was most alarming. It appeared human.

Max turned the branch to ash with just a touch, and the reaction continued to every inch of the wood until there was nothing left of the spell. The creature's blubbery weight splattered as it hit the ground. Max flexed his right fist again and again. His body was going numb. But even on the threshold of death, Max was curious. He ignored the pain coursing through his body, and examined the creature up close. Its opaque eyes stared vacantly at the magician. Max opened its jaw to reveal rows of shark-like teeth. Its tentacles were barbed. Max considered himself fortunate he hadn't been skewered in the brawl.

Max, there's trouble, Charlie warned, appearing through the tunnel wall.

He painfully returned to his feet using his cane for support. "You're a bit late, Charlie," he said, this time as a whisper. It hurt too much to scream. He dismissed the orb as power returned to the Edison bulbs, and light cascaded on the blubbery mess sloshed at his feet. "I already took care of it," he said, poking at it with his boot. The wintry chill of his demonic adversary had finally dissipated, along with the pain. He would live to fight again.

No, Charlie urged, *there are other spirits here, dozens of them. All around us. The spirits of children.*

"What are they doing?" Max asked, clenching his cane, bracing for what was next.

They're all pointing at you.

But Max realized too late the attack was coming. The Edison bulbs flickered around him. In the corner of his eye, he registered the shadow of a small figure tossing what must have been a live wire into the water near his feet. It felt like a German stick grenade had exploded inside his body. But before the pain could register, the shock had blown him back several feet, and rendered him unconscious.

CHAPTER EIGHT:
EVERY BIRD IN ITS PLACE

It was a long and trying return to consciousness; his insides felt like a fried fish on Friday. Max awoke inside a man-sized birdcage suspended over an endless black pit by a central chain; one that didn't look like it would support his bodyweight for long. He threw himself into a panic, inadvertently causing the rusty cage to sway violently to and fro, an action Max immediately came to regret as the chain groaned in protest. As his prison spiraled around, he caught glimpses of a sandy-haired boy and a dark-skinned child standing watch on a platform several yards away.

"Hurry, get Mista Fey," the sandy-haired boy commanded, and watched as the child vanished into the adjacent tunnel.

Max guessed Mister Fey was their master, or, at the very least, his jailer, and he knew he probably didn't have very long to get his bearings before the new problem presented itself. "You there," Max called out, gripping the bars of his cage, "help me down." But the sandy-haired boy simply turned his back. Max hadn't expected it to be that easy, but at least he now knew the boy was no ally.

"Mista Fey told me I'm not supposed to talk to you."

The cage slowed its excessive swinging, and Max was finally able to face the child. The cage was too small to stand; the tall man could barely sit upright. He had been stripped naked, his cane was taken, even his ring. The coarse metal was cold on his skin. His every adjustment for comfort inflicted a new scrape and bruise on his tender flesh, but he finally managed to manoeuvre himself into a better vantage position.

He couldn't see the bottom of the pit, but a fall from that height surely would kill him. He saw other cages suspended from the ceiling. From what he could see, his neighbours were rats and the bones they gnawed on. The large area had four other tunnels that led into the chamber. The walls were fitted with a cross-stitching of thick pipes, which splintered off into every direction. Most had valve wheels to control flow, and, by the stench of long-standing water in the air, Max guessed he was dangling above a rainwater run-off used to redirect excessive levels towards the rivers.

The cage door would have been a simple matter to undo, but even if he could escape the cage, he was too far from any ledge to jump, and he couldn't swing to safety without snapping the chain. Morbidly, Max admired his prison's efficiency. He saw Charlie floating next to his cell, frantically trying to speak. Some thing or spell had silenced the spirit, which, within itself, was impossible magic. Max knew he was truly trapped, and undoubtedly going to die, depending on his jailer's mood. "I'll make you a deal, kid: free me from this cage, and I'll help you flee from this place."

The boy defiantly turned back around. "I have no reason to help you," he said, pointing at the captive with a stump that was once his left forearm.

"Your arm," he said, motioning towards the wound, "I know what that means. They took it from you when you returned empty-handed." The boy didn't falter. "You'd reject freedom over the people who did that to you?" he stressed, with a practised sympathetic tone to win his trust, mindful not to antagonize the boy.

The child grimly surveyed his own affliction, and then simply looked upon Max with sullen eyes; eyes that reflected years of horrid pain and abuse. "Yes," he said, plainly. "I live to serve my keepers."

"Attaboy," thundered a gruff voice from behind the child. "That's the kind of loyalty I like to hear from my kids." The dark-skinned child had returned with a stocky man with wild, curly black hair, but bald completely down the middle. His crooked, hooked nose must have been broken and set at least a dozen different times in his lifetime. His white shirt was speckled with what looked like grease and blood. His eyes glared at the boy with a contained madness, as he affectionately rubbed his sandy hair with a strong, calloused hand.

Max wasn't even sure a gunshot could stop him. One punch from that man would have shattered a grown man's jaw, let alone a child's. Max knew his kind well. He was a brute. And, by his age, most certainly a Knave. The magus immediately found himself shouting, "I demand—"

"Shut your goddamn mouth," the stocky man screamed with unyielding authority. His voice thundered around the chamber, making him sound like an angry god. He turned his attention back to the children, and tightened his vice-like grip on the boy's head, torquing it towards the African. The man lowered his voice to a whisper, "Loyalty, I reward. Loyalty, I respect. So, I need to know if you are still loyal to me, young one."

The sandy-haired boy nodded.

"That's good," he said. "Yet I heard you talking with the prisoner, even after I specifically ordered you to keep that little mouth of yours shut," he bit.

"But he talked to me, Mista Fey. He tricked me," he pleaded. His eyes glistened with tears.

The man simply nodded. "Ah," he said. "He tricked you."

"Yes," the boy stammered, looking at his friend for support. But the dark-skinned child wouldn't dare defy his master.

"Don't look at him!" the man howled into the boy's face. "I'm the one talking. Me!" But the man's frenzy eased when he noticed the child had piss running down his leg. He just shook his head and shushed the trembling sandy-haired boy, drawing him in for a loving hug. "It's okay, if you said he tricked you, then he tricked you. You're just a stupid kid who didn't know better." As the boy calmed down, the man held him out at arm's length. "In life, we all make mistakes. Them's the breaks."

But the man dug his grip deep into the frail shoulders of the boy. His eyes glared like a carnivore cornering its prey, as he inched him backwards towards the edge of the pit. The child struggled against the man's might, but it was like trying to push back against an avalanche. "Yours was disobeying me, and I can't have discord amongst my kids." With ease, he pushed the boy over the edge, and down he fell into the blackness. His screams erupted from the pit until he splashed hard into a body of water below.

"You monster," Max screamed.

But the man paid his prisoner no heed. Instead, he stepped to the edge and listened. The boy screamed and begged and cried for help, but his shouts became muffled as water entered his mouth. Soon, only the thrashing sound of a one-armed boy trying to remain afloat was heard until there was no sound at all.

He turned to the only boy left in the room. "Now scram," he shouted, watching with a smile as the child nearly fell in retreat down the tunnel. "And tell the others what you saw." A moment later, the two adults were left alone. "Let me make one thing abundantly clear," he said to Max, but with his eyes still affixed to the darkness of the pit below. "I loved that boy... I did," he lamented, "I love *all* my boys. But it's true what they say: spare the rod, spoil the child."

"You didn't have to kill him," Max thundered back.

"Kill him?" the Knave repeated, incredulously, finally turning to look at the man in the birdcage. "Nah. I did nothing of the sort. I simply gave him a little push. Mama birds do it all the time. Sometimes the little birdies fly," he said, using both hands to simulate flapping wings. "Sometimes they don't. That one didn't. If the boy had both arms, he might have survived," the man shrugged. "But he failed as a thief and failed as my child. So his bloated corpse will simply spill out into the East River by morning, never to be seen again. And I will mourn his loss, as I've mourned all the others."

Max studied the Knave. The man was resolute with his barbarity. There would be no reasoning with him. "And what will you do with me?"

"Good question. With you, I'm not so sure," he said, pacing the platform. "My name is Augustine Fey. Men should know each other's names."

"I'm... Max, Max Thanatos," he hesitated to return.

"Greek?"

"Romani."

"Well, Max, my boys found you snooping around where you don't belong. That, we can't have. Me? I'm a reasonable guy. I believe in fair play. So it might have been an honest mistake, maybe not. You look like one of those dirty tramps from under the bridge, with that thing dangling from your chin," he said, mocking the man's long beard with his hand. "Maybe you stumbled down here three sheets to the wind, but that, I'm not so sure. This place ain't exactly easy to find, and I thought nobody'd be stupid enough to try. So my money's on being one of those brats' old man, looking to bring 'em home, or maybe you're a copper."

"Do I look like the police?"

Augustine laughed at that. "Nah. A bit old, I'd say. Pervert, maybe. But it don't matter what you are, Max. In the end, you'll probably be joining the boy for a swim. Depends on your tone. Keep me laughing, and you might just stick around for a while. But if I leave this room unhappy, no one's coming back for ya. You'll die of thirst long before you die of starvation, so you'd best have a reason to keep me here," Augustine warned. He reached into his right pants pocket, and removed a tarnished pocket watch. "You got sixty seconds."

Bastard, cursed Max. He wished then he was Houdini. No trap could ever contain him. Unfortunately, Max was just an artificer without his trinkets. "I didn't stumble into here by accident," he declared. "I know exactly where I am, and I know exactly who you belong to." He hoped his confidence would have struck a chord with the man.

"Good for you. Clock's ticking."

"You belong to the Murder Society, a guild of thieves as old as this city." Max said, observing the bastard, who didn't even flinch at the mention of the name.

"You brand every child's right hand with your insignia: a crow within a gear, signifying each child is a cog in your machine." The magus saw that got a reaction.

"Lucky guess. Thirty seconds."

"I bear the mark on my right hand. I was one of you. I bear the same curse. And, before you reached into your pocket, I saw that you do, too."

"We all do," he snorted. "Part of the deal. Ten seconds."

"I can break it," the mage bit.

The brute finally took his eyes off the watch. "Yeah, how?" Augustine dead-panned, not even bothering to hide his sceptical tone.

"I'm a magician."

His grin was gone. Augustine stood in place, and studied his prisoner with a stoic glance, revealing neither belief nor suspicion. "Nice knowing you, pal," he finally said, and made for the exit.

"Look," Max commanded, half-begged. The man had no reason to believe him: a naked loon trapped inside a birdcage, but his jailer turned around anyway, awarding him one last chance to win his freedom. In response, the magus gripped the bars of the cage with a fierce intensity, and muttered again the incantations of the ancient Persian illusion. The corroded steel slowly transformed into gold, and spread out until its entirety was consumed by the precious metal. And Max hoped the oaf wasn't smart enough to realize the weight of authentic gold would have snapped the chain like a twig.

But greed was the sickness of all weak men, and Max knew it immediately took to Augustine. He could almost see the machinations twisting inside the brute's bald head. "Free me, I'll break the curse, and I'll turn your entire world to gold."

"You saying I'll be richer than a Rockefeller?"

"No, dear sir, I'm saying you'll be so rich, even the Rockefellers would beg *you* for money."

Augustine clasped his hands together in delight. "See, now you're talking." But that delight quickly faded as he took a step into the long shadows of the room, which twisted his face into something sinister. "But you're not too bright, are ya? You missed us that much you just had to come back for more?" he asked, wagging his finger. "You got out of this place. You should have stayed there," he snarled. "See, I heard stories of the old days. Compared to now, you had it good. There's a new order around here, and you ain't going to like it. But you think that trick won your freedom? Nah," he said, shaking his head. "You've just gone and traded yourself one prison cell for another. You'll never see the sun again, that I promise you. Welcome back to the Murder Society, you stupid son of a bitch."

CHAPTER NINE: THE MURDER SOCIETY

Max learned his brute of a jailer wasn't so stupid after all. The magician's hands were shackled tightly behind his back, which would have been simple enough to unlock if he had the ability to speak, but his mouth was gagged with a cloth that tasted heavily of machine grease, barring him from his power. Spells weren't all waving one's hands about like a vaudevillian. Magic was more like verbally picking a lock; some spells were far more complex than others.

Augustine paraded him naked through the twisting corridors of the Nest. The thick, steel chains clanged with his every step. The younger children turned away as Max passed. They had seen this particular disgraceful walk several times before, so the nakedness wasn't why they averted their gaze, it was out of fear of the Knave that shoved him. The older lieutenants were the cruellest. They laughed as they slapped his buttocks and thighs, howled as they pulled on his manhood as he passed in vile acts of dominance over the lowly prisoner. Others yanked his long beard, nearly dragging Max to the ground.

Fey swatted the lieutenants away from his prize. "Back, you dogs."

But the older boys returned the insult with barks and howls, winning a smile from their master.

The magician had suffered far worse humiliations before, and shame was something that lessened with old age. Instead, he focused on how he would kill Augustine when the chance presented itself. Until then, he would endure the march. Finding the girl was the only thing that mattered. But he was in a poor position to rescue anyone, including himself.

The brute pointed to the tallest of the boys. "Where's my *daughter*?"

"We were told to bring her to Madame Doubleday, Mister Fey," he replied, surprised his master didn't already know. "The dinner bell rang when you were in the Aviary. You didn't hear it?"

"No." The boy got a backhand for his tone. Fey was no longer amused. "*I* told you to keep her separated from the others until she was processed." The man snorted like a bull on the verge of a rampage, but even he understood no one could refuse the sow Doubleday. Not even him.

Max knew "processed" meant preparing the girl for servitude before being distributed to the knaves as a chew toy. He guessed Augustine had just lost his prize.

Charlie floated in an uneasy silence, mouthing words Max didn't have the luxury to interpret. But if he were to guess, they were probably along the lines of an 'I told you so.' And Charlie would have been right. He was always right. His younger brother was aware of something he was not, that was plain, but neither men were in a position to have that conversation. The blood ritual had taken its toll on his strength, but with the incident at the Electric Circus and his battle with the creature in the tunnel, Max was beyond exhausted. His mind was sluggish, every fibre in his body cried for mercy. And now he was well behind enemy lines, without his trinkets, armed only with the wits of a man begging for rest. But there was no rest for the wicked, not in that place, and so he was marched on.

Max had been away from the Murder Society for a long time. It was like walking through a brave new world. He remembered a medieval place of lit lanterns and gruel and having to drink filthy rainwater that seeped down from above. In his day, they were scavengers, pillaging for any subsistence just to survive. Now, every inch of the Nest had been urbanized. Tapped water mains provided fresh running water. Above Max's head, multiple vacuum tubes shot orders to and fro in an intricate mailing system.

As he passed deeper into the complex, children chipped through bedrock with pickaxes, expanding their world even further beneath New York. Complex pulley systems hauled supplies and barrels of food to floors above and below. He walked past a galley, and the scents of seared meats filled the halls. Max even heard the cries of babies echo through the corridors. There was no telling how far this new Nest could have reached, but it could have been all across the city, now occupied by hundreds, if not thousands of children. They no longer needed the world above. The Murder Society had become more than just a guild of thieves, it was a thriving city.

But his generation was trained, disciplined, and treated better than property. They were assets. While the material side of the Nest had evolved into something better, Max saw shrouds of fear masking the children as he passed, tormented by tyrannical men stalking the halls like monsters haunting the dark, and he imagined Augustine was just the tip of the iceberg. But a pickpocket needed steady hands to work, not ones trembling in fear. Around him were a new generation probably more concerned with surviving the night than stealing from marks, and he wondered if this new utopia on the surface was really crumbling underneath.

Let it all come toppling down, he cursed. Max didn't have a single cherished memory from that place, except for escaping. But his masters had taught him how to live. Theirs were only teaching them how-to live-in terror.

"In here," Fey commanded, shoving Max down a long corridor, away from prying eyes. Once he felt they were alone, he removed the gag from the magician's mouth and continued. "Can you really break this curse?" he asked, looking at his own scarred hand.

"Yes."

"Then do it right now."

Max readied a spell to make the man swallow his own tongue. All he needed was another moment to catch his breath. "It's not that simple, I need—" He tried to finish, but got Fey's thick trunk of a forearm pressed up against his throat for his trouble.

"I don't have time to play games, magic man. You think this is all about the gold? I can have my boys steal whatever I want, when I want. Either you break the curse, or I break your neck," he seethed, shoving his branded hand into Max's face.

The magus struggled to speak, "I-I need something you took from me. My cane. With the wolf's head."

"That's it," Fey spat, his patience had been spent, and drove his boulder of a fist once into Max's solar plexus, then again, and with a thrust of his hip, delivered a third and final strike to the aged man. Augustine stepped back, and allowed his prey a moment to gasp in air.

The magician's mind spun like a top. His thoughts were jagged. The spell was lost in the haze. In-between sucking thick air back in his body, he wheezed, "It's enchanted. My totem. It holds all of my power," Max lied, but it was a fib he hoped would bring him more time. The air came a bit easier into his damaged lungs. "Reunite me with it, and I will break your curse. Do you have it?"

Fey looked at the man with more surprise than suspicion. "Yeah," he returned, uncomfortable with sharing that knowledge, "It's been sorted with the rest of the goods."

"Thank God," Max exhaled, with the spell on the tip of his tongue once again. But it was too late. The gag was shoved back into his mouth, and then he felt Augustine's thumb press up against his right eye.

"Do you also need your eyes to break it?" he threatened. "Because if you're wasting my time, I'll pop them like grapes between my teeth," he threatened, mashing his blackened choppers together. "But I don't got time to make two trips. See, I gotta talk to my boss about a girl. Just so happens, she also has your cane, so that means two birds, one stone. I'll bring you to it, then you'll do what *you* said, or I'll do what *I* said."

***

Max had finally returned to Chinatown, but beneath its streets. He crushed vines and weeds underneath his bare feet, which had wildly overgrown most of the natural bedrock. The magician would have thought the sight serene if he wasn't in such a frightful place. Max stood before the central chamber of the Nest, the wretched heart known as the Inverted Church. Two stories tall, the modest limestone building was older than Max knew. Its Gothic design had a Palladian arched window in the front of the structure, and thick ivy growing on its walls. Its once-pristine façade remained fractured from the collapse. A pair of copper-capped towers framed the structure like sentinels watching over the church. It twisted his stomach to know his mother once found religious solace within its walls. Now, it remained like a dead thing God had abandoned.

Max felt the warm, foul stench of Augustine's rotten teeth as he breathed upon his cheek. "You think you're the only one here with tricks?" the brute warned, with a tinge of anxiety in his voice. "You'd best mind your manners in there. I've seen all types in my day, but my boss?" he said, letting the last word linger. "She even gives me the heebie-jeebies."

Augustine knocked three times on the large wooden door and waited. A moment later, a series of latches were unlocked from the other side, and the heavy door creaked open revealing a figure draped heavily in a black cloak. The identity was hidden behind an antiquated plague mask, with its long crow-like beak and glass lenses. A man's muffled voice said, "Madame Doubleday is in ceremony and cannot be disturbed," and went to slam the door in his face.

"You miserable shit." Augustine wrapped his massive hand around the man's frail neck, and tore the plague mask off of his face, revealing the reddening, sheepish face of a ginger boy on the cusp of manhood. "You want to slam the door in *my* face?" He wrangled the ginger's head up against the frame, and gripped the heavy wooden door with his other hand.

"No, please," he squeaked, barely getting the words out from his crushed windpipe. The authority lost from his voice.

"'No, please,'" Augustine mocked. "Not such a bigshot now, are ya?" He saw the boy hastily shake his head. "I'll tell you what, you go and inform Madame Doubleday that I have a guest worth entertaining, and I won't use this door to bash your ginger head in. Deal?" The brute released his grip, and the boy immediately struggled to suck in air. But off he went, ushered on with a stiff kick to his rear end by Augustine as he went. With a grin, the brute turned to Max and said, "Some people forget their place."

Max was shoved through the door, and onward he was marched through the belly of the building. He had never been inside before. It was the inner sanctum of his former masters, a hallowed place said to be the end of all those who enter. The entire building smelled like incense and bird droppings. He couldn't even temper the stench by breathing through his gagged mouth. Its walls were lined with mouldy tapestries, the floorboards were warped with age. It was a place of decay.

Charlie flailed his arms with urgency, trying to warn Max of an unknown danger ahead, but Augustine continued to shove the magician deeper inside. He stood at the threshold of the sprawling worship chamber. The air was crisp like winter. There were no pews, no bibles, and no resemblance of a place of God. Instead, a hundred crows fluttered uneasily in birdcages that filled the entire room like tiny iron maidens. The chamber was hazy from the smoke of burning black candles, each positioned below a birdcage. Their flames heated the metal trays beneath the creatures' feet, causing them to slowly suffer as they constantly lifted one leg and then the other.

In the centre of the room were four tables. Each had an assortment of stolen goods being catalogued by the plague priests: money, jewellery, valuables, clothing, and, there, amongst the loot, was his wolf's head and clothes, and also with the assortment was his vest of trinkets.

Something stirred at the far end of the room, Max saw the ginger-haired boy from before whisper into the ear of a slender, dark-skinned woman, draped in a silken robe thin enough to be see through in the soft candlelight. But the woman became agitated, and gripped the boy's wrist. He tried pathetically to break loose, but she gripped a black feather from her altar and stabbed it into the boy's neck. The change was almost immediate. He winced and fell, clawing at his stomach. His skin blackened, his face went pointy. The bones in his arms cracked, his legs broke in two. As he collapsed hard to the floor, tiny black feathers coated his entire body, and further he shrank until he was no longer a young man, but a crow, fluttering its wings in a panic, as if trying to fly for the first time. In a tormented chorus, the other crows cawed their shared misery. All were cursed, like him.

"Meester Fey," she said, with a thick African accent, not turning to face or look at him, "You have disturbed me this late evening. Why?"

The knave was quick to answer. "Madame Doubleday," Augustine said, like an obedient child, "Look, I'm real sorry for interrupting your, um, ceremony, but I brought you a prisoner who can turn metal into gold. I saw it with my own eyes. He's a magician, like you." But the brute barely got the last word out before the woman's shadow had serpentined across the room, and lifted him up effortlessly by his neck.

The shadow was independent from the woman, but still acted to her will. Max had never seen magic like that before. He wasn't even sure she was human.

"No one is *like* me," she hissed, and slammed the man down to the floor.

Much to his disappointment, Max saw Augustine stir after the impact. That blow would have surely killed a weaker man.

The woman stepped away from the altar. Just on the edge of the candlelight, Max saw a girl, an early teen by his guess, bound to the slab of rock by spikes driven through her hands and feet. There was no mistaking who she was. Her blonde, curly hair was matted to her face from sweat. Her skin was olive. An image of Uriel's daughter flashed in his mind. He had found her. He had finally found the girl.

The slender woman raised a stone dagger high above her head. Down she drove the weapon, carving the soft forearm of the olive-skinned girl who struggled vainly to break free from her confines. Max saw the glistening glow of golden ichor trickle down the girl's arm. The woman lurched her head back, and then clasped her jaws down on the wound like a biting cobra. Heavily she drank, and Max thought the girl would have been completely emptied of her life elixir. But a moment later, the woman lurched back, and smiled as the girl's wound healed itself completely.

Max understood why it was a feast.

That was when the girl looked wearily up at the magician, and they saw each other for the first time.

"Augustine," the woman oozed, "I have decided to keep the girl for my own. She is unlike the others."

The man was in no state to argue, nor could he. He could barely move. But Augustine was a stubborn as he was durable. "With all due respect, that ain't our way. She's my kid to train."

"Your children are cattle. Nothing more. I allowed you all to play your games." She took the dagger, and drove it down through the palm of her right hand.

The blow was felt by everyone in the room, including Max, who dropped to one knee in absolute agony. His blood ritual wasn't strong enough against her magic. He even heard the unified screams of pain from the children outside the building, even far beyond the thick walls of the Inverted Church. Screams that echoed throughout the halls like a chorus of suffering. The curse linked them all through pain, akin to a vastly powerful voodoo doll. Any pain inflicted upon her would have been felt amongst them all, if she willed it. Any fatal blow would have been theirs.

"Your tools freed me from my earthly prison long ago. From its belly, I was reborn into a world of meat. And Mister Fey, I am forever hungry. So remember," she said, "that you and your *daughter*, and all of your children, are alive because I allow it." Her words resounded across the room, startling the crows. "Or should I simply feast on you all?"

She finally turned to face them. Her wrinkled skin was obsidian. Her sunken pupils were stone white, her hair was braided and coiled around her head like a snake. Her body was sickly thin, as if a rubbery layer of skin had been stretched taut over her bones and skull. Her body was a patchwork of grotesque scars that Max knew from experience were self-inflicted to punish others.

"You," she said, pointing a crooked finger at Max, "How did you feel my blessing? You are too old. You are not my child." She waved her bony hand, and the gag loosened and slipped from the magician's mouth. He had his words at last.

But a wiser man would have chosen his words with more care. "I'm here for the girl," he shot back, almost threatened, nodding towards the Fallen's daughter, earning even a curious glance from Augustine.

"No," she laughed. "She is food."

He had dealt with her kind before in the Congo: cannibals that fed on the flesh of their enemies, believing they'd absorb their power and strength. He had hunted with them, feasted with them. It was why the Cult of Ten Heads took Charlie's heart. The body had power. The diseased would drink the blood of children, hoping an unspoiled life would cleanse their impurities. "And I bet the girl's blood tastes sweet."

"Sweet like nectar!" the woman snarled.

Magi blood was far more powerful than a normal man's, but ichor's magical properties dwarfed that of even magi's.

The room grew colder with her every step as she drew closer to Max. As she passed the sorting tables, he noticed a tiny stream of smoke appeared from the pile of jewellery, as if a glowing ember had caught. Max saw its source. A ring blazed with such intense heat, it scorched the wood beneath it. Not just any ring; it was his onyx ring, burning in the presence of insidious evil. Whatever she was, it was no human. He had to break free, to give himself a fighting chance. But Max sensed her power from even across the room. Was she stronger than Sexton

Graves? Even more than Ammon? He couldn't tell. But her presence forced him to take a step back, and he used every ounce of willpower to keep from running.

"Unlock," he said, and he was finally freed from his bonds. When it came to power, Max was no slouch, either.

"Magic man," the woman squealed in delight.

Despite the hellish cold that bit at his naked body, despite the immense power that emanated from the figure, Max approached her. He had already experienced death too many times; Max had nothing left to fear. He saw Charlie trying to beg him to flee, but the magician knew he couldn't leave such a vile thing alive, especially one that treated children like livestock, one that cursed them into birds. Max balled his hands into fists. He didn't have to live a life of a saint to be a good man. He already had blood on his hands. But, while he was still alive, he wouldn't allow evil, any evil, to continue unchecked. To Max, he'd rather do good than be good.

But the magus wasn't the only one who had a revelation. Augustine, who had the moxie of a prize-fighter, and was already back to his feet. The broad man's nose was terribly broken again, and had shifted under his right eye. His face was bruised and swollen, his eyes watered. He bared his black teeth like a wolf. He had gone mad with rage.

"Thirty years of your madness. Since I was a tyke," he screamed. "I won't let you feed on my kids no more." He brandished a stained shiv from inside of his boot and charged at the woman like a freight train.

She didn't even defend herself. Instead, she turned fully towards him, and allowed his knife to penetrate her neck. But the blade did not pierce her skin. Max saw it cut through the back of Augustine's neck, like a mirrored reflection. The big man stumbled back, clasping the wound as it spurted blood with each heartbeat. The man couldn't speak, instead, he fell to the ground gargling his last words, which Max knew would have been as vile as the man himself. Strangely, Max felt pity for Augustine. If the magician had never escaped the Murder Society, he, too, could have been that man.

"A pity," was all she said.

But Augustine's death might have just saved Max's life, for it confirmed his hunch about the curse. "You must know why her blood is sweet," he said, nodding at the girl. "Magic runs in her veins, as it does mine. I've been casting magic since I was a small boy, so if you think her blood tastes like nectar, my aged blood would be as sweet as sugar. Even sweeter!" he taunted.

Max saw the woman's white pupils widen with gluttony. Much like Augustine before her, greed was the sickness of the weak, and it had claimed her too. "Come," he dared, holding out his forearm, "take it all."

But the woman swatted his arm away, and dug her fangs deep into his neck. He felt light-headed as the blood left his body with every swallow. And that was exactly what he wanted.

The woman recoiled back, sensing something was wrong.

"How does it taste?" Max spat.

She clawed at her throat.

"Spoiled?"

Blood dripped from her eyes and nose. She clenched her stomach as the blood worked its way down. She dropped to a knee, then fell onto her belly. "What have you done?" she screamed. Her voice was phlegmy, as she began haemorrhaging.

"Unfortunately for you, I, too, am a master of primitive magic," he said. "I spent a lifetime learning its dark, forbidden secrets. Including one particularly nasty spell that turns my own blood into acid."

"No," she wailed.

"Don't fight it, my dear. You're already dead."

She knew it as well. Her every cough spat out blood and torn, fleshy bits of her oesophagus. She clawed herself slowly towards the olive-skinned girl, desperately tried to grab out with her last bit of life. "Save… me."

Max stood over her dying body, still melting from the acid. "A pity," he mocked. "Your curse was brilliant in every way except one: you were vulnerable on the inside. Ponder your mistake as you freeze in Hell until the end of days."

But the volatile woman had crawled just close enough to dip her finger into the girl's ichor that had spattered onto the floor. Even a drop was powerful enough to begin healing her grievous wounds, much to Max's horror. His trick was not enough. Before his eyes, her body was already repairing itself. It would only take another moment for her to heal completely, and then another moment for him to die.

Terror had taken Max utterly; he just stood and watched as the woman became nearly complete again. She was too strong, and the girl's blood was too powerful. He couldn't stop her. Max didn't know how. His body quivered in fear. He wasn't going to survive this. That he knew. He saw the hideous face of the slender woman curl into a wicked smile, for she realized it, too. The naked and battered man had only one gamble left. There was nothing else left to try. He filled his frail lungs until they hurt, and let forth a thunderous cry, "Uriel, I have found your daughter!"

All of the room shook, and felt like the entire fabric of reality was vibrating itself asunder around Max. The birdcages rattled, the candles were nearly blown out. The stained-glass windows shattered to pieces. Max covered his ears in a pathetic attempt to block out the high-pitched wailing of a Fallen breaking through the space between spaces, but it did little to ease the intensity.

"What is this?" the woman screamed, and she crawled back to her feet.

The all-too-familiar blinding light washed out the room. It was the brilliance of a thousand daylights crashing over the magically-diseased creature that had once fed on the blood of children. Its heavenly power completely and utterly obliterated her into nothingness. Max saw the singular wing stretch forth and then wrap itself around the body of Uriel, standing over him.

"Where is my daughter?" thundered the Fallen.

Max pointed a shaky finger towards the altar.

Uriel put out his arms, and the spikes impaling the girl vanished. She floated into his embrace.

"How is she?" Max asked, looking upon the girl with concern.

Uriel cradled his unconscious daughter. "I will make sure she won't remember any of this," he said, tenderly, "and I've already healed the darkness in her heart. In the morning, her mother will find her sleeping in her bed. Neither will remember she was ever gone. Now tell me," he said, the tenderness in his voice boiled into fury. "Who did this to my child?"

"She was taken by a guild of thieves, but her torturer is no more. She was a creature of darkness. You killed her the moment you arrived."

But that wasn't good enough for Uriel. A father wanted vengeance for his daughter. Needed it. Someone had to suffer. "Then I will smite this 'guild of thieves' until not a single person remains," the Fallen proclaimed.

Max knew it was no bluff. "You can't," Max begged. "They're children, nearly all of them."

"I don't care," he said, looking at his daughter. With a single nod, the remaining plague doctors, who had been watching the entire ordeal from the shadows, exploded into bits.

"No," Max screamed.

"This no longer concerns you," he warned.

If the Fallen lost control, there'd be no stopping him. "Uriel," he pleaded, dropping to his knees. "I will forfeit my meeting with the Devil. In exchange, just spare all of their lives. Please, I beg of you. They're children," he stressed again. "Taken from their mothers, their fathers."

The Fallen looked down at the feeble man. As always, he was impossible to read or predict. But something must have struck a chord within the ancient being. He looked up, seemingly at nothing. "Father," he lamented. After an impossibly long, tense moment, he nodded. "I believe that ends our contract." In a blink, Uriel and his daughter were gone, leaving the two brothers alone in the Inverted Church.

But Max, your deal, Charlie finally was able to say, joining his brother.

But he flashed a weary smile at his brother, just happy to hear his voice again. "I must have just picked up one of your bad habits, that's all."

What bad habits? Charlie returned.

"Morality," he quipped. His voice was soft, defeated, but there was no regret. Uriel would have killed them all without hesitation, and he needed at least one happy ending that day. He would just have to find another way to find the Devil, he knew. But there was one thing he could do. "Unlock," he commanded. Each cage door sprang open in unison, freeing the crows from their torture, but not from their curse. But at least they were alive. "I was in a bad place without you," he said. "I needed you, Charlie."

His brother certainly agreed. *One minute, my voice was there, then it was gone. Silenced by a power I have never felt before. It was like a fire had gone out inside me. I haven't felt a presence that strong since Sexton Graves.*

They both looked at where the woman had been. "Maybe the spell died with her?" he asked, unsure. "She was unlike anything I have ever met before. She was monstrous, and I was weak," he admitted, "weaker than I'd ever been."

You went through Hell tonight.

Max dismissed the excuse. "No," he exhaled. "I'm just an old man."

You'll live for another hundred years.

Max just smiled. "No, don't wish that on me. Knowing myself, I'd *still* be looking for a way to save you, at this rate."

Charlie shook his head. *There was something else at play here, Max, but I'm afraid I'm too thick to see it. I missed something. We both did.*

"If *you* missed something, then all is lost," Max said, as he gathered up his things from the sorting tables. As he redressed, he noticed ichor was still fresh on the altar. With a just a touch, he could have healed his wounds from that day, his lungs, his old scars and weathered body. But he just shook the thought away. The pain was a reminder, that no matter how powerful he was or wasn't as a mage, he was still human.

At least we solved the case, Charlie said, trying to cheer him up.

"At least," he repeated, with a sigh. With its cruel masters dead, the Murder Society would struggle to fill the ranks. Perhaps many would use the opportunity as a chance to finally flee that wretched place, as he had. Tomorrow, he would reach out to his contacts within the police, telling them the guild was vulnerable enough to liberate. Perhaps they could even reunite the lost with their families once again, he thought.

Perhaps, the next time he passed the bakery, they'd be fewer posters on the window. Or maybe none at all.

***

The sun was already up by the time a worn and beaten Max finally returned home to his apartment, stinking of smoke and the New York underbelly, and the only thing on his mind was a deep, deep slumber. But there was a sound he hadn't heard in years when he walked inside: his Graham Bell was ringing. He picked up the receiver, and didn't quite remember how to answer, "Ah—yes, hello, you may speak," he stammered. A familiar voice came through, one he also hadn't heard for almost as long.

"Max," a man's voice said on the other side, "It's Theo. Houdini is dead."

BOOK II
-
THE DEVIL & THE MAGICIAN

CHAPTER TEN:
THE TURNING OF THE DAWN

The labourers worked under the darkness of the new moon. Shovels removed dirt loosened by the endless thrashing of their pick axes. They didn't tire, never ceased their work, for the dead did not care. Deeper they dug into the plot at the Trinity Church Cemetery; its covering made heavier by the snowfall; its coffin buried three feet deeper than most. The hardest part was breaking through the protective wards designed to keep out all manner of thieves. But their master was an academic of the arcane arts. He had seen the rudimentary wards before, authored by the Golden Dawn. To Sexton Graves, it was like dismantling a child's puzzle.

The shovel scraped against wood. His prize revealed itself at last. "Hurry," he commanded, eager for the treasure within.

With undead strength, the labourers easily pried off the coffin lid with their hands, revealing the skeleton inside, garbed in the remains of what was once its finest suit and tie. The black man's corpse possessed by Sexton climbed down the ladder to join the others, reached in, and separated skull from body. He cradled the trophy in his hand and smiled. "Hello, Charlie."

***

New York's Grand Central Station was vast and void of nearly all of the normal hustle of a Tuesday morning. Sunlight speckled through the windows of the vaulted main floor of the Vanderbilt Hall, chasing away the darkness of the vacant ticket booths and barren platforms. No porters ushered along brass carts, toppling over with luggage. No newsies bellowed out the day's headlines. Not even a steam whistle sounded, for only one train would arrive that early morning with a body destined for the soft earth of Machpelah Cemetery. It was to be a simple operation, but when it involved members of the Hermetic Order of the Golden Dawn, a secret society of mages tasked with the protection and study of the mystic arts, there were always complications.

The snow fell heavy and constant, and did little to keep the press away from the 42nd Street entrance. Max heard the dismayed shouts, offers of bribes, and threats invoking the "freedom of the press" even from across the other side of the Park Avenue viaduct, but the coppers were steadfast, denying them the rich bounty they sought: a photograph of the coffin.

But the panicked pleas of the press slowly hushed as the detective approached. It was a reaction he had grown accustomed to over the years. One by one, they turned to see a man akin to a demon, dressed all in black, emerge from the snow flurries with his long, pointed nose and waxed bald head visible whenever he adjusted his tall top hat. His extraordinarily long, greyish beard was wrapped around his neck like a scarf. His eyes were masked behind heavily tinted spectacles. His appearance ignited a fury of curiosity.

"Who are you?" asked a reporter.

"Are you a friend of the departed?" shouted a second, competing against the others.

Max was bombarded by more questions, as the press parted to allow the strange figure through. He tapped his top hat with the tip of his walking cane, its handle a wolf's head carved from Indian ivory. "Gentlemen," was all he said, as the bewitched coppers allowed him to pass into the building, much to the protest of others denied.

Seldom did Max consult for the New York police, and he did so with great caution. He preferred they knew nothing of his real work with magic, or of the numerous macabre trinkets sown into several hidden pockets all over his person. Instead, he used his knowledge of the occult to help those helpless against the supernatural, to bring light to where there was none. Working publicly as a detective allowed him to discreetly search out his own cases, and it made him far more approachable than advertising as 'master of the arcane arts.' To Max, it was better than rotting away in his apartment from grief.

Max was no sooner past the entrance when a portly man, with a thick Long Island accent, finally screamed over the crowd, "Did you know the victim?"

That stopped Max in place. "Victim?" he involuntarily replied out loud, damning himself for being baited. The question ignited a fury amongst the reporters. Harry Houdini's brother, Theo, had called him days ago to help escort the coffin from the station. That's all he knew. Yet the press knew more. Max found it humiliating. "Let the dead rest in peace, you vultures," he cut under his breath. With a sly flick of his finger, he summoned a powerful wind to torment the reporters, nearly toppling them over where they stood. The magus just shook his head despairingly and soldiered on, careful not to further fan the flames.

That was a terrible idea, parading yourself in front of the press like that, Charlie said. *I thought you wanted to keep a low profile?*

Max didn't appreciate the tone. "My enemies already know my face," he was emboldened by hubris to say. "The press are locusts. They will move on to feed on the next catastrophe."

Max, if just one of those reporters wanted to learn more about you, who knows what they'll find by overturning a few rocks. The press is one enemy you don't need.

The detective didn't bother to return his dead brother's worried glance, although it was hard to ignore his ghostly visage hovering about. "I am hunting the Devil; do you think something like the press intimidates me?" he bit out, white-knuckling his cane. "I have only one obligation, dear brother, and that is to you. Everything else is absolute pish posh."

But—

"If the press wants to burn the world down around me, so be it, Charlie. I have bigger fish to fry." The words came out more harshly than Max intended. He loved his brother more than anything, but frustration tore at him that day. Houdini was a great friend, one of the few he had left from the Dawn. After the war, they had lost touch. Houdini became a famous escape artist, and Max never saw him again. "I will be more careful," he finally said, and left it at that.

"Mister Thanatos," Max heard someone call from the other side of a vendor's booth. The detective recognized the Irish accent almost immediately. He was one of the detective's contacts within the police department, one who knew Max's secret, for they had fought together in the war. He was a confidant.

"Officer Ronan," Max returned. He saw the patrolman resting his back against the news stand. He was as wide as he was tall, with a bright ginger mane of hair bulging out from underneath his police cap, which he removed respectfully in the detective's presence. "Did the train arrive yet?"

Ronan fidgeted with his hat, rotating it in his hands. "Aon," he answered, in Gaelic, shaking his head. "Things went a bit mad when your friends discovered the body." Ronan respected the man, but always found him rather intimidating. He shied away from making eye contact. "Don't know much about it, myself. Something ghastly, I heard. I was asked to wait for you."

"Friends?" Max asked, ashamed to be the last to know once again. He was only to meet Theo at the station.

"The famous guy's brother, Theo Hardeen, and another fella. I didn't catch his name. Bald, like you— no offence," he quickly added. "They arrived not too long ago."

Max nodded, reaching into a vest pocket. "Here, I owe you for last time." He removed three tiny carvings of native women with colourful baskets, and held them out for Ronan to take. "You mentioned your daughter was having terrible nightmares. Place these Chilean worry dolls under her pillow when she goes to bed tonight. They will help."

The copper plucked them from Max's hand, flabbergasted by the gesture. "I can't thank you enough for this."

Max gave him a curt nod of his top hat. "Give your family my regards. I'll be seeing you."

The mage had never seen the train station as empty as it was that morning. It felt like he was trespassing on sacred ground, and it made him feel intrusive. His every step echoed across the marble as he made his way towards platform 13. Most of it had been cordoned off with white sheets erected like curtains. Privacy for when the body arrived… or was it for something more ominous, he wondered. He saw silhouettes of men fluttering about on the other side of the sheets. Max also saw two coppers watching for trespassers, but they kept their distance, fiddling with their rosaries in prayer. He saw the glint of enchantment in their eyes. Even bewitched, it was clear something had them spooked.

There was a heavy aroma of something sweet, like honey. But there was also something else resonating in the air, as if the entire building was in a state of unrest. Growing up in the city, Max had studied and explored every corner of the station; he knew its every sound, its every scent. Yet the air felt queer, the station unfamiliar.

"Max, you're here," said a figure emerging from behind the curtains. He had a slight Hungarian accent, one softened by living in America for some time. Before Max stood Theo Hardeen, the second most famous escape artist in the world. He was husky, and his chubby cheeks reminded Max of a baby's face on a man's body. Thank you for coming," he said, greeting Max with a firm handshake. "I wish it was under better circumstances."

"Anything for an old friend. I'm sorry to hear about Harry. He was a great man. The best of us, really." It came off more rehearsed than sincere. Condolences were never easy. "I noticed the protective wards when I entered. For the press?"

"No, not just for the press," Theo returned, somewhat distant. He gave the detective a sorrowful glance. His eyes were worried, heavy. He just shook his head. "The Brothers Houdini are no more," he said, as if saying the words aloud finally made it true. "The doctors," he muttered, "they said Harry died from drowning. Can you believe that nonsense? That man was a proficient swimmer. I've never seen a fitter man than my brother," he said. "He survived peritonitis years ago, but this? We suspect something else happened to Harry."

"What? Like foul play?" Max asked sceptically, wondering if grief had taken its toll on his friend.

Theo nodded, and looked around, as if someone would overhear what he was about to say. "We believe… Hexenhammer has returned."

Max flinched at the name. It was taboo amongst magi. "Those witch hunters haven't been seen since the war in Europe, Theo." The idea was too fantastical to make sense. "Why now? Why Harry?" he asked.

"As a warning to the rest of us," Theo said.

Max just shook his head. The idea that Hexenhammer was back was as absurd as it was terrifying. Magi had been hunted by Hexenhammer since the English Civil War, and had been slaughtered almost to the point of extinction.

"I don't know," Theo admitted, trying to make sense of it all. But the man shook the thought away. "Max, don't listen to the ramblings of a grieving man," Theo smiled, trying to ease the tension. "There'll be plenty of time for us to talk later today. Right now, we could use your expertise, as a detective."

"*You* needed his help," corrected a British and gruff voice from the other side of the privacy curtains. "You're the one who asked him here. Not me."

Max's blood went cold. The magus knew exactly who it was. He could have recognized the English bastard in his sleep. "What is Crowley doing here?" the magus spat.

Theo held up his hands in a vain attempt to stem the detective's fury. "He arrived last night for the funeral," Theo replied. "Even though Harry broke away from the Golden Dawn, Aleister still insisted on being here when the body arrived, and you know how he gets when he *insists*."

He knew the man's vanity all too well. Crowley had no desire to be upstaged by Houdini's funeral, and would, no doubt, find a way to make the day all about him. But Max wasn't petty enough to say that in front of Theo.

He had come to the station at the request of his long-time friend. He had no idea he'd be walking into a social ambush, one that made him impossibly uncomfortable. Max thought about walking away, but he then remembered why he was there.

Two decades and an ocean between them wasn't enough to heal their rift. The man was pathological, a parlour magician, a spoon-bender. Crowley cared more about being a celebrity than the arcane arts, and yet he was the man in charge of the Golden Dawn. Not to mention, the very same who had banished Max.

"What exactly is going on here?" Max asked, looking for a reason to stay.

"Something astonishing," Crowley replied. "And something frightening." There he was, stepping out from the curtain, Aleister Crowley, now as bald as the detective. "Christ, you look pug-ugly," Crowley laughed, as he gave

Max a once-over. "And old. What is that blasted thing around your neck?"

Time also had not been kind to the Golden Dawn's leader, Max noticed. He had known him as a young man from London, but now he was someone well past his prime. He was pudgy, his squidgy face reddened like a tomato with every word. His forehead beaded in sweat. His tweed suit was one size too small, and his polka dot bow-tie was one size too big. He looked like a blowhard ready to burst like a balloon.

"Come, you might as well see for yourself," Crowley said grudgingly.

It felt like confronting a childhood bully after years of being victimized just to pity him in the end. A wry smile flashed across the detective's face as he parted the curtain and walked inside; yet the moment was fleeting when Max laid eyes on what Crowley was examining.

"And don't you dare touch a thing," Crowley barked.

But Max ignored the man's second verbal lashing. His attention was too fixated on the corpse suspended next to the train tracks. It was tall and frail; it had unmistakably curly, blonde hair and olive skin. Its singular feathery wing was as lifeless as the body. The figure was a Fallen, an angel who has been banished from Heaven. Max once knew him as Uriel.

The body was impaled on the extended vertical lower part of a Chi-Rho, one of the oldest depictions of the Christian cross used by the Roman emperor Constantine. It was constructed from train tracks torn from the ground, impossibly bent to form the 'P' at the top. The arms were attached to the upper section of the 'X' below the 'P'. A sweet scent of honey was in the air: Uriel's ichor, the blood of magical beings, which had dried all over the brutalized body from extensive wounds. But there was no blood pool at the base of the Chi-Rho, meaning he had been murdered elsewhere and placed in the station.

Was this intended for us? Charlie asked. *Who could he have done this, Max? To an angel!* The fear in his voice was clear.

"I don't know," Max whispered. His mind raced to connect a thousand possibilities.

"I've never seen anything like this. Have you?" Theo asked Max. "It must be another angel of some kind. An actual angel, Max, crucified," he stressed, hardly believing it, himself. "Crowley and I have been examining it for the past hour. Even he's clueless."

"Not entirely," Crowley said, trying to save face. "I have prophesied about this in my books: a war between good and evil. The devils have finally struck!"

But Theo ignored his leader. "We were hoping you might know something; anything."

Of course, he did. But would he share? As Max approached the body, he felt his knees buckle under the weight of it all. Uriel was by no means a friend, but the Fallen had trusted him, confided in him. He had seen him just days ago, alive and reunited with his daughter. And now he was dead.

"I told you he would be of no help. You might as well have recruited a vagabond off the street. By the looks of him, you already have." Crowley's tone was filled with spite. He removed a long golden rod from a black bag, and began sweeping the crime scene, humming as he went.

Max was thankful, but not surprised, the British buffoon knew nothing about the Fallen. But it did nothing to put him at ease. Neither Crowley nor Theo understood the gravitas of what was before them. Uriel was immensely powerful. To see the angel beaten and broken, let alone killed, was unfathomable. Horrifying. Sexton Graves was an incredible mage, probably the most powerful of them all, but even he was incapable of killing something divine. The very notion that there was something out there that *could* do so made him shiver.

He wondered if it was retaliation for keeping the daughter a secret. Maybe his own kind had turned against him? Did the angels learn of his secret? What of his daughter, he worried. Was she still alive? Or was it about something else? Max looked at Charlie, but he was lost in his own thoughts.

"Burn it," Max demanded. He felt himself swelling with rage.

Crowley's face turned a deep crimson. "Are you mad? We will do no such thing! This discovery changes everything."

"Burn it, or I will," he threatened. "The body, the blood. All of it. No one should have access to them, not even us. The press is right outside. If one of them took a photograph—" Words left Max when he saw a look of protest on Theo's face, someone he once considered reasonable.

"And you think no one would notice a pyre burning in the middle of a platform?" Crowley shouted. "If you even think of giving that *thing* a second glance, I'll lock you away in the deepest fathom of my Glassworld, personally."

"Oh, do shut-up," Max shot back. "Harry's train will be here any time."

"I can erase the memories from their minds," Theo insisted. "I planned to do so anyway. We'll never have an opportunity like this again, Max. Think about what we could learn," he stormed, bubbling with anger.

"I don't care." Max removed a silver lighter from his pants pocket and began to utter a small incantation, but before he could even finish the first word, Theo slapped the lighter out of his hand.

"You selfish bastard," Theo flared. "Crowley was right. Asking you here was a mistake." He balled his hands into fists.

Max, he should be given last rites, at last.

The detective couldn't believe it. Even Charlie was against him. Max shook his head in disbelief. Crowley, the opportunist, would have turned it into another one of his ludicrous novels. He took note of the look on Theo's face. It wasn't one of grief, or of a man tasked with burying his brother. His face was twisted by wrath.

Max could have told them the truth, but he really didn't feel like sharing. Instead, he felt like pummelling both men with his cane. He felt the frustration boil like a slow eruption, and he was eager to let it loose. He didn't know why. The hatred was infectious; he saw it twisting the faces of those around him until his vision blurred. He heard his brother call his name, but it was too late. A metal rod connected squarely to his temple, knocking off his top hat. Max fell to the ground. He heard Crowley scream over his body, but the words were muffled. Blood got into his eyes. The world went red. He heard fighting. Then a gunshot.

Max propped himself up on his forearms. He was dizzy, but fought hard to stay conscious. Charlie continued to scream his name. His vision blurred, but he saw the coppers restraining Crowley. Theo struck one over the head with a club. But then Max fell back to the ground. His hand had slipped on his own blood. He was badly hurt, and didn't realize it until he started to move.

Everything around him was swallowed by a quickening madness, and that was when Max remembered something his father once told him as a boy: all insanity, all hysteria was inherently demonic. Hellish things left a trail of madness behind them like a wake from a large ship. Max turned his head towards the crucifixion. No man had the power to kill an angel. Something sinister had murdered Uriel. It was the only explanation. His companions were caught in the wake of the being's destruction. He heard their bestial shouts as they tried to tear each other apart.

He rolled himself over onto his back, and reached into a hidden vest pocket. Demonology was not his strong area of expertise, and there was very little he could do against their primal abstracts, like rage. It was like trying to knock out a tornado with kind words. But he had a metacarpal bone from St. Gaius, and an array of Catholic prayers his father had beaten into his memory. He gripped the bone fiercely in his hand and prayed. Max dipped his index finger into the pool of his own blood and painted a cross on his forehead.

Faith was a powerful weapon, but only for those who believed. Max didn't need faith. He had encountered both angels and monsters in his long lifetime. He knew Heaven and Hell weren't merely stories to keep the masses in check. The very air around him was saturated in black abhorrence; the only way Max could fight back was by channelling his love for his brother. He flooded his mind with happy memories of his time in London, of his master Ammon, of his mother. If evil fed on hate, Max would try to rob it all of its sustenance.

It was incredibly taxing. To Max, it was like tensing a muscle; he could only do it for so long. The bone burned his skin until it caught fire. He tossed it hard to the ground, and watched as it skipped over in the direction of Uriel, ultimately stopping at the base of the Chi-Rho. The world around him fell quiet. He no longer heard his brother call out his name. As his vision returned, his battered colleagues released their holds on each other. All of them shared looks of disbelief.

Theo looked at his bloodied hands and screamed, dropping the club to the floor. Crowley took several steps back. His eyes were wide, fearful. He saw Max on the ground, bleeding from his head.

The leader of the Golden Dawn, removed his green pocket square from his suit, and applied pressure to the detective's head. "What the hell just happened?"

The detective watched Theo as he put the two coppers under an enchantment likely to contain the situation. "You don't remember hitting me with your rod?"

Crowley shook his head, causing his jolly cheeks to roll with the momentum. "Believe me, I've spent many years fantasizing about bashing your head in, but... I would never hurt any of my brethren," he admitted, with great regret, "especially with so few of us left." Crowley realized his moment of weakness, and motioned impatiently for the detective to apply his own pressure. "But I'm not your bloody nurse, either," he finished, getting back to his feet. "Keep the damn handkerchief."

"I took care of the police," Theo said, finally, trying to make sense of what had happened. "When I break the trance, they won't remember what has happened. I won't be able to explain their wounds, but I'm sure Crowley and I could think of something." The last word was barely a whisper.

"Theo, what happened here wasn't your fault," Max said, using his cane to get back to his feet. "I'm almost certain this platform was possessed, and we walked right into it. I managed to subdue whatever it was…I hope."

"The platform was under demonic possession?" Theo repeated, dumbfounded. "That's impossible."

"No, very rare, but not impossible. Demonic spirits can possess anything or anyone, even buildings."

Max, something's happening, Charlie screamed, pointing towards the body.

The metacarpal bone from St. Gaius twitched subtly at first. It bounced in place, once and then again. It fell back to the ground, and began to spin around faster and faster until it finally came to an abrupt stop and snapped in half. The air around the magi became incredibly cold. Uriel's abdomen quivered and then protruded, as if something was moving around under the skin. The bulge slowly worked its way up the torso until it reached its throat and then up to its cheeks, which ballooned in size. Max heard the buzzing sound even before thousands of black flies ruptured from Uriel's mouth in a continuous stream, and swarmed at the men.

As Crowley and Theo tried pathetically to swat them away, Max retrieved his silver lighter from the ground, whispered a small incantation, and tossed it at the corpse. In an instant, the mangled body was engulfed in a blazing inferno of white purifying fire, and quickly turned to ash. Only the skeletal frame of the Chi-Rho remained.

The three magi watched as the swarm buzzed and swayed in a singular motion until it finally took the shape of a person. "Max," it said, in a thousand voices speaking at once.

Against his better judgment, the detective stepped before the aberration. "Were you the one who killed the angel?" he accused, more than asked.

Its head cocked to the side. Whatever it was, it ignored the question. "You have been searching for the Father of Beasts, and you will not find Him," it began. "Not until you are ready, and He is convinced."

"I don't understand," Max pleaded. "Convinced?"

"What the devil is that?" Crowley spat. His every spell against the manifestation fizzled away to nothing. Theo's magic fared no better.

But the magus ignored them.

"Of your commitment. Our Father wants the abomination. You know where it is," the thing oozed.

The Nephilim, Charlie gasped.

"It is beyond our sight, and we see much," the flies all said.

"But not her," Max said, relieved the ward Uriel placed upon his daughter was still active, even after his death. In his final act, Uriel had sacrificed himself to keep the girl safe, and he wouldn't dare betray that. "And you never will see her," Max affirmed.

"*You* will," it mused, touching Max's head. "The Fallen made sure of it." The face of flies twisted into what looked like a smile. As it finished uttering its taunt, all the flies dropped to the ground in a black heap, returning the platform to normal.

The questions came fast and constantly from the other magi, but Max paid them no heed.

What did that mean? Charlie asked, looking at his brother.

"It means Uriel's case just reopened."

Somewhere in the distance, a train whistle cut the air. Max removed a flask from within a hidden pocket of his peacoat, popped the lid with a flip of a finger, and took a much-needed swig of tonic. It wasn't his beloved spiced rum, but it had to do. He had just been targeted by a demon, something powerful enough to kill a Fallen, and now demonkind wanted the girl. He looked over to at his concerned brother with a sigh. He knew that Charlie knew what he had to do. Max had no say in the matter. The girl was still in trouble. "You know, Charlie," he bemoaned, "one day, that bad morality habit of yours is going to get me killed."

CHAPTER ELEVEN:
A FUNERAL FOR A FRIEND

What have you gotten us into? Charlie asked.

It was a fair question. One he couldn't answer. Instead, he gazed out across the field of Machpelah Cemetery, coated by heavy snow melting in the sun.

Uriel and Houdini. The day was already full of great loss, and it was just noon. Max couldn't shake away recollection of the creature from the platform. He had fought monstrosities before, even as recently as beneath Chinatown, but the latest dark entity felt stronger than Uriel, if that was even possible. He had summoned minor demons in the past, conversed with them. For creatures of absolute malicious intent, he found them strangely good company. But Hell had its own hierarchy. His rituals merely skimmed the surface of a bottomless abyss. The true horrors lurked beyond his reach, far beyond his education. He wondered that afternoon if something from the deepest fathoms of Hell had boiled its way to the top, and onto his trail.

Max inhaled deeply. The wintery air felt good in his lungs. The ugly brutality that morning gave way to a welcomed pleasantness. But it hardly put him at ease. The day now felt like the eye of a still-growing storm, for he knew the real terror had yet to come. He exhaled. One problem at a time.

The sunlight glistened off the snow, the perfect conditions for saying goodbye to an old friend. Houdini would have loved it, he knew. The escape artist was the Dawn's greatest public figure, much to Crowley's dismay. His magic was simple, yet beautiful. No chains could restrain him, no lock could hold him. Charlie used to say that even death wouldn't have been able to keep him for long. The idea made Max smile. If only that were true.

Hundreds lined the streets, and even more mourners waited at the gates. It seemed as if nearly all of New York had turned out for the funeral, suffering through the unyielding, New York winter chill just to say farewell. But all stood in silence, grief weighing heavy in their hearts. Occasionally, the wind carried the soft sounds of sobbing, but it all felt quite still, as if even time had stopped to pay its respect to the great man. But the public display made things nearly impossible for a secret society of magi to send off one of their own. They had enemies, ancient and resourceful. And this was the first time in decades they had all gathered publicly in one place, just to break a wand over Houdini's grave.

Max watched the authentic funeral from the shadow of a mausoleum just up the hill, which contained a modest plot for a man so big in life. But for the service to be held in secret there was Houdini's last wish: The decoy funeral was being held by Theo and Houdini's widow, Bess, on the other side of the cemetery, for the crowd and the press, while the Golden Dawn laid the body to rest here. This funeral, conducted below where he stood, was not extravagant, by design. The modest ceremony kept eyes away, along with the wards and spells of protection.

Crowley crushed a yellow rose in his hand, ruffled the petals from the stem, and held them out on his cashmere-gloved palm. He uttered a short phrase from an ancient time, and off they flew, one after another, waltzing in the breeze across Houdini's plot. As they touched the ground, the snow instantly melted away from the grave site, retreating into a perfect ring. The greyish grass beneath was rejuvenated into a luscious flower garden of every spectrum of colour. Crowley nodded his head, content with the modest gift for one of his own. Houdini always loved beautiful things.

You should be down there, Charlie insisted.

Max stubbornly shook his head. There were far too many ghosts from his past saying goodbye, and he counted more adversaries than friends from his time with the Golden Dawn. "I am quite happy with where I am."

They were your friends.

Max scuffed at his brother's naive sentiment. He saw Baskerville Downes, Crowley's personal lapdog, hiding underneath his signature red umbrella. Max guessed Baskerville still hated him for slighting his master so long ago. Lynn Lin was there, too, dressed more for a soiree than for a funeral, in her azure-coloured dress, refusing to surrender to the cold for the sake of being seen. The unconventional Chinese woman was surprisingly very traditional with her views on magic, and fought vehemently for his dismissal after she discovered his study of blood magic.

You'll probably never be together like this again.

"Except for the next funeral," he said snappily.

Max, don't be like that, Charlie soured.

"Like what?"

Spiteful, like father.

Max turned away from Charlie, pulling his peacoat closer to block out the strong winter chill.

"I'm only here to support Theo and Bess," he said, curtly.

Then why are you here, and not with them?

Max wished his brother would stop pressing the point. "You wouldn't understand."

You'll be surprised, Charlie returned. *I still remember what it was to be alive.*

Max gave his thumb ring a twirl. "When I buried you," he said, softly, for it was a taboo topic between them, "Ammon and the Brothers Houdini were the *only* ones who came to pay their respects, and Ammon *never* leaves Edinburgh. But he made that exception, for you," he stressed.

Charlie didn't know what to say.

"They did what was right," said Max. "But to show you how petty the Golden Dawn has become, that's not even the real Crowley," he said, pointing to the buffoon making a speech. "The fat oaf sent a magical projection of himself in his stead, just like he did at the train station. Solid enough to clock me in the head. The real one's probably too busy grovelling over some MP in London, barking for favours."

I don't see the difference between Crowley hiding in London and you sulking here in the shadows, Charlie snipped. *At least he's making an effort.*

"If you want to go, go," Max shot back, nodding towards the funeral. "I'll be here," he finished, crossing his arms.

You're impossible.

"So you often tell me," he said. The two brothers continued to watch in silence.

Charlie was right, of course, but Max would never admit it. His stubbornness had ended many friendships over the years; his pride had ruined even more. When it came to relationships, Max destroyed everything he touched, and he hadn't grown wiser with age. He had spent a lifetime running towards unspeakable things, dreadful creatures that would have given any rational person reason to flee, but socially, he was a coward. "One day, I will make amends, Charlie," Max said, apologetically, and he meant it. "But that day is not today."

It was more than just simple cowardice. Max hated many things, funerals especially. He was old, and had buried nearly his entire family, including his mother and his brother. His cousins were gone, lost in the war. His aunt died in a fire. His uncles died in a murder-suicide. He had no nieces or nephews, and his grandparents died long before he was born. Max was grateful he had no children of his own, for he feared he would have buried them as well. The only one left alive was his father, not that it mattered to Max, for he hasn't spoken to that bastard in decades.

Charlie was the only one who still cared.

He fondled the locket around his neck. Max's bloodline was cursed, or so he passionately believed. He thought it would have been best if the Thanatos name died with him. Given the events of the day, that conclusion seemed closer than ever. He looked over to his brother, still stifled with frustration. Max fought so hard to save him, because he wanted at least one Thanatos to rest in peace. Max shook the thoughts away. His still mind always went to dark places. Funerals had a way of reminding people of what they had lost, instead of what they still had.

Max, Charlie said, seeing his brother tense up for another argument, but then caught a glimpse of something curious. *Who are they?* he asked, pointing to an outcropping of white oak trees behind the service. *More Golden Dawn?*

A dozen figures slowly marched in unison towards Houdini's funeral. They wore purple cloaks with a golden pentagram. They approached as if towards a vigil, holding lit, red candles in their cupped hands. Cowls concealed their faces, but Max recognized the insignia. "No, they shouldn't be here," he whispered. "The Society of American Magicians. They petitioned to join the Golden Dawn after the war, but were only Vanderbilt performers and academics with no real magical abilities. The Dawn rejected them, rather unceremoniously," he added. "Made something of a spectacle about it. They hated us since, and did much to make our existence public."

If they have no magic, how did they get past the wards?

Max gripped his cane.

Are they here to cause trouble?

"Of that, I am most certain. No one has heard from them in years."

Why?

Max tensed. "Because Crowley imprisoned them all in his Glassworld."

But it happened before he finished his sentence. The leader threw a metallic cylinder into the crowd, shining ever so briefly in the midday sun. "Get down," Max shouted at the mourners, but he was too far away and already too late. He saw the explosion before he felt the shock wave. Baskerville expanded the magic of his beloved umbrella to absorb the impact of the blast, saving their lives, but the detonation knocked Max hard into the snow. He wasn't even back on his feet before he heard a second explosion sound in the distance. The public funeral was also under attack. "Theo," he exhaled. Even at the opposite end of the cemetery, Max heard the people scream.

Their assailants didn't care who was caught in the attack, magi or civilians.

He watched as the attack put his former guild mates on the defensive, and against his better judgement, Max ran towards the fray to help. The cloaked assailants were fearless as they continued their march towards the Golden Dawn, slowly and methodically. The funeral site had become engulfed in a spectacular display of colour as spells exploded like shrapnel. Max ducked and wove his way around tombstones to avoid the wilder shots. But the magic from the Dawn members never found its mark. Their enemies continued undeterred, unchallenged.

The Golden Dawn realized it, too. The cowardly Crowley commanded a hasty retreat and was the first to flee, vanishing as he dispelled his projection. Baskerville took to the front, alone, planting his umbrella down as a barrier. Max remembered it as a simple artefact, but one undoubtedly powerful. To his enemies, it would have been an impregnable wall. "Go," he commanded, in his soft English voice. "I will buy you time." He stood at the ready, his hands wove a complex spell, ready to rain hell upon those who threatened his family. But his heroic display was not enough. Lynn Lin screamed as she saw a bullet hit the magus squarely between the eyes, piercing through a barrier that should not have been pierced.

She commanded the leaves of grass to twist into emerald serpents, but they did not heed her call. "Who are you?" she shrilled towards the undaunted men, as they crunched Baskerville's umbrella beneath their boots.

But the men did not reply; they did not falter in their approach. Max heard the pop, pop, pop sound of gunfire, forcing him behind the mausoleum for cover. He had very little defence against a bullet. "Charlie, what do you see?"

Bodies, Max, he returned.

Charlie confirmed his worst fears. "How many?"

Some managed to portal out, but…I—don't know. It's ugly.

"How many?" he screamed over the battle. There were already too few of them left. Any more loss that day would have been broken him.

Too many. You have to run, Max.

Max rummaged through his vest with shaky fingers, looking for something, anything. All reason had left him. Panic took him. Visions of Ypres flooded his fragile mind. He didn't know whether to fight or flee, and decided the first trinket he pulled from his vest would decide his fate: a cinnamon lozenge for his lungs.

"Unbelievable," he muttered to himself, and lobbed the pill over the mausoleum. But the tiny, crimson orb quickly expanded from a pea into a blistering fireball propelling itself towards the combat. "No," he gasped, thinking he had just doomed both friend and foe.

He ducked for cover, and counted down until the imminent explosion, but none ever came. He peeked again to see nothing was scorched, that no man had been burnt to cinder. "Thank God," he said, but immediately realized the real danger, "wait, my spell!" he balked under his breath. Magic had failed him, too.

But the fireball had been impossible to ignore. It had caught the attention of the leader, who ordered the rest to break rank and pursue. Who wasn't left for dead was dying or had already fled. Their assassins did not care for prisoners and methodically shot the bodies in the head for good measure. Max knew he wouldn't be the exception, and so he fled. Portal spells were granted only to active members of the Golden Dawn, quick bridges that led directly back to London. Max had no such luxury. As he cast a spell to hasten his step, even that, too, had failed. His assailants negated magic, and so he was nothing more than an old man running for his life.

As a wild shot shattered the tip of a headstone, Max was thankful the men were no marksmen. But he knew his lungs would give out long before their munitions. He thought of Theo and Bess, and prayed they had survived. Police whistles and sirens cut through the screams of the crowd. He darted through a narrow passage between two gaudy mausoleums of angels with trumpets. Two pursuers cut around, one tumbled hard to the ground when his feet slipped on ice. Another shot fired out, this time grazing Max's shoulder. But as his body surged with adrenaline and fear, he hardly felt it.

Max reached the perimeter of the cemetery, and dived into the panicking crowd. It was a torrent of hysteria, Max was ensnared in its ferocity. But that hardly deterred the men's bravado as they fired blindly into the masses. It only furthered the chaos around him. Bodies fell as he ran, each catching a bullet designed for him. He cut through an alleyway, and crossed over Cooper Ave. He was nowhere near his apartment. He hardly even knew Queens. Please, God, don't let me die in Queens, he prayed.

More copper whistles sliced the air. Max could no longer see his pursuers through the living wall of people blocking his view. But he wouldn't dare stop then to try. Max felt like a marble in a bagatelle table, violently ricocheting off those around him fleeing from the madness of the day. He finally broke through into another alleyway to catch his breath. He grabbed his shoulder to feel the wet, cooling blood from his wound.

Max, Charlie urged, pointing to where they had entered.

He turned to see two of the purple cloaked men follow him in, guns raised for a clear, straight shot. Max knew he was a dead man. He had no strength left to breathe, but he ran anyway. He had just reached the end of the alleyway when he felt the first shot enter his back, followed by a second, singeing slug that pierced his lung. The impact was enough to stumble him forward in a daze, off the curb and onto the street. He heard the cries of his brother, realizing at that final moment he was still alive, only to see a flash of green and chrome from the corner of his eye as a two-ton motor bus struck him, launching him into the air.

His broken body tumbled and skidded violently along the street. The black pavement ripped away his exposed, pale skin. He didn't hear the screams of the onlookers, or the blaring automobile horns. He didn't feel it when his broken ribs skewered his lungs, or when the jagged bones of his arms and legs pierced through the soft flesh. Or even when his shattered body eventually came to a stop some fifty feet away from the point of impact.

Max was only alive in the academic sense, for his heart struggled to pump what little blood still remained within his body. But, even with his brain battered to mush, whatever cognitive power he had left told him he was dying. Those precious few moments of life were all he had left. His body grew cold. He couldn't breathe. His world was black. His eyes were pulverized. Max couldn't even see his distraught brother kneeling besides him, or the bus driver flailing for anyone's help.

In the end, there was no bright light. There were no angels waiting to collect him. No loved ones. He was simply falling asleep. His mind was flushed with a spectrum of colour until, that too, faded away into stark nothingness.

CHAPTER TWELVE: TO HELL AND BACK

In the end, there was darkness.

A droplet fell into the black abyss creating ripples that expanded ad infinitum.

Max stumbled out from the dark into a subway tunnel dimly lit by the soft, electric glow of an Edison bulb, flickering its final moments from above. He looked down at himself, expecting to see a mangled corpse of a man. But he was alive, naked, but alive, trekking barefoot through the muck.

His legs gave out. He collapsed against the brick wall of the tunnel just to keep himself from keeling over. The coarse masonry stones felt cold against his bare skin. No, it wasn't just from the stone. The chill came from everywhere: the air, the ground, even radiated within himself. He called out for Charlie. His voice echoed down the tunnel, and was swallowed by the blackness beyond.

And so he walked. Down the tunnel he went. Through the muck, through the inescapable chill. The world seemed at a slant. He struggled to move. It felt impossible to continue. His legs refused to obey. He tried again for his brother, but words also failed him. Max grabbed his head. He tried to remember where he was, how he got there. Above, the dismal light flickered again. It would not last.

He willed himself forward. Or was it back the way he came? Each direction brought him again to the junction. Always the same junction. He thundered a primal roar from frustration, but there was only silence. Nothing made sense. All he knew was he couldn't stop shivering. His beard was coated in ice. His feet and hands were blackening from frostbite. Then the pitiful light wavered for the last time, bursting the bulb into a hundred little shards. Max was thrown again into blackness. His every step gashed razor glass into the bottom of his tender feet. But on he pressed. Alone and deep within the strange tunnel. He tried to mutter words, unique words—a special language that once helped him light the way, but those words were forgotten so long ago. Ma…gic, he struggled to remember. Words escaped him. His thoughts escaped him. The only thing certain was the gloom.

The ground sucked at his bare feet. Max struggled to break free, but each step sank him deeper into glutinous mud. Eyes wide, he desperately clawed for the wall. His fingers tore at stone, scraped the mortar, hoping to find something, anything to clasp onto. But it was no use. He fought just to keep his head above ground until skeletal hands grasped his feet, and forced the magus down deeper into the abyss with the unbridled strength of the dead.

He gasped in his last bit of air, but it would do him no good. His body forced itself to suck in the clinging muck, and the blissfully cold filth filled his damaged lungs with every draw of breath. But the torment of dying never ceased. Max drowned in the blackness of the mire for hours, days, years.

***

Through the veil, the magus felt a small, firm hand slip into his.

Max's stilled heart sputtered once, and then thundered like American artillery fire as icy magic pounded through his body. Ripped arteries stitched themselves whole, coursing warm, fresh blood through his veins once more. His pulverized bones popped and twisted themselves back into place like a jigsaw puzzle. His chest rose and fell as he sucked in the putrid air of New York industry into his restored lungs. His back arched off the street, his legs flailed to life; every fibre of every muscle spasmed as they attached themselves back onto bone. And the once gangly, stringy flesh left shredded by the road surface patched itself over the wounds, leaving them as if they had never existed at all. As his strength returned, he grasped the stranger's hand with a crushing grip.

Max had been remade.

The colours slowly returned within his mind, then the light to his eyes. His thoughts had returned, his hearing, his vision. He opened his eyes, and saw the radiance of the city, the overcast sky above. Life had been filtered back into the dead. Rebirth was a violent process, but Max was among the living once more. He saw dozens of people encircle him as he remained where he had died. He heard the chaos of what he had left behind, the screams of violence, the sirens, and the cries for help in the distance. But Max still felt the hand clinging onto his. He slowly turned his head to see an olive-skinned girl with curly blonde hair kneeling over him. She looked neither shocked nor scared, as if bringing the dead back to life was a menial task.

"It could have been worse, considering," she said, placing her clammy palm on his forehead, satisfied with her work. "The men who did this left you for dead, but they haven't gone far." She reached underneath her winter coat, into her wool, blue dress, and removed a fuzzy seed, and forced it into Max's mouth. "Swallow," she said. "It'll help with the shock."

Max tried to shake the image away, thinking it was another malicious creation of the mire. "This isn't real," he exhaled, spitting it out. "This isn't real!" He pulled away from the girl. He wouldn't fall for its tricks again. Max then felt a calming, familiar chill over his shoulder. He was so enthralled by her, he didn't even notice Charlie was floating at his side. He thought he had lost him for good. "Charlie," he cried, almost in disbelief.

You're alive! Charlie could hardly believe it, himself.

"There's no time for this," the girl urged, failing to get the heavier Max back to his feet. "We have to leave before they come back."

They had attracted a score of witnesses, and more gathered by the moment as drivers abandoned their automobiles to gather around the duo, with hats over their hearts. No one said a word. Max saw most drop to their knees, crossing their chests in silent prayer. Others simply ran away in fear, thinking the devilry from the cemetery had found them, too. Even Max didn't understand it all. He had studied magic from the most learned men around the world, dealt with angels and fought against vile malevolence, and even he was left speechless. They had all witnessed a miracle.

"This is really happening, isn't it?" he asked, turning to the girl. His mind thick with cobwebs.

She nodded, throwing a worried look around.

The magician turned to see the instrument of his destruction idling several yards away. The International bus's chrome chassis was wet with blood. His blood. "How long was I gone?"

Minutes.

"Minutes?" he whispered, incredulously. Terror washed over him. "No."

"We have to go. Please," she urged again.

But the strain of being brought back to life was too taxing. The words barely registered. Max was frantic. He ignored the crowd now begging for answers. He ignored the ginger-haired bus driver pleading to Max for forgiveness. He struggled back to his feet, pushing her hand away. His clothes were tattered, his tinted spectacles were smashed, and he was covered in his own blood.

He had been gone for years, drowning in that muck. But it was only for minutes? "Oh, God," Max exhaled. He looked at his brother like a teary-eyed child waking from a nightmare. "Charlie, I was in Hell. Hell," he choked, trying to swallow down the fear. "After all that I've done, it was always Hell that awaited me," he whispered, afraid the darkness would hear him.

Calm yourself, Max, his brother pleaded. *Listen to her. You can't stay here.*

"If you won't listen to me, listen to Charlie," she said, handing Max his wolf's head cane.

"Charlie?" he repeated. Hearing her say his brother's name aloud was like taking a burning torch to the cobwebs. Clarity had finally returned to the magus, who shook the death terrors away, and looked upon the girl properly for the first time. He realized only then it was

Uriel's daughter before him, now dressed in a simple shift and sandals. How did she find him? How did she know Charlie? He had questions. Too many questions. For once, the magus was the one without answers.

Word of his resurrection had already spread. The familiar fizzle sound of a flashbulb ignited as someone in the crowd snapped a photograph. He heard the coppers blow their whistles. They were already too close. "Perhaps you are right," he admitted, nodding towards the girl, "it would be best to flee." The last thing Max wanted to do was explain to the police how he was brought back to life. Questions would have led to more questions, and then things would have spiralled out of his control. Magic to heal wounds was rare, but not unheard of in certain circles. But to resurrect the dead? That was something even beyond his education. Was that the power of a Nephilim? Hell flooded his mind again, and he panicked. Max cast a spell of flickering bright light, and used the disorientation to slip away through the crowd, taking the girl by the hand.

If one foolhardy optimist was left alive in the world, he would have said the only silver lining to be found after the attack on Houdini's funeral was that no one paid much attention to another bloodied body running through the streets. Once Max was a few blocks uptown, he and the girl retreated between two buildings. He tossed his blood-soaked coat into a metal garbage can. Max patted down his vest, and, to his horror, removed smashed trinket after trinket from their hidden pockets, including the locket around his neck. He pried open the latch, smashed shut from the impact, and saw a piece of the lock had punctured his mother's faded photograph. He had no spell to repair the damage.

Charlie noticed it, too.

In a fit of rage, Max didn't even bother to unbutton his vest, instead he simply tore it off and trashed it alongside his coat, and then kicked the metal can for good measure. A fine collection, ruined.

Do you remember what the entity said at the station?

Max couldn't forget. "Not now," he warned, tossing the girl a cautious glance. Under his coat, his linen dress shirt had got the worst of it. Once white, its entirety was nearly dyed a crimson hue, and the cold, wetness of it all clung obnoxiously to every inch of his torso. He thought he must have looked like a crime scene. With a word, the shadows elongated and criss-crossed through the alley, providing cover from any prying eyes. "What's your name?" he asked. The gentleness of his voice was a complete contrast to his bloodied person.

"Helena," she said, watching as he tore off the crimson-stained sleeves from his shirt, and used them to wipe his face. He then peeled the rest of it off and tried his best to wipe himself clean. But it was like drying himself with an already damp, bloodied towel.

He paused when he noticed all of his cutting scars from his days in the Congo were gone. Every last one. "My mother was always strict about etiquette, when Charlie and I were boys," Max said, "one might even say obsessed, really, but I'm not quite sure there's a rule for being brought back to life. I can't imagine a thank you would suffice, Helena, but it's all I have to offer, at the moment."

That goes for me, as well, Helena. Thank you for saving my brother.

"It's quite alright," she said, in a voice tinged with embarrassment.

But Charlie still wasn't done with his brother. *Max,* he repeated, but more commanded.

The magician skipped up the side of a brick wall for a boost, and clung to the railing of the fire escape above. His bodyweight brought the ladder crashing down with a clang. With a quick ascent, his heeled boots pounding against the metal, Max commandeered a starched dress-shirt from a low-hanging clothesline, and shrank it down to a comfortable fit with an incantation. It would have to do. He couldn't run around Manhattan half-naked. It was bad enough running around Queens covered in blood.

But Max felt good. His breathing wasn't laboured. The swift climb didn't even wind him, as any exertion normally would have. "You even healed my old war injury," he said towards the girl, with a grateful nod. Just how powerful was she? He breathed in as deeply as he could, and held it for a long moment. It had been years. "Remarkable," he said.

Max, Max, Max, Charlie persisted, hammer-and-tongs.

But the magus was at his limit. "What it is?" he growled. Below, his brother was relentless with his concern, so he joined him once more, if only to shut him up. Charlie was impossible to ignore for long.

The spirit shook his head in disbelief. *Are you all right?* he asked, softly. *You just suffered an ordeal,* he said, not knowing if 'ordeal' was the best way to explain someone returning from the dead. *You're in a shambles, whether you're aware of it or not. You're shaking.*

"It's just the adrenaline," he lied.

Max let the words linger. Charlie was right. He was always right. Every city block had seemed a monstrous creature of its own. He had hesitated at every street corner, every intersection, paused at every automobile and large green motor bus that sped by. He had watched as the traffic crossed once, twice, and upon the third time he white-knuckled his wolf's head cane just to keep his hands from trembling. By the time the fourth cycle of traffic went, Max had finally summoned enough courage to step off the curb and onto the street, and it was a process he had repeated for several blocks more until he finally retreated into that alleyway. He had become a grown man too afraid to cross the street.

He finally turned to his brother. "Charlie, you are right," he admitted. "About what you said. I *am* in a shambles. But not from fear of death, but of the Hell that awaits me. But the living press forward. There's no other choice." Habitually, he reached to adjust his spectacles, but remembered they had been smashed to bits alongside his body.

Charlie simply nodded. He just had to know.

Max felt completely defenceless without his trinkets. He had relied on them for far too long and often that he had neglected rudimentary spell craft, the essence of all magic. He had settled into a comfortable pattern with his ancient relics over the years and couldn't deny that they had made him lazy. Easy magic was not magic; it was stage performance. And theatricality would not be enough to best Hell when it would eventually come for the girl.

He turned to Helena, his expression softened, "I apologize for my state," he said, readjusting his beard around his neck, realizing, it, too, had been spotted with blood. "It has just been a really trying day." How remarkable the girl was, he noted, to remain steadfast after it all. So composed, for a young woman, during a crisis. "Where are your parents?" he fished. "Your mother… father?"

"Mister Thanatos, please drop the pretence," Helena said. "I know about my father."

The magus found it more of a relief than surprising. It would make things easier. "Then I need you to come with me, back to Manhattan," he said. "To my sanctuary. You'll be safe."

"Safe?" she repeated, not truly convinced. "I saved *your* life."

She wasn't wrong. "So allow me to return the courtesy. We need to talk."

On that, she agreed.

His thoughts raced back to the attack, Hell, the girl. Even Uriel. He couldn't sort them. He had to go home. That's all he wanted, and to make it back across town, he'd have to face his fear and commute, for, in his state, walking home would take all damn week. He sighed. One problem at a time, as his mother used to say.

"May I recommend a taxi?" she asked.

"You've read my mind."

***

Officer Ronan gripped his navy-blue custodian helmet over his heart. "What kind of man would do this at a funeral?" he asked himself. The fresh snow from the morning had been blackened to ash everywhere the grenades hit, red snow contrasted with rows of bodies underneath white sheets fluttering in the strong afternoon wind. He watched his brethren collect chunks of arms and legs like firewood scattered around Machpelah Cemetery. He hadn't seen so much carnage since the Battle of the Somme. Ronan smoothed back his thick, ginger mane, and solemnly returned his helmet to its place. His squad car had arrived too late. There was no one left for him to save. The people who had come to mourn that day would now be mourned themselves.

Heavy footsteps crunched snow behind him.

"There's a special place in Hell for the monsters who did this," said Lieutenant Henson, placing a hand on the broad man's shoulder. "And I promise, I'm gonna send them all there, personally, when we find 'em."

"I thought we fought to end this kind of evil in the world," Ronan said, turning to his colleague. "What the hell did we accomplish over there? The world's just gotten madder. Even my own daughter's too afraid to leave our home. And you know what? These days, I don't blame her."

"Your little girl might be on to something," he agreed, striking a match and relighting his pipe. "People here are saying the Devil was behind this. They saw black fire erupt out of nothing, tombstones thrown like rocks, even the ground balled into a fist. If you can believe that malarkey."

"Like magic?" Ronan asked.

Lieutenant Henson just shrugged, blowing out a cloud of smoke. "Not my words, lad. Theirs," he said. "But sure." He turned to the big man. "Look, why don't you go help direct the ambulances. Johnny's making a mess down there. You don't have to be here."

Ronan shook his head. "I am where I need to be. It wouldn't be right to them," he said, nodding in the direction of the dead. He walked down the hill towards the bodies. Magic, he thought. He knew it was real. He had seen it for himself, and from the same man: a good man. But good man or not, in his eyes Max Thanatos was a suspect.

CHAPTER THIRTEEN: HEAVEN AND HELL

Towel-drying his beard, Max Thanatos felt human again. He walked across his apartment, over the frayed Turkish rug, pressing the open palm of his hand against the air, as if upon an invisible wall. "Unlock," he commanded. The air rippled like a disturbed puddle, and Helena watched with visible amazement as the once modest apartment in Alafair expanded up and out into something beyond the confines of the building space. New hallways appeared, and walls twisted and reshaped themselves into a massive foyer. "Please make yourself at home," he said to the girl. "My real home. I have something I must to do before we talk."

Helena just nodded, as she stepped deeper in his sanctum, mystified.

What do you want me to do?

"Just watch her," he instructed Charlie. "Let me know if anything happens."

Like what?

Max shrugged. "Like Hell, perhaps. I won't be long."

He entered a small parlour full of divination artefacts he had collected throughout the years: crystals, reptile bones, cursed coins. Some he had even confiscated from around the neighbourhood, taken from confidence artists for their own good, but the crown of his collection was a fortune telling machine he built with his own hands. Inside, an animatronic puppet of a gypsy woman, fashioned after his mother, sat at a table with a deck of tarot cards ready to be dealt. He dropped a penny inside the coin slot, and watched as the puppet's eyes flashed a fiery crimson, her head rattled to life, and then cocked to the side, as if waiting to hear his command.

"Do you wish to know your fortune?" she said, like static noise played from an old record within the box.

"Show me the Golden Dawn."

It nodded. With a pop and a click, a wooden arm clunked down to scoop up the deck. In their golden age, the Dawn kept only twenty-two members, each represented by a card of major arcana. But the cards represented living members, past and present. Even then, the number of cards rarely went up. They were a dying society. Hexenhammer had made certain of that throughout history. Some, they had even lost in the war. Max had never seen the deck dealt in full in his lifetime.

The first card drawn was The Fool, much to Max's relief and regret. Crowley was still alive, naturally. Only the good died young. The coward, he cursed, sending even his projection away instead of staying to fight. But then Max saw the fortune-teller's hand reach for another card.

The next card drawn was of an old man holding forth a red lantern. "The Hermit," Max exhaled, relieved to know Ammon was still among them.

The fortune-telling machine then drew his card: Death. Max nodded, for he knew he was still alive, thanks to Helena. The hand then reached for another. Thank God, he thought, for he had feared he would have been last.

The Empress and Wheel of Fortune were dealt next. Lynn Lin had made it out, which didn't surprise Max, for the woman was a survivor in every sense of the word. But the news of Theo did. He was glad his friend survived the attack, especially after being isolated from the others.

But when he saw the fortune teller's hand stall, his heart sank. Excluding himself, the blowhard and his master, "Just two?" he cried, pounding his fist against the machine. He expected bad news, but nothing like that. "Only two survived?" Houdini was gone, and he had seen Baskerville die for himself, but seven members had come to pay their respects that day, and five magi didn't make it out. The Golden Dawn had been decimated.

But the hand sputtered to life one last time, slowly, at first, and then reached for the deck once again, as if even the machine was uncertain. She pulled the card from the top of the deck, and drew The Devil.

"No," he gasped. Sexton Graves was still alive.

***

The last time Charlie saw that look on his brother's face was when their mother passed away. *Dire news, I take it?*

Max stumbled into the foyer, lost in his thoughts, and nearly tripped over the girl who had taken to a pile of books on ancient deities on the rug. He had entirely forgotten she was with them. The bad news came in droves; he didn't even know where to begin. Instead, he just nodded. But the news about Sexton, he would keep to himself, for now. His brother would have just panicked, and at least one of them needed their wits about them.

Is Theo alive? Charlie asked.

"Yes," he returned, regaining his composure.

Bess?

"I don't know," he admitted. "But Theo would have protected her with his life." That, he knew.

So what now? the ghost asked, looking at Helena.

It was a good question. Max sat down on his worn, leather sofa, one of the few items intentionally left unchanged by the unlocking of his sanctum. "Helena," he began, "do you... remember me? Do you remember ever seeing me before?"

The girl abandoned the thick tome, and walked over to join the brothers, watching as a plush armchair materialized from nothing before her, which certainly looked more comfortable and posher than the sofa. "No," she said, planting herself down. "We met for the first time today, on the street."

Max looked over to Charlie, thinking the same thing.

But earlier, you said you knew about your father. Then that means you—

Max interrupted, fearing his brother would give too much away. "Could you tell us about him? There's just something we would like to confirm."

Helena just nodded. Her face was about as unreadable as Uriel's. "We may have met for the first time today, but I know much about you."

Max leaned forward in his seat. "And your father?" he insisted.

"Uriel," she replied, plainly. "The angel."

Again, the brothers glanced at each other. *And your mother, where is she?* Charlie asked.

"Gone," Helena said.

"As in, she passed?" Max asked, respectfully, only for the sake of clarity.

Helena shook her head. "No," she returned, "simply gone. As if she never existed. Not a picture remains, nor a letter. Not a single person remembers who she was, except for me."

Max remembered Uriel's warning about his brethren wiping the woman from time. But, if that was the case, why wasn't she purged alongside the mother? One problem at a time, he reminded himself.

And your father revealed himself to you?

She nodded. "He appeared to me a few nights ago, when was I asleep. He was so beautiful, a thing of light," she said, in awe. "I wasn't even scared. It was as if I knew no harm would come to me in his presence. He touched my head, and that's when I knew everything."

"Even about us?" Max confirmed for himself.

She touched her forehead, and wrinkled her brow in concentration. "I don't understand how, but I was able to find you, like I always knew you were going to be on that street today, at that very moment in time. As if it were—"

"Destiny," Max finished.

"Yes," she said. "Like destiny."

The thing at the platform was right, Charlie exhaled, looking at Max. What else did it know?

"Then do you know who attacked the cemetery today?" he begged.

She just shook her head.

"Or anything about a man named Sexton Graves?" Max implored again, hoping for anything more, but only earned another concerned look from his brother.

"No," she apologized, looking a bit flustered. "My father told me you were the only person I could trust, Mister Thanatos. That I had to find you—and that I shouldn't trust your brother Charlie."

Max balked at the idea. "Your father never liked my brother," he confessed, annoyed that the Fallen instilled his prejudice onto the girl, "but, believe me when I say Charlie is my better in every possible way." The pride he had for his younger sibling was clear, but then he turned to Charlie and teased, "But don't you dare repeat that to anyone."

I hardly believe you said it, myself, Charlie said, with a smile.

Helena shifted in her chair, tucking her legs underneath. The atmosphere in the sanctum soured back to reality, "But my father's dead, isn't he?" she asked.

He didn't hesitate. "Yes," the magus said. "Murdered."

Max, Charlie protested. *Show a little tact. That was still her father.* His brother was never one for beating around the bush.

"What?" he said. "Better the girl knows the truth."

"In a way, I already knew," she said, touching her chest. "I sensed that the light I felt that night had gone out. But who could kill an angel?" she asked, more to herself.

Max looked at his brother, hoping to avoid another remark. "My dear, the real question is why? Helena, I must ask: did your father tell you *who* you are? How is it you are able to bring the dead back to life?" Max stopped speaking abruptly as the shame of his actions washed over him. If he hadn't burned the body back at Grand Central, Uriel might have been able to tell them the identity of his killer. He could have been brought back to life by his daughter. Max shook his head. He had no way of knowing what awaited them all. At the time, it had seemed the right move.

"Father called me a… Nephilim."

Max nodded. "You're incredibly special," he admitted. "Unique, even. As far as I know, you might be the only one of your kind."

"In New York?"

"No," he said, "in existence, and your father went to great lengths to protect you."

"Protect me? From whom?"

My brother and I believe Hell is after you.

The girl shifted again in her chair.

"As you already know, Heaven and Hell are very real, but much closer than you imagine. There is no great city in the clouds, no icy pit below our feet. They are alongside us. Always. Many deities exist, some far older than Christianity, but Heaven and Hell deal with the piety and sin of souls. And they work in balance, one keeping the other in check: nature and man, good and evil, light and dark. Neither win nor lose," he lingered, thinking of what Mahesh had told him many years ago, "they simply just push and pull at each other. That struggle is what we call life."

The girl just blinked in response.

"Tea? Milk?" Max asked abruptly. She shook her head. The magician reached out into the air, summoned a crystal glass into his hand, and watched as it filled itself with a brown liquor. After a much-needed sip, he continued, "But I strongly believe you exist outside the domain of Heaven and Hell. In a way, neither have any claim over you, nor rule you."

"I'm upsetting the balance?" she asked.

"Yes," Max replied. "An anomaly would be closer to the truth, but that is why you're in danger. Your father shielded you from their eyes, but both sides have many allies in this world. If just one finds you…" he let the words dangle, hoping she finally understood the consequences.

"And whose ally are you?" she insisted, shifting uncomfortably in her seat.

"That of my clients," he said, with a wink. "I am a magus and a detective, and I take neither side in this little eternal skirmish of theirs, but Uriel has been a client of mine in the past, and even trusted me to… find you once before." He had nearly said too much. "Now, you have been left alone in a very dangerous world, my dear, and in a far more precarious position. So, because of that, I have decided to extend the agreement I made with your father by placing you under my protection."

"How can you protect me against Heaven and Hell where my own father failed? He was an angel."

The girl didn't beat around the bush either, Charlie noted.

"For starters, we're one step ahead of both sides."

"How do you know this?" she asked, sceptical.

"Because you and I are still alive," Max said, giving his thumb ring a twirl. "And if we are to stay ahead of this, I need to seek an audience with my informant."

Don't tell me, Charlie moaned. *The hat?*

"The hat," Max confirmed. The little treasure he had procured in the Deep South was a card he decided it was time to play in his pursuit of the Devil.

And you think that's wise? With our guest here? he whispered.

"As long as we remain within the walls of my sanctum, we are well beyond the reach of our enemies." He downed the rest of his liquor and dismissed the glass with a pop. "Or so I believe."

Charlie put his hands on his hips.

Max shrugged. "Just don't sin or pray to anyone while I'm gone."

I'm not coming with you?

"No," he said. "Don't forget, Hell wants you, too, and I want you here. Keep our guest company."

And do what?

"I don't know," he said sardonically. "She's a girl. Exchange feelings excessively."

***

The wall split in two, allowing Max to walk through unhindered, and closed itself off again to the hallway. He had many vaults tucked away in his sanctum. Each harboured its own death contraption, its own element of ungodly wares designed to maim and steal away the lives of men. But this vault housed a rather plain top hat, one still covered in a bit of orange dust. Deep within its magical space was a creature that had once possessed a young girl named Marie. The Dawn called them vorghouls, a minor demon that latched itself onto children like a spectral leech, slowly becoming them until death. But it wasn't the children they sought. Vorghouls fed on the despair of parents as they watched their sons and daughters die a very slow and painful death.

With a wave of his hand, the hexagon-shaped room rotated clockwise, facing both the east and the west, then another portion closer to the room's centre rotated separately counter-clockwise, locking into place. The entire room was unravelling like a puzzle box until it finally came to rest. Wards and glyphs burned themselves into the wall like graffiti until not a single blank space remained. He placed his right palm onto the floor, and a seal stretched out to every corner.

Upon release, the demon would find itself trapped inside a cage within a cage within another cage. It would take the creature years to break through them all, decades even. He was confident in his magic. He had trapped it once already, and that was in a dusty shanty. He was now in his sanctum; its every inch answered to his beck and call. If it somehow broke free, he could do it again.

He reached into his vest, and retrieved a leverlock knife. With a flick and one slash, his palm was wet with blood. "Release," he commanded. The top hat quivered on the floor, then quickly bobbed from side to side before it flipped itself over entirely. A black ooze seeped from the opening, and puddled over the seal. The anamorphic blob whipped out like black tendrils and folded into itself, but as the figure took shape, the vault was thrown into a supernatural darkness. Then his thumb ring burned.

Max was so preoccupied with the seal, he had forgotten all about the restraints. He leapt backwards, and commanded manacles and chains to hold back the beast. He hoped his folly wouldn't be his last. He heard the clanking of metal rapidly drag across the floor, followed by the sound of chains being pulled taut as they reached their limit. The putrid smell of rotted meat filled his nostrils.

"Is that Max?" a little girl's voice piped inches from the magician.

Max heard the laboured breathing of a large animal, then a step with tremendous weight behind it. "Max,

Max the eater of sin," the girl's voice sang. "He'll steal your soul with a toothy grin."

He summoned light to return to the vault, but the creature was so vile, so full of darkness, that the rays simply couldn't survive fully. Even the flame from his lighter failed to illuminate the room. It was as though he had stumbled into a room of pale moonlight. "I need information," he said, puffing out a cloud of mist into the frigid room.

He saw the chains slither across the floor like serpents. The demon didn't want to be bothered, and was retreating to the other side of the room. As Max's eyes began to adjust, he saw the large outline of a figure hiding in the far corner, sniffing the air like a dog.

"I smell Hell on you," the creature said. "How?"

"You don't ask the questions."

The vorghoul stirred at the sound of his voice, rattling the chains as it shifted around. It sniffed again. "I smell something else… grief," it purred. "You have lost much today, hu-man. It smells like honey. Let me have a taste. Just a little. I am famished."

Max clenched his fist, and all of the heavy chains wrenched the creature hard against the wall.

Max approached the monster. It was twice his size, and covered in short black hair that shone in the soft light. The arms were elongated, and dragged across the ground. Its legs were inverted like a dog's, but hoofed like a horse. The face was hideously scarred, as if diseased by smallpox. It was sickening to look at, but Max didn't turn away. It was very nearly a beast in every sense, except for its blue eyes, which looked human, but reflected a stark hatred for him.

"Who killed Uriel?" he demanded to know.

"You did," it said.

Max growled, already tired of its games, "You are of a hive mind. If one knows, you all know."

"Then find another demon," it returned.

"I have you. The Fallen, Uriel, who killed him? Was it your kind?"

"You did," it insisted again.

Max reached out and drew a cross on the creature's black chest with his index finger, burning the symbol into its flesh like acid. The creature howled, but not from the pain. "Hell *is* suffering," it called out, as if begging for more. "Pain is our symphony, and you don't have the instruments to play."

"Pain won't work? Then how about I read you last rites, and free you from this plane?" he threatened. "You will be locked away in purgatory, cut off from the Hell you so dearly love, and wither away for all of eternity. No grief, no torment. You will never see the Father of Beasts again!" His voice rose to a shout. "That, I promise."

"No," it whimpered, like a broken child.

"Then tell me who killed the angel," he ordered.

"No, no, no," it continued to cry.

"Tell me!"

"You did," it finally said, once more.

Max rolled up his sleeves. "Then so be it."

"...when you betrayed him."

He paused. "Betrayed?"

"Yes, betrayed," it nodded, "to the necromancer."

"Sexton Graves?"

The vorghoul smiled, brandishing its rotted fangs. "He struck a deal. Promised us the abomination. We gave him more time to die. But the hu-man struck two deals, so sayeth others. Another with the 'Doves.'" The creature smiled again, and let out a 'coo-coo' like the bird.

"'Doves'? He's playing demons and angels against each other?" Max asked.

"Smart man, stupid man," it chuckled. "And he doesn't like you very much."

"Then why kill Uriel and not me?" he asked.

"He wanted that pleasure for himself," the girl's voice purred. "Of course, we can make a deal of our own, Sin-Eater. On the side. Just between you and me. No one will know. I protect you; you just release me," it said. "I just want to see Hell again. Send me home."

Max stroked his beard. "I have a counter-offer of my own: rot in purgatory."

"No," it shrieked, flailing against its iron bondages.

***

Max left the vault speckled head-to-toe in the black bile of the creature. Last rites for a demon were always a messy affair. But Max had answers at last; he finally understood the danger. Heaven and Hell wanted the girl, and so did a very dangerous enemy. Max was overpowered and outmatched, and now in possession of the most sought-after thing in all of creation. He would need help, but not before another shower.

CHAPTER FOURTEEN: LAZARUS

New York was still. The life of the city had been ruptured like a burst pipe after the attack on Houdini's funeral made every front-page headline. No one left their homes. The streets were barren. Morning had come, and with-it misery and despair.

Officer Ronan walked W. 95th Street like Death, silent and undeterred from his task. He had parked his Packard police car, taken without permission, several blocks over, for this was something he had to do alone. He wanted to walk, to think. No copper would have walked Alafair alone, but he was a veteran of the Great War. He had seen many things much worse than a gypsy ghetto. He had lost family and friends, and by week's end he would have buried even more.

War hardened a man's heart. The lucky ones came home numb, human but not really so. Husks of men pantomiming what it was to be alive, trying to find their place again, while locking away the burden of sympathy so deep down inside, it would never see the light of day again. But not him. Ronan remembered them all. He was cursed with perfect recollection. Innocent lives were lost: twenty-three people, including seven children, and five police officers. Their bloodied faces seared into his memory. It didn't just break his heart, it made him angry. The perps were still at large, gone like the wind. Vanished, as if by magic… or… by magic?

He stood outside the brownstone building, gripping the newspaper furled in his hand. He was about to confront a magician, with a Colt on his hip and a bobby stick on his belt. The city wanted answers. The lost deserved retribution.

He demanded justice.

***

"Breakfast is served," Max said, placing a plate of pesarattu before Helena. "This is Charlie's favourite Indian dish." He smiled as the girl winced at the sight of the green omelette before her, just as he had the first time it was served to him. "It took me years to work up the courage to try it, but I was glad when I did."

It tastes better than it looks. Believe me, Charlie added.

"Believe me" was a phrase someone said when they were lying, she knew. "Thank you, Mister Thanatos," she responded, eyeing the food with suspicion.

"Please, just Max."

'*Mister Thanatos reminds me of my father,*' Charlie parroted, in Max's voice.

"Exactly," he said, glaring at his brother for stealing his line. "Since we are going to be together for a while, there is no need to be formal." He draped his linen napkin over his lap, and began privately saying grace until he caught himself, instead concluding with "Bon appétit."

Helena sliced off the crispy part at the edge, and cautiously took a bite. Her scepticism warmed to approval. "This is delightful," she beamed.

"Cooking and magic are more alike than one would think," said Max. "A cook might not necessarily make a great magician, but every magician would certainly make a great cook."

Except for Ammon.

"Maybe except for Ammon," Max reluctantly agreed.

"My mother used to bake the most wonderful walnut bread," the girl boasted, but a shadow fell over her when Helena realized she was alone.

Max realized it, too. "Maybe you could bake it for us tonight, for dessert?"

It was a weary smile, but a smile nonetheless. "Yes, I would like that very much," she agreed, returning to her pesarattu.

"Then it's settled."

Charlie floated to the far end of the dining table, watching them enjoy his favourite meal, one he could no longer taste. It was a bittersweet torture, one of many he had endured throughout the years. He heard Max tell her a story about a monkey he once saw play a hurdy-gurdy at a wedding, and they laughed. His brother was a reserved man, one might even say cold, except when it came to children. He knew there was a tempest raging within Max's heart, but he wore a brave face for Helena's sake. The poor girl needed his strength, feigned or not. He found it to be a touching scene, but one that would not last.

Max would burden himself again to save her, and at great sacrifice. He knew him too well, whether it was to repay Helena for bringing him back to life or to honour the Fallen, a creature his brother didn't even like. And despite the uneasy happiness at that table, Charlie had to remind Max of what was to come.

You've been quite aloof since your meeting with your… informant, yesterday. I believe now would be the perfect time to tell us about your plan, Charlie said. *Or is she going to live with us in the sanctum indefinitely?*

Max took a sip of water. "No," he replied. "That was never my intention. The girl deserves to live a long and happy life, that is most certain, and it will never be possible chained to my side," he looked at Charlie. "No offence meant."

None taken.

"So, I need to broker a deal between Heaven and Hell."

Charlie laughed.

Wait, you're serious?

"Do you think I'd jest at a time like this? Attacking angels with magic would be like throwing stones at a mountain. And demons are just abject horrors, sins given flesh. Banish one, two more appear. I can't fight them, Charlie."

Then what can you possibly offer in place of a Nephilim?

"It's not the girl they want," he said, looking at Helena, "it's for the balance to return."

His brother wasn't convinced. *You would think one side would finally like to win this war of theirs,* Charlie stated.

"And you would be right," he agreed. "But one side fights vehemently for the Greater Good, the other deals with pride and wrath. To spite the other's victory, either one of them would much rather keep the balance than let the other win."

They'd rather stalemate than concede defeat? In its own way, that oddly makes sense.

"And I have an idea as to how to exploit that, but it's the longest of long shots, and I can't be the negotiator in this transaction. There are rules to this kind of game," he said. "Human representatives from both sides need be present: one who consorts with angels and another who considers himself the Great Beast."

Charlie laughed again. *You mean Crowley? You want to bring in the one man who hates you above all else to… defend your case against Hell? To fight in your stead?*

Max shrugged. "Like I said: it's a long shot. Crowley is all about self-interest, and if either side gets their hands on our guest, there wouldn't be much profit to be made in a world that no longer exists as we know it. Imagine if nature won? Or darkness?"

Would it be so bad if Heaven won this war? Charlie asked in Latin, so the girl wouldn't understand. *There'd be no more monsters for you to fight. No more evil in the world.*

"What are you suggesting, exactly? That we serve her up to those things?" Max shot back, testily, in Latin.

No, he returned. *I-I don't know.*

"They'd smite every sinner in a heartbeat, Charlie— no matter how small the infraction, myself included, and then I'd never be able to save you. No one could, because everyone would be gone," he returned in English, tired of their argument. "Crowley would see my point, merely to further his own self-interest. He is a simple creature, fuelled by simple desires. And, as much as I hate to admit it, his particular and very vocal hate for Christianity has given him some clout amongst demonkind. They'd listen. Plus, there's a third party involved in all this I would very much like to avoid."

Sexton Graves is still alive, Charlie guessed correctly.

Max didn't bother withholding it anymore, and just nodded.

Do you think he'd still come for her?

Max wasn't so sure.

You're afraid to face him again, aren't you? he asked, but there was no blame in his voice. He had felt the man's malice at the Nightshade for himself, and that was before Max burned his world to the ground. He knew a reckoning would eventually come for them both.

"Who wouldn't be?" Max said. 'But one problem at a time."

The spirit just shook his head, but after a pause went on. *And who is to be the one consorting with angels?*

"And ruin the surprise? After breakfast, you'll find out," he teased, with a wink. "I've been charging a very special spell since last night."

What spell?

Their conversation was interrupted by three knocks at the door.

The trio exchanged worried glances, but the girl was the first to panic. "Don't worry," Max said to Helena. "Hell doesn't knock." His sanctum was synched slightly out of reality, but he kept his front door always tethered to the real world, just in case he needed a lifeboat from a spell gone sideways. But that didn't mean anyone could still come through. The door had no lock to pick and was heavily warded. "Nothing can get in unless I allow it," he assured the girl.

The knocks came again, this time with more heft.

"Mister Thanatos," came a gruff, Irish voice from the other side. "It's Ronan. It'd be best to open up. Your neighbours said you were home." He banged again. "I can do this all day."

"Who?" the girl asked.

If he wants to knock, let him knock.

"He's an officer in the police department," he answered. "We assist each other, on occasion." He turned to his brother. "He's no enemy of ours. In fact, he might even know who attacked the funeral," he said, reverting his sanctum back to his modest apartment with a twist of his hand.

Or maybe he's here with the entire police force.

Max balked at the idea. "Why?" he asked. "I've done nothing unlawful, except maybe flee the scene of the attack. And that was only to save myself. I'm going to let him in."

Charlie crossed his arms. *What about Helena?*

"If he asks, she's here for violin lessons."

You don't even own a violin.

"Then I'll conjure the damn thing up," Max bit, before opening the door with a forced smile. He hadn't seen his friend since Grand Central. He was eager to hear details about the funeral, and about what happened with the thieves' guild beneath Chinatown. With the chaos raining down around him, he was just happy to see, at least, one of his friends was alive and well. "Officer Ronan," he said, "how may I help yo..." but the words had barely left his mouth. With a clubbing blow, the copper got the drop on Max with a bobby stick right between the eyes.

Max stumbled backwards. The big man didn't pause for a moment, as he rushed through the door like an avalanche, pinning the aged magus hard against his coat room door. Before the magician even realized he was being attacked, handcuffs were already tightly clasped around his wrists, and had a Colt jammed into his ribs. It was almost like being brutalized again by Augustine Fey, but this man was supposedly his friend.

Ronan promised himself he would be stern, promised to see it through— no matter how intense, how heartbroken, it made him feel. But he saw the shock on the magician's face, the blood trickling from the man's wound, and he wanted to take it back. He wanted to wish his actions away. He wanted to begin the day anew, to find another way. But he only tightened his grip. He could not waiver, not then. He was a solider, a cop, a man, and a father. He would not falter in his task. "I'm really sorry about this, Mister Thanatos, I am, truly, but you're coming with me back to the station to answer a few questions. And I can't have you turning me inside-out before you do," he said, securing the handcuffs even tighter than before.

A million questions assaulted Max's mind, but only one stuttered out. "Why?"

"Because I took an oath to the city of New York, to protect and serve. And a lot of good people died yesterday because I did neither. I'm doing this for them," he said, but hesitated. "No, I'm doing because I'm selfish," he confessed. "I'm doing this because you got a second chance, and they didn't."

"What are you talking about?" he shot back, confounded by it all.

"I'm talking about this," Ronan returned, wrenching his friend back around to face him. He pulled out the day's edition of the *New York Liberty* from his pants pocket. In big bold print, the singular headline read "Lazarus," with the photograph taken of Max and Helena after his resurrection. "A crowd of people saw you come back to life." From over Max's shoulder, he saw Helena peer out from behind a worn leather sofa. "Saw *that* kid bring you back."

He dropped the newspaper. "See, I put enough of the pieces together. There was an attack, you ran, got broadsided by a bus, and then she brought you back. And I got to thinking: why couldn't she do the same for the others? Why do they have to stay dead?" He then turned to speak directly to the girl, "I know this seems scary, but I'm not here to hurt you, lass. I'm a copper, one of the good guys. It's my job to help people. Do you understand?" he asked.

Helena shook her head, clearly frightened by the man.

But Ronan didn't care. "Look, I'm gonna need you to come with me. You can't stay here by yourself."

"She isn't going anywhere," Max warned, and was wrenched hard by Ronan for his trouble.

"I don't want to," she said.

"It doesn't matter what you want, it matters what I want, and that is for you to come with me. If you brought Mister Thanatos back, you could do the same for all of the victims. There was a kid—younger than you—who was caught by a grenade. You can help him. His name was Edward Wilcox. Another: a mother of two, Sylvia Welsh. Bled out in the snow, right in front of her kids. You can help her, too."

But Helena shook her head, taking a step back.

"Why?" Ronan cried out. "If you could bring people back from the dead, why wouldn't you?" he growled at the girl, incredulously.

"She's not a tool, Ronan."

But the copper wouldn't hear of it, and shoved Max back against the door. "Think about the friends we've lost in the war. Family. Your brother. Her gift is a miracle. She has no right to pick and choose who gets to come back. It should be her duty."

Ronan was no fool, Max knew. Subduing him as quickly as he had was a smart tactic, one he never expected from the man, but he had made the critical mistake of not gagging his mouth. Unlocking the cuffs would have been as simple as uttering a single word, but, despite the suffering the man's brutality, he couldn't bring it upon himself to harm his friend, who had been struck mad with grief. He had lived it all before in Bombay. But the man was seething with rage and armed, and more telling was that he had now turned his attention onto Helena. If Max couldn't protect the girl from a single man, he had no right to try and protect her at all. He had considered Ronan his friend, but he had no choice but to treat all threats equally.

Her safety was paramount. He couldn't let Ronan take her from that place, Hell would literally break loose upon them all.

"Ronan," Max pleaded, "I'll tell you everything. Everything about the attack, about the girl, about how to save them all. No one deserved yesterday. I've lost friends, too."

Max! Charlie protested.

But, as usual, he ignored his brother. "Just shut the door, and give me five minutes to explain. That's all I need to make this right. We'll talk, you deserve that much." His words were soothing, calculated. Deceiving.

Ronan looked at the mage. "Five minutes," he agreed. "Only because you helped my daughter. But then everyone's coming with me," he said, slamming the door shut with a shove.

"Unlock," he said. "I'm sorry, Ronan." The officer was caught in the middle of a twisting room, like a funhouse, as they found themselves in the mage's sanctum once again. The floor expanded, nearly knocking the Irishman off of his feet. The steel cuffs popped open and collapsed hard to the floor with a clang. Max had turned the tide on his friend. With a command, the front door swung fully open, and the magus summoned a powerful gale of wind. With the force of a hurricane, it blew the big man out of the apartment, slamming the door shut behind him.

But Officer Ronan did not find himself back in the brownstone's hallway with the frayed red carpet. He had been flung onto a busy street at night, and nearly crashed into a hundred Chinese bicyclists swerving to avoid a collision as they peddled their way through a busy marketplace in Shanghai.

"He won't be bothering us anymore," Max said, more ashamed than proud of his deception. "Not for a long time, anyway."

What did you do?

"Moved the apartment," Max replied, plainly.

You what?

"That was going to be my big surprise," disappointed it was spoiled, "but we're currently on our way to visit my old Master. Ronan just took a detour along the way."

To where?

Max shrugged. "He could be anywhere, honestly. I just hope it's somewhere… inconvenient," he said, touching his forehead. "Once he cools down, I'm sure he'll figure something out." Or, at least, he hoped.

"He hurt you," Helena said, reaching up to heal his wound.

But Max pulled away. "I don't mind," he said to the girl, gently. "It'll serve as a great reminder of today. After all, isn't that what scars are for?"

He scooped up the paper from the floor, and scanned the article. It didn't mention his name, but he knew anyone in Alafair wouldn't hesitate to identify him for a reward. Charlie was right once again. The press was one enemy he didn't need, and now the police were involved. New York, his home, may be lost to him for good.

CHAPTER FIFTEEN: AMMON SAFAR

Max walked across North Bridge towards New Town. Unlike the sprawling metropolis he had left behind, always with its eyes on tomorrow, Edinburgh hardly changed. The monochromatic, medieval city flirted uneasily with modernization, stubbornly clinging to the old ways. Even in the Age of Tesla, the idea of motorbuses on Princes Street was more fantastical to the Scots than the faeries in the Highlands or the banshees haunting the western shore. And in another hundred years, he doubted very much that would change.

A wintery gust carried the scent of approaching rain in from the ocean, then an icy drop splashed atop his very bald head. As if the sky could no longer hold itself back, it all came rushing down at once. But it did not cause him to hasten his step, nor did it of those around him. The drops felt lighter in Scotland than anywhere else in the world. He found them soothing as they spattered against his smooth scalp. He wore no hat that day. The unpredictable Scottish gales never allowed such accessories to be kept on anyone's head for long. One simply had to endure the wetness of it all. That was the Scottish way.

Marble-coloured Shetland ponies hurried carriages past Max. Their hooves clattered rhythmically across the cobbles as they went. A vagabond begged for coin nearby. A train whistle cut the air from below. It was a comforting sound: the sound of civilization at work. Beneath North Bridge, Waverly Station was a beehive of activity. Porters shouted new arrivals. Thick plumes of white clouds puffed in the distance. The magician smiled. Edinburgh was exactly how he had left it, and he wished he had never left at all.

Past the Balmoral Hotel and close to North Bridge was Calton Hill, and in the shadow of Calton Hill was a narrow antique shop much older than people knew. Some legends said the shop predated the city, and that Edinburgh was built around it. But only one man was old enough to know for sure.

Max stood before its front window, one so smeared with soot and grime that he could hardly see through the glass. Next door was the same tea shop from his youth. Before he stepped through the door, the scent of vanilla flooded him with memories of an earlier time. As he reminisced, people walked by without giving the shop a second glance. It was magically warded to be ignored. It was bad for business, but critical for the owner's discretion. The antique store once had a name, but it had been forgotten with time. No one but a select few even knew it existed. To Max, it was a sanctuary. It was a second home.

I won't be joining you inside, Charlie said, rather bluntly. *I'd rather wait out here.*

Max shook his head at his brother's stubbornness. "Suit yourself," he returned. "But you should reconsider. He would be happy to see you again."

That would make one of us.

The shopkeeper's bell jingled as Max opened the door, igniting a smile from the magician. The very notion of a bell above the threshold struck him almost as comical. "As if you didn't already know I was here," Max announced his arrival.

"I sensed you the moment you stepped onto British soil, Maximilian. I'll join you in a moment. I'm just waiting for the kettle to boil," called a man's baritone voice from the back room.

"You're a magus. Command it to boil," Max mused.

"Never waste perfectly good magic on the mundane," lectured the voice.

Max unbuttoned his wool peacoat, heavy with rain, and draped it on the worn brass hook by the door, just as he had done a hundred times before, and waited. He breathed in the dusty, stale air. Every inch of the store was protected by incredible magic; wards prevented evil from manifesting outside the walls and within, and even his new pair of raven-black-tinted spectacles revealed invisible runes inscribed on the walls, runes that eluded even him.

But the shop was as quaint as it had always been. His Master could have forged a paradise with a thought, crafted a world to his likeness, shaped it to his every whim or desire. To everyone else, reality was but a locked door, yet Ammon Safar held the key. Yet, despite the man's incredible gifts, he always chose to live a modest, earnest life. A life most selfless.

Max walked down a narrow aisle, studying the priceless antiques from civilizations long extinct, ones preserved and protected. Each piece of the assortment radiated magic and history: a vial of ash from Pompeii, wood from the Trojan horse, even a scale from a white dragon. The first trinket he had ever collected was from the shelf before him: a pygmy skull trapped in amber. It was as a gift from his Master. It sparked a curiosity that ignited his lifelong obsession as an artificer.

"Anything you'd be willing to part with today?" Max half-joked, eyeing the collection like a child in a sweets shop. He loved baiting the man, who was too charitable for his own good. "Take whatever catches your eye," Max mumbled under his breath, knowing his Master far too well.

"Take whatever catches your eye," the voice said, predictably. "I have a fellow coming by today with a new acquisition."

Max tried to pick up the small vial of ash, but it held fast in place.

"*If* you can break the enchantment," the voice added, also well-versed in his pupil.

His Master never made things easy. That would have been like deciphering a language yet to be invented, he realized, so Max smiled despairingly instead. It was truly a pity. He would have loved to brew the volcanic ash into his coffee.

A thump echoed from the back of the shop. It was an all-too familiar sound of a heavy book being shut. "Why hello there," said a soft, English voice from the back of the shop. A sandy-haired young man sat at a small table, dwarfed by a pile of books. "You must be Mister Maximilian... Thanatos, I believe. I heard Master Ammon say your name when you arrived. He often speaks highly of you."

It was strange hearing someone else call Ammon his 'master.' It made Max feel a bit territorial. "Who are you?"

"Oh, right. Please forgive me. My name is Howard," he said, blinking behind a pair of thick spectacles. "Howard Dove. It's a pleasure to make your acquaintance."

"His student?" Max asked, but more stated. He felt betrayed once the realization finally sank in that Ammon had moved on. "Are you a magus?"

The young man shook his head, seemingly disappointed with himself. "Sadly, no. Just a historian, I'm afraid, cursed with an insatiable curiosity. Grimoires and symbology, curses, and creature *compendiums,* most of your culture's history has been diluted over the ages by legends and myths."

"So young Howard here is learning the oral history of our people," Ammon continued, as he finally emerged from the backroom, "as how I lived and witnessed it. The volume would be the first written account of its kind."

Max watched his Master walk across the room holding a cup of tea that rattled in his shaky hand. It was the first time he had seen his old mentor since he had left the Golden Dawn. The mental images of the great magus Max had carried in his memories for so long were replaced with the person he now saw before him. The Egyptian was lanky and balder, his aged, dark skin looked coarse, and he looked almost feeble, like a gentle grandfather. A far cry from the man he knew before. He still dressed simply, like a labourer, but the man was far from simple. "Why have him author it?" Max asked, more insulted than confounded. "Why not one of us?" he stressed again, hardly put off by the young man's presence.

"Because the boy reminds me so much your brother," he lamented. "I see he's not here with you. Is he still—"

Max simply nodded, answering the question before it was asked. His heart wrenched a little when he saw the man's disappointment. "He doesn't hate you," he wanted to reassure. "He just still doesn't—"

"Forgive me for teaching you magic," Ammon finished.

Max nodded again slowly. He had first met the Egyptian in New York, when he was caught trying to pick his pocket. It was a chance encounter that set him on the path of a magus, which also uprooted Charlie's life for good.

Ammon returned the nod with a weary smile. He turned to Howard, "Continue with your studies. Expect to be tested on Sumerian when I return. Sumer was a particularly intense period for my kind," Ammon stated, ushering Max to join him at the front of the store, and casting a dampening spell for privacy.

"Sumerian? Poor kid," Max said, remembering his own lessons. As they walked, Max observed his former Master. His eyes were cloudy, his skin cracked in patches on his neck. Decades made up a sliver of Ammon's life, but during the years Max had been away, his Master hadn't only come to look older, he looked ill. "Why are you recording our history now?" he asked, insinuating something more.

"I am in the winter of my long life, young Maximilian. When I go, so does our history. I just thought it was time to settle all of my affairs, if you will. The world should finally know our story, and our struggles, before history tells another version."

It sounded impossible, coming from his Master. The idea of death. Ammon had witnessed history like no other. He never confessed his true age, but claimed to have been born before Christ. He had seen religions rise, empires fall. Ammon had spent a hundred lifetimes preserving the past. In every sense of it all, he *was* the past. Any book, any object he touched, he instantly knew its contents and history. His Master spoke every language known and unknown to man. And according to legend among the magi, he was the inspiration behind Merlin, a claim he never refuted.

"You can't die," Max gasped.

But Ammon chuckled, knowing better. "It is true magic prolongs our life, but always at a great price. Sometimes, it rots us from the inside, like a vicious disease. In rarer instances, the power corrupts us fully, and turns us into monsters."

"I have fought such a creature, not too long ago."

"Then you already know. Magic is our beginning, and our end. Even I can't escape it." Ammon rubbed his weak chin with his index finger and thumb, "It takes much of my power these days just to maintain this form," he said, but more confessed. "I adopted this face centuries ago, never guessing then just how poorly dark skin would be received by the civilized world. Yet you wouldn't want to see this old mask of mine slip, not even a little. You wouldn't like what lies beneath this gentle persona."

Ammon moved across to join Max at the shop's counter, and placed his cup and saucer down. "Now; it has been far too long, criminally so," he said, placing a loving hand upon Max's shoulder. With a raised eyebrow, Ammon appraised Max's extraordinarily long beard, still kept wrapped around his neck like a scarf. "The beard, I don't like."

But as his former pupil dug down for a rebuttal, Ammon warmly silenced him with a playful pat on his face, "Whatever the reasons are for not seeing me, they are yours and yours alone," he said. "After what happened to the Golden Dawn, I feared I had lost you, too."

Max slumped a bit. He had rehearsed countless excuses on the walk over.

"I've buried enough friends in my lifetime," Ammon said, "but I did send Bess a wreath. I met her once, at the wedding. She and Erik made such a nice couple," he frowned, pointedly refusing to ever refer to the magician by his stage name. "As lovely as it is to see you again, I know this isn't just a social visit. But I'm afraid time is against us this day. I have an appointment with Howard's father, and you know I never break an appointment," Ammon took a sip of his already-tempered beverage. He tapped the rim of the tea cup with his fingernail, and the milky brew rapidly started to steam, earning a disapproving glance from his pupil.

"Do as I say, not as I do," Ammon smiled, innocently taking another sip. "We have precious time to talk, so what brings you all the way back here to me?"

"I'm in trouble, Master," the magus blatantly confessed, slowly shaking his head at the understatement.

Ammon felt nostalgic. He had heard that exact same statement from his pupil at least several dozen times before.

Max noticed, too. "Proper trouble," he reaffirmed. "But it's far more complicated than that." He walked over to his peacoat, and retrieved a rolled-up newspaper from an inside pocket. Max unfurled Ronan's copy of the *New York Liberty* atop the counter, revealing the front page.

"*Lazarus*," Ammon read the headline aloud, touching the paper with his index finger.

Max pointed to the curly-haired girl in the photograph. "That girl there? Yesterday, she saved my life, Master. Quite literally, brought me back from the dead after I was hit by a bus."

"I... did not know that," he revealed, regretfully. His expression softened. "I knew about the attack, but no one has seen or heard from you in weeks—"

"Weeks?" Max gasped. "This was yesterday's paper."

Ammon shook his head, pointing to the newsprint. "This is dated November. It's nearly Christmas. Where have you been?"

He honestly didn't know, and worked it out aloud. "I phased my apartment to Edinburgh this morning. It was the only way to see you, but the spell was cast very hastily. It must have been miscast."

"Yes, I know that spell quite well, having authored it. You're fortunate lost time was your only casualty. That miscast could have blinked you out of existence." But then Ammon gave him a sly smile. "Miscasting, at your age. It's never too late to retake my instruction."

He waved his palm over Max's heart. "But you are no un-dead," he said. "You are still among us: one man, two souls. It was no necromancy that brought you back. This girl's magic you speak of is impossible. No magus has ever returned anyone from death."

Even with the protection of the dampening spell, Max lowered his voice, "That's because... the girl is the offspring of a Fallen."

"She's a Nephilim? Impossible!"

Max shook his head. "I knew her father. Someone murdered him to get to her."

Ammon had seen much in his long life, but the news twisted even his stomach. "A lot has happened while you were on your way here," he said. "I heard about the girl, through certain circles, vague rumours, really, but it wasn't until I touched this paper when it all made sense. Nikola Tesla ignited a firestorm by posting a reward for any information leading to magi, and to the girl. The Rockefellers, Edison. All of the industrialists. They incited a witch-hunt in America, and it didn't take long for it to spread here."

Ammon shook his head in dismay. "You didn't live through the witch-hunts, Maximilian. Children, women, my friends, all were strung up or burned, persecuted out of fear and hate. And now it's happening again."

"I think that is the least of our problems," Max admitted. "I may or may not have just doomed all of Creation." He felt his mentor's wintery eyes appraise his face as he spoke, as if they searched for something beyond words.

That was a first from his pupil. "Go on," Ammon said, cautiously, waiting for the other shoe to drop.

"Heaven and Hell are also after the girl, and I'm hiding her in my sanctum."

The Egyptian just shook his head at this.

"I need you and Crowley to negotiate for her safety on my behalf."

"Do they even know you have the girl?"

"Hell already suspects as much. I can ward myself against minor demons, but there's nothing I can do against an angel, when one finally comes for us. Whether they know I have her or not, I can't just wait around to find out. I need your help."

There was a rare panic in the ancient man's voice. "I don't know what you expect from me, Maximilian."

"Anything."

"I can't just ring angels on my Graham Bell."

"They come to you!"

"Yes, like moths are drawn to the flame. It's my age that stirs their curiosity. Nothing more."

"There must be something you could do. Don't you have an artefact that could protect us? A spell? Her father shielded her from their view. So, there must be a way." He watched his Master survey his face again, as if all of the answers lay between his eyes. "Master," he pleaded. "The girl didn't just bring me back, she healed me: injuries I sustained in the war, old scars covering my body. If you meet with her, I know you'd change your mind. I could even ask her to heal you."

"No," Ammon shot back, pounding the counter with his fist, nearly toppling over his tea cup. "I have earned my right to die."

The two men, more akin to family than friends, sat in awkward silence for what felt like an aeon. The Egyptian just simply looked down at counter, unable to face his former pupil. His capacity to help others was limitless, but in that rare instance of instances, Ammon was powerless and ashamed. "Max," he said, softly, "If you wanted me to trap this city inside a bottle, I would. If you asked me for a palace of gold and diamonds, it would be yours. But what you're asking…" he said, allowing his words to float. "There's nothing I can do. Even if the angels came for tea, I couldn't change Heaven's mind. I rarely ever changed yours. I have no power here," he said, with great regret. "I'm not even Christian. I'm sorry,"

Max felt like he just took a punch. "Fine. Then I'll go and ask Crowley."

"You will not find him," Ammon warned. "After the attack, he and the survivors took the Golden Dawn's Palace out of reality."

"Then give me my skeleton key, and I'll find them," he growled. "You still have it, don't you?"

Ammon nodded. "I am its keeper, yes. But you were exiled from the Golden Dawn. The backdoor is closed to you. Crowley made that quite clear to you, and to me. If that man knows about the Nephilim, about how she brought you back, or even that magic made the front pages—and I'm quite sure he does, knowing his resources— he will throw you into his Glassworld the moment you return. We have enemies, ancient enemies, ones we've done our best to elude for as long as I can remember. But this," Ammon said, lamenting over the headline. "The girl may have doomed us all, good intentions or not."

"You mean Hexenhammer?" he said with loathing, remembering Theo's warning back at Grand Central Station. But the magus didn't believe it then, and certainly didn't believe it now. "No one has heard a whisper from them since after the war," Max said, but weary of speaking the name aloud. "The girl deserves to live a life. I'm doing everything within my power to protect her, but it feels like I'm trying to look left and right at the same time. I can't do this alone, Master."

"If you believe the Golden Dawn will help you, then you are naïve."

"Let that be my problem. The skeleton key is the only way to reach them."

Ammon sighed. "You are in quite a terrible predicament, Maximilian. Crowley is more stubborn than you will ever be, and will offer no safe harbour for you or the girl. That man still hates you for sleeping with his wife, you must know that."

"They were divorced, at the time," he corrected. He always corrected.

Ammon just shook his head. "Listen to me: no more of your nonsense. If I give you the key and you return to the Golden Dawn, especially after you exposed magi to the world, he will imprison you until the end of your days. Who knows about her fate, but you will never save Charlie or the girl locked away within the Glassworld."

"I will save them both," he vowed.

"I have lived long enough to see patterns repeat themselves in history and in people," Ammon warned. "Right now, you are playing the part of the fool. No, you cannot save everyone. One learns certain truths in old age."

"I *am* old."

"Everyone is a child to me," Ammon said, patting Max's shoulder. "You must find another way. Consider this my final lecture. And with that said, I will not give you the skeleton key. Believe me when I say it is for your own good." Before his pupil could interject, the shopkeeper's bell rang.

"Please forgive my intrusion," said a soft English voice. "I didn't mean to interrupt. If you'd prefer, I can come back."

"No, that won't be necessary, Mr. Dove. My guest was just leaving."

Max left his stool. He had hoped the events of that reunion would have been far different. It felt like a betrayal, to get the 'bum's rush' for some 'rube', just for the sake of his Master's integrity of never breaking his word. He hurried for his peacoat in retreat, hoping Ammon wouldn't see his scowl. But the Egyptian held him with a firm hand upon his shoulder. Max felt the man's energy seep through his palm.

"I may seem heartless now, but one day you will come to realize the wisdom of my actions and appreciate it. You know me best of all," he said. "I only help those who cannot help themselves. And you, young Maximilian, are most capable of saving us all."

And there were times when his Master knew exactly what was in his heart. "I don't know what to say," Max said.

"Just say good-bye," Ammon returned, with a smile.

Max felt more alone than ever on his quest. The magus gave Ammon a nod as he helped him on with his heavy peacoat, and together they walked towards the door. He observed the man his Master called Mr. Dove as he passed. He was an immaculately well-dressed, well-groomed gentleman about half his age. In an ocean of black coats and black hats, the man was decked in a crisp white suit and a white bowler hat. The man looked like a banker, possibly a lawyer. And in his hands was a golden lantern with an intricate metal frame like a birdcage. Inside was a thick, red candle. Max balked at the idea he was usurped by a business transaction. If only he had more time with his Master. He wanted to part on better terms.

"Apologies, old chum," the man said at Max, tipping his hat. "What a beautiful shop. So many antiques, I could get lost in here for weeks. I trust Howard hasn't been a handful?"

The man made Max's skin crawl, and not merely because of the casual familiarity of his attitude.

The rain eased into a light mist. He had left Ammon's shop behind, probably for the final time. He shook his Master's hand, but hardly a word was said in parting. As far as Max was concerned, there was nothing left to say. He stood on the pavement and tilted his head back. The sun was masked behind the overcast sky, and the rain smelled of the ocean. It felt clean as it sprayed his face. His eyes followed gulls as they playfully darted over the buildings and he envied their freedom. Max breathed in the Edinburgh air deeply and held it in his lungs. He was never good at good-byes. Then he simply sighed, and began his walk back towards North Bridge, back towards the apartment.

He would need a new plan.

CHAPTER SIXTEEN: OLD BOOGIEMEN

Mr. Dove ran his white-gloved finger along the antique shelf, frowning at the dust. He would have to burn the glove later, perhaps along with his clothes. "My son has told me a great deal about you, Mister Safar."

"Please, just Ammon," the Egyptian said, with a welcoming smile. "Your son has taken to my lessons like no other, and I am eager to teach. Tea?"

"That would be splendid. Black, if you have it. No milk. I have an affliction."

"Of course," the magus replied, with a nod. "Howard is nearly done for today, if you'd care to wait for him at the counter." Ammon walked into the backroom, and came out a moment later with a cup. "What luck, the water was still hot."

Mr. Dove surveyed the stools, and choose not to sit. He would not besmirch his handkerchief by wiping away the filth. "I think it might be serendipitous, meeting you today of all days. Divine providence, even," he said, looking at the door.

"Why is that?"

"That chap, with the excessively long beard."

Ammon smiled warmly with pride. "Yes, a very dear friend of mine."

"Shame he had to go," Mr. Dove, admitted. "He's quite famous, you know. Been in all the papers. Maybe

I'll catch up to him in the city. Maximilian Thanatos: former member of the Golden Dawn.," he said, setting the lantern upon the counter, and facing it forward for a better view.

Ammon's smile was no more. "How do you know about the Golden Dawn?" he asked, eyeing the lantern.

"Oh," he said nonchalantly, removing a silver lighter from inside his coat pocket, and igniting the wick. "We know everything about your dear friends. Or, to be more precise, those left alive."

Ammon brow glistened with sweat.

"Feeling a tad under the weather?" asked the man in the white, crisp suit. "That's the beauty of this relic," he mused. "The lantern, itself, is just a piece of rubbish. The real power is the candle. We jokingly called it Hell Wax, on the account of its colour, but the name eventually did stick. It does something miraculous—"

The Egyptian dropped down to a knee, then collapsed hard to the shop floor. "What have you done?"

"I stopped the devilry in your veins. Simply put: no more magic."

Ammon summoned a gust to blow out the flame. "Don't," he begged.

But Mr. Dove grinned at the pathetic attempt. "It will continue to burn until the candle is no more. It's a quite resilient little thing, wouldn't you agree, Howard?"

The magician turned to see his young pupil step over him like garbage to join his father. "I apologize for the ruse, *Master* Ammon," Howard said, coolly. "But it was the only way for my father to gain entrance to your shop: one has to be invited." His voice was cold, indifferent: far unlike the kind young man he had taken under his tutelage months ago.

"I almost tasked the boy with your capture, but he wasn't ready. I fear he was actually beginning to like you," Mr. Dove said, with disgust. "When my master had the most curious epiphany overseas, as if God himself had graced him with divine insight, it led us to where we are today. Led my men and me directly to you. He knew quite a bit about your passion for teaching, love for children sympathetic towards your kind, and told me how my son could win your trust, which was hardly a challenge, honestly," he said. "My master was right about you, Ammon Safar: you are a gentle fool."

"The world's most powerful mage, oblivious to those around him, reduced to nothing in just a flick of a light," Howard said, with the same distasteful tone as his father, trying to make him proud.

"No. You don't understand," Ammon slurred over the pain rippling through his body. "Go. Save the boy. Before it's too late."

Mr. Dove disagreed, as he removed a Webley revolver holstered behind his back, and pointed it at Ammon's skull. "Before it's too late? Devilborn, this was over the moment I walked through your door."

***

Well, that didn't go so well, did it? Charlie overstated.

"You eavesdropped?"

I didn't have to. Your expression said it all when you left his shop.

"Ammon declared he was unable to help. We are on our own," he confirmed angrily, bitterly disappointed and bewildered by the attitude of his Master.

Maybe we could make it work—living in the sanctum. We could be in a new city every day—they'd never find us. Bide our time.

"I want to go back home to New York," Max went on. "Our home. It's where mother is buried. Where you are buried. I will never abandon that," he said, touching the crushed silver locket around his neck. And he continued to walk. "I wish you were by my side, Charlie. You could have changed that man's mind. He always listened to you. Ammon was adamant—he told me his refusal was for my own good, but I think I can convince Crowley. But without the skeleton key, even he is lost to me."

There was a rare trace of defeatism in his voice. Max was hardly a tactician. Annihilation was often his best motivator. But his situation was quite different from that of searching for the Devil. It wasn't about self-preservation for either himself or his brother. This time, Max had been burdened by another, one he had no real obligation towards, but still carried determinedly because of his own perverse sense of honour.

"I'm sorry," Max said.

Charlie turned to his brother. *For what?*

"For this. For everything. I make everything difficult."

We are brothers, Max. Despite my reservations about the chaos that has inevitably found us once again, ultimately, I will never leave you to suffer alone, as taxing as it is not to. And trouble certainly finds you.

It wasn't something to smile about, but Max found himself doing it anyway. "I don't know what I'll ever do without you."

Sunlight crept through a break in the clouds, cascading the wet capital for a brief moment. Max silently agreed.

It was no revelation. Trouble was a certainty, as if divine forces revelled in testing his resolve time and time again, like Job.

You were a thief, once. Couldn't you just steal the key? Charlie asked, doing what he could to change the topic, and to leave behind the awkward moment of compassion between them on North Bridge.

Max rubbed his beard. The thought seemed impossible: robbing his Master. But, still the suggestion was a bit out of his brother's character.

Would it be so wrong, stealing back what is already yours? Charlie added.

Even the antiques were enchanted well beyond his education. He dreaded to learn what magic awaited him with the proverbial keys to the kingdom. "The first time I met Ammon, I tried to pick his pocket, and failed famously," he said, with a smile. "The man never sleeps. He can sense me at will. Ammon cannot be trifled with, bested or tricked. I doubt I can even get past that shopkeeper's bell."

Was that a joke from Max Thanatos?

"It must be the end of days," Max mused, but was so involved in the conversation he hardly noticed the faint sound of screams carried by the wind. Then North Bridge trembled beneath his feet. Everyone, including the magus, stopped to gaze in the direction of Ammon's shop. "Master," Max exhaled. Before he took his next step, a wave of energy rolled across the city, shattering nearby windows and gaslights lining the bridge. Chaos erupted on the streets of New Town.

Max was already in motion, rushing through the panicking crowd back the way he had come. An explosion sounded by Calton Hill, spewing black smoke into the overcast sky. Gunfire popped. It sounded like he was back in Ypres, like he was back at Houdini's funeral again. Several bullets whistled past his head, forcing him to duck between two buildings. A woman wasn't so lucky, as she caught a stray bullet and fell down dead just a few feet away.

Max, Charlie called out. *Helena isn't here to bring you back.*

"I don't care," he blurted. He only cared about his Master. Another explosion thundered through the city. This time, there was no smoke bellowing from the blast, no concussive shock that followed. It felt seismic. As Max readied himself against the building to brave the gunfire once again, he felt the structure at his back rumble.

Max knew the pain of a gunshot, had experience the shell-shock of munition blasts in the war, but even his jaw dropped as a colossal hand emerged from the smoke of battle, and clasped the side of neighbouring building, crumbling the brick into nothing under its wicked grip.

What is that? Charlie panicked.

"I don't know," he rasped, summoning enough willpower to run towards the thing. Giants were creatures of Germanic fairy tales, of lore. Pure fantasy. But Max had seen and fought creatures also once believed to be of myth: monsters that fed on blood; men that turned into beasts. Ghosts were real. Demons were real. Even a Nephilim. But that creature, if it was a giant or not, was still not his true concern. He knew had to reach Ammon. That was all that mattered, even if it meant blasting through it.

Single shots turned into the rattle of automatic gunfire, as a barrage of bullets came from a Vickers machine-gun, one of the most feared sounds from the war. A sound he could have identified in his sleep. "Christ!" he cursed under his breath. Fear crept its way in. The attack on the funeral clawed at his frayed mind, one already frail from dying. He shook the memory of Hell away. He could not waver, not then, not even in the face of the murder device designed to rip a man in half.

And it did just that. Max saw innocents caught in the crossfire, shot in the back as they fled. Blood covered the cobbles, dust from the debris made it hard to see the extent of the carnage, but Max knew it was bad. The ground beneath his feet shook again, as the thing in the distance took another step. There was nothing he could do. All he could think about was Ammon, whose shop was at the epicentre of the war zone.

His mind raced as he tried to make sense of it all. Was the giant after Ammon? Did he summon the creature to his defence? The man's power was limitless. Yet, why did Max feel such dread in his heart? Magic made the papers. Now, a beast was unleashed upon the streets of Edinburgh. The secret world of magi was no longer a secret.

Another volley of machine-gun fire tore through the street. Max risked a glance from the cover of a building, and his heart sank. There, in the middle of the block, was a monstrosity that stood three stories tall. Its dark skin had swollen into a deformed, pulsating mass of muscle and sinew, as if its entire body was consumed by gout and turned inside out. It was more creature than human, except for the face. "Master," Max breathed. Was that the thing underneath Ammon's mask? Had he been that beast all along?

Its entire body was battered and riddled with bullets cutting through the air. Black bile oozed from every wound. Yet the creature took the barrage and held its ground against the men in crisp white suits he could now see manning the Vickers. The grotesque mass stretched its body as widely as it could. Its arms reached out, easily touching buildings on both sides of the street. The thing that was once Ammon had no intention of running. No, it was using its girth to try and shield all that he could from their assault, taking every bullet; every blast.

The old fool was sacrificing his life for others. "Fight back," Max pleaded from the shadows. But he knew the truth. He and Ammon were outnumbered, and magic could do little against machine-gun fire. If he fought back, the block would have been decimated. More lives would have been lost, and it was clear his attackers cared very little about collateral damage. Ammon was their prize, and he took every shot. He didn't move, he didn't even try to shield himself. The splattering sound of each bullet piercing his skin was sickening.

"Cease fire," Max heard someone cry out. And the command was repeated down the line multiple times until the streets were filled with only the tormented cries of the wounded and the dying. Out from Ammon's shop came the man he knew as Mr. Dove, obviously the commanding officer, followed by his son. He twirled a brass ring of skeleton keys around his index finger as he walked with brazen calm out onto the street, and stood arrogantly facing the creature before him, hardly reaching its knees.

Max.

"I know." The well-dressed man Max had walked past in the shop, the same man Ammon trusted enough to allow entrance, was a Judas all along. The boy with the thick-spectacles was also involved. Max had been so caught up with the emotions of seeing his Master once again, that he hadn't even listened to his own instincts. Now that enemy had the skeleton keys in his possession; the literal keys to the Golden Dawn. Had that been their goal all along? Max couldn't have imagined a worse scenario.

"Ammon Safar," the man projected, seemingly for all of Edinburgh to hear, "you have been judged by the Order of Hexenhammer, and have been found guilty of the practice of witchcraft, which is high treason against the throne of God, our Lord. In His name, and in the name of all things holy, I banish you from His realm by penalty of death. May He have mercy on your soul."

As commanded, Howard lifted the lantern before him. Ammon no longer stood like a quiet sentinel protecting his city. Instead, the lumbering mass tottered against the building, shattering the entire front facade, as both he and rubble collapsed onto the street. The thing that was once a man convulsed on the ground in wretched agony, Max wanted to call out to his Master, but such foolish action would only have resulted in his own death. How Ammon flailed in pain! His howls resonated deep within Max's soul.

"Now," Max heard Mr. Dove command in the distance, motioning for all men to fire.

The beautiful Edinburgh afternoon was no more. A dozen men opened fire, two blasted the beast with Vickers guns. The barrage was relentless, as it systematically blew the creature to pieces. But the thing never fought back, didn't resist. It was as if all hope had been beaten from his essence. The creature he once knew as Ammon struggled as he turned his head toward Max, as if he knew his pupil was watching all along, and they looked fixedly at each other. The soft, wintry eyes of his Master were the only thing that remained unchanged, and Max dared not turn away. He watched as the last light in those eyes faded away to nothing. The most powerful magus alive, perhaps in their history, was nothing more but a corpse in the shadow of Calton Hill, and Max ran back towards his apartment as fast as his feet could carry him. "Hexenhammer," he said to himself. They had definitely returned.

***

Max saw the hushed pauses as the news of the attack spread like wildfire into Old Town. The quiet capital was now in turmoil. How could anyone make sense of it all? His every step was like crossing a chasm. Max's history lay dead in the street. All of that knowledge, gone. Ammon's stories, gone. His former Master savagely executed for all to see. It was an impossible loss.

He heard his brother beg him for answers, but Max had none. Terror shot his mind point blank, as if the men in white suits were biting at his heels. The image of Mr. Dove hung heavily in his thoughts. He felt Hexenhammer everywhere. He dared not risk a glance backward. Max ran until his lungs screamed for mercy, then he pushed even more. He knew the danger. Breath was a luxury he could forgo.

Mr. Dove had seen his face, and by extension, so had Hexenhammer. That man had them both cornered in the shop. So why was Max allowed to leave? Why? his mind screamed. But the answer was apparent: Ammon was their ultimate prize. He should have fought back. Why didn't he just fight back? His Master's death haunted his every thought. There were too many questions. He found it difficult to focus. Every building looked the same, every street. He knew Edinburgh as well as New York, yet fear had perverted that familiar city into something foreign.

At least he had the sense to double-back through Waverly Station, ultimately towards Grassmarket, a small avenue of shops in the shadow of Edinburgh Castle. It was a risk; the city was mad with crowds. Passengers were flushed out of Waverly in droves. Every train ceased operations in the wake of destruction. It was easy enough to hide amongst the milling crowds. Max had to be certain he wasn't being followed, or he would have brought a siege to his doorstep. Charlie was an extra set of eyes, but agents of the ancient order could have been hiding anywhere and everywhere, all within an arm's reach of the magus. Hexenhammer were predators. Their strength lay in numbers and deception, and they were always ready strike with a knife in the back.

The city was a labyrinth of dark corners and alleyways. It offered a plethora of places to lay an ambush. As he went, paranoia struck at him like a fist. Every shadow was his end. Every corner hid a monster. Max shook his head to clear his thoughts. He was frantic. Reason failed him. He had to regain a measure of control. His imagination was running dangerously wild, and the old, stuffy magus knew imagination was for children. He had to calm himself. He had to think.

Charlie's voice snapped him out of it.

Max, did that man recognize you, back there in the shop?

"No doubt," he said, sucking air into his lungs as he spoke. His association with Ammon Safar was damning.

He hardly believed Mr. Dove was a fool. At the very least, he would have been pursued for information, tortured for a confession, executed if found guilty, and all magi were found guilty. If captured, he would have been as good as dead, and Hexenhammer were historically thorough with their prey. But unlike Ammon, Max wouldn't go down without a fight.

They had the skeleton keys. They had the means to enter the secret headquarters of the Golden Dawn, a society charged with the teaching and protection of the arcane arts, but having the keys wasn't enough to simply walk through the door. But if they knew about Ammon, what else did they know? His old friends, even the blowhard Crowley, were in grave danger. In one fell swoop, the world's most powerful magi could be snuffed out like a candle. Ammon hadn't stood a chance against them, and he was the strongest of them all. Max had to warn them, somehow.

His lungs were spent. Even renewed by Helena, Max was still old and well past his prime. He stopped to catch his breath within a crowd gathered in front of a small café. The Grassmarket was open, exposed, but also a perfect place to scout for pursuers. As he sucked down the air, he observed. Afternoon tea brought patrons by the dozens, filling every wrought iron chair in the square. Families and loving couples sipped from porcelain tea cups and snacked on a prism of geometric pastries. The place was untouched by the anarchy he had left behind him, but probably not for long. It was an oasis in the middle of a jungle on fire.

The magus reached into one of his many hidden pockets sown into his black vest, and removed a handful of sunflower seeds. In the cup of his palm, he held them out before his mouth and whispered a short incantation in Apache, an old shamanic spell for hunting. He tossed them out a few feet away, and watched as little birds with blue and yellow plumage spiralled down to the street for an easy meal. "I need you to be my eyes," he said, and the birds plucked them into their beaks, and swiftly disappeared into the overcast sky in every direction.

It felt like an age before his lungs slowed down. The crisp air felt good as he took it in. Even his heart slowed to something less than rampant. His thoughts were his again. He closed his eyes and concentrated onto his aerial spies. The spell was meant for one beast, not several, and birds were especially erratic. He could only see through their eyes. At best, he could influence them, not control them. But he saw enough.

Agents had crossed over the bridge in pursuit, but they were scattered across Old Town, unorganized. That was the good news. One or two men, Max could handle. Any more that that would have been a problem. The bad news was that magic, as brilliant as it was in many regards, still couldn't stop a bullet. Only the sanctuary of his apartment could truly save him that day.

You know how I feel about Ammon, Charlie said, *but he hardly deserved that.* His words were soft, compassionate, but more for his brother's sake than for Ammon's.

Max nodded, as he sucked in more air. "Thank you," he said, appreciating the sentiment.

But the lantern's light, he stressed. *It was the same as at Houdini's funeral.*

Max had noticed, too.

How could that man've bested Ammon Safar? I thought he was beyond deception. His voice turned demanding.

"The light. It must nullify magic somehow. It's the only explanation."

But that was a well-planned ambush. Vickers machine-guns? They were organized. To bring artillery into a major capital city? Those men were waiting for him. How did they even know about Ammon, Max? I thought he was your kind's best kept secret.

"I don't know," he spat, already tired of the line of questioning. He didn't want to hear someone else say his Master's name, not even his brother. Across the square was a dark-haired lady selling a variety of crystals and small mirrors from a three-wheeled cart. Max didn't have time to haggle, nor the pounds sterling on his person, so he easily lifted a circular looking glass in a brass frame with a simple distraction technique. He was already destined for Hell, so petty thievery hardly concerned him.

One block over, he gazed into the mirror, and then shattered the glass into pieces behind a bakery.

Well, that was seven years' bad luck.

"They'll have to wait their turn," he said. A moment later, as many Maxes as shards materialized on the street, identical reflections down to the minute detail. He didn't quite like the eccentric men standing before him. "Maybe Ammon was right about the beard," he retorted, but only caught himself saying his name afterwards. The wound was still impossibly fresh in his heart. "Go," he instructed the reflections. Without hesitation, each doppelgänger ran into the wilds of the city boulevards, hoping to take their pursuers along for the chase. That should buy him some time.

The apartment had manifested itself inside the East Suffolk Road Hostel, which made Max's comings and goings that day particularly scandalous, considering it was the University's newly opened dormitory for girls. But the joyous mood he had left behind that morning had soured upon his return. The news had reached even them. Some consoled each other in wet, sobbing groups, while others fled the building with suitcases in-hand. Gossip of a monster filled the hallways along with the fragrances of floral perfume and clove cigarettes. Their pretty faces scowled as he passed, a look he had grown quite accustomed to throughout the years. "I'm just visiting my granddaughter," he said many times as he started his way up towards the fifth floor, issuing curt nods in a poor attempt to defuse the intrusion.

A chorus of shrills ignited throughout the hostel's foyer. Max heard the commotion from the third floor. Heavy boots pounded the moss-coloured stone floor as men in white suits stormed their way indoors, shoving aside girls like tin soldiers. As soon as he leaned over the stairwell banister for a better vantage point, he was spotted by the burly man leading the charge.

"There," he shouted to the others, who hastened their pace. Strong hands fiercely gripped the brass banister, thrusting the men upwards to the first landing.

How did they find him? They were close. Too close. It was a race Max wasn't going to win. They were fit, enraged, and fuelled by duty. He cursed himself for allowing his enemies to get so near. His adversaries had him cornered in that seven-story building. And now those young girls who did not flee in time would, no doubt, be caught in the coming exchange.

Dawn, he thought. He only had to hold out until then. That was when the spell would recharge, and take him far away from Hexenhammer. But he had led those men straight to the apartment, straight to the girl. The thought of her in their possession was too much to bear.

From his vest, he removed a velvet pouch plump with marbles. It was childish, he knew. Ammon would have disapproved. But each colourful sphere was painstakingly incanted with their own spell, some deadly, others were just a nuisance. There was no time to sort them. Max simply turned the bag onto the steps, and one by one they fell and bounced and found their way down the stairwell. Max had already reached his floor when he heard the first concussive blast sound, followed by the thumps of grown men slamming into walls. That one was his particular favourite.

Another marble exploded, spewing blankets of cobwebs over every inch of the third-floor landing, ensnaring anyone in the tangle until the spell expired in one month's time. Marbles of fire and ice popped like firecrackers, excessive gales howled through the stairwells, followed by debilitating flashes of light. The agents of Hexenhammer had no defence against attacks that hit them from all sides. Each brought a unique agony, and Max wanted them all to suffer.

But Max miscalculated. He had forgotten all about the second stairwell at the far end of the hallway. As he approached the door numbered 506, a second group of men in white suits exploded from the other doorway. They wasted no time before drawing their revolvers. Max raced down the hall. Just two more doors until he reached his apartment. His neighbour, a dour blonde and spectacled girl, stepped into the hallway carrying a bouquet of wilted sunflowers destined for the trash. The first bullet hit her in the shoulder. She instantly spun around, and the second shot pierced the side of her head, blowing out a piece of her skull. As tragic as it was, the girl had just saved Max's life.

Three steps later, Max threw himself inside the room and slammed the door behind him. Even if they kicked it in, they wouldn't find Max's world on the other side. His apartment existed in the same plane as the dormitory, but they were out of synch with each other. Only an adept magus would have been able to cross that threshold, even if they suspected it at all, and then there would still be the matter of the lock that only Max could open. To Hexenhammer, it would have been as if he simply vanished into thin air. They punished all magi, but they hardly understood the intricacies of magic. He had finally made it. Trouble would not follow him here.

CHAPTER SEVENTEEN
TEETERING ON A KNIFE'S EDGE

Max sat like a sentinel at the door, waiting.

On his left rested Smite, his wolf's head cane carved from Indian ivory; once a sinister instrument from his past, now purposed with devastating power. To his right, his old service-issued Webley revolver, never once fired. Their light might negate magic, but he doubted very much it would stop a bullet. Glyphs were intricately drawn in blood across the scuffed door and floor, encircling his body; blood from a gash on his palm that throbbed with every heartbeat. A score of spells sealed the entrance, and a score more reinforced them. They were a complex tapestry of protection. It would take hours for Max to undo his magic, and they were of his own design. Still, Max sat with his eyes firmly affixed on the door, unsure if even that security would falter.

His nostrils flared at the sudden scent of lilac.

"I hope you don't mind," Helena said, as she entered the room. "I found a perfume while exploring. I liked the bottle."

"It reminds me of my mother," Max lamented. "It… was her favourite flower." His attention was so fixated on the door that he did not hear her approach until she appeared beside him with a plate of sliced green apples.

"You must eat," she said. "You've been sitting there for hours."

"Thank you, Helena, but I don't have much of an appetite."

As she dangled the plate before him, his grey eyes caught the juices glistening on every slice, and it ignited a roar within his belly.

"Your stomach betrays you, *Mister* Max," the olive-skinned girl smiled, stressing her newfound nickname for the man. "Quickly now, before I take them all as my own."

Even with the gravitas of the day, Max felt himself smile. "Then join me," he said. The temptation was too great to resist. He plucked his share of the little tart treasures from the plate, and a moment later, he and Helena gobbled them up just as quickly as they had appeared, sating his uneasy appetite for the time being.

"You're injured," she said, noticing his hand, and cradled it into her own.

Her touch was firm, warm; her palm smooth. He felt compelled to pull his hand away. Everything he touched he destroyed, and wanted to spare her from his curse. Yet it hardly took any time for the slit to heal over, erasing all evidence of his self-inflicted cut. "Your gift is miraculous, my dear, but you needn't waste your powers on frivolous things."

"Frivolous?" she repeated.

"You didn't have to heal my cut."

"You're right," she mused, "I didn't *have* to." She flashed another modest smile, and sat down next to Max, just outside the circle of blood, careful not to stain her white dress with it, and together they watched the door.

It all felt queer to him: waiting impatiently for his world to end, as if his pursuers were being rude to keep him. "How are you finding my sanctum?" he asked, just to break up the tension. "Making yourself at home?"

She cocked her head, unsure how to answer. "It's big, but lonely," *she said.*

"When you have lived a long life, you tend to collect a great many things. Even I find it difficult to navigate, at times," he said. "This place can have a mind of its own."

"Where is Charlie's room?" she asked.

Every room is my room, the spirit joked. Sometimes, I even share one with Max, when he's a good boy.

But Max wasn't in the mood for his brother's humour.

"Are you a magician, too?" she asked Charlie.

The spirit laughed. The only trick I know is how to sour my brother's mood.

"But you're still… alive," she stated, *as if trying to solve a grand mystery.* "More magic?"

Both brothers exchanged an uncomfortable glance, but Charlie nodded his permission, knowing full well how protective Max was over their tale.

Max sighed. "Many years ago," he began, *"something terrible happened to my brother, and I wasn't there in time to save him. So I used magic to keep him at my side until I could."*

"Like how I saved you?"

"If only, my dear," he exhaled heavily. "Helena, I will tell it to you the way it was first told to me," he found himself saying, turning to face the girl. "Angelic beings perform miracles. Your father's blood flows through you, which is how you saved my life. But the magic I practice is considered… Devilborn," he finally said.

"Devilborn," she repeated, barely above a whisper.

Max nodded. "That has been our understanding since the very first of us learned to weave magic. Of course, only the Devil would know for sure," he added. "When God created nature, the Devil bestowed upon men the power to pervert it, in the ultimate act of defiance."

Helena brought her knees to her chest, and tucked them tightly with her arms, as if it would keep all of the world's evil away. "Then is magic wicked?"

"Wicked?" he repeated, smiling slightly. "No," he immediately answered, but then pondered the girl's question. He had encountered sinister people throughout his long life. Sexton Graves played the dead like puppets for his own personal gain. The woman he had fought below New York fed on her blood for its power. Even Crowley abused magic to influence his social standing. But did magic really seduce good men into something dreadful, or was it like a demon's poison, which brings out the evil already in their hearts? He truly did not know.

"A dear friend of mine once used magic to mystify crowds around the world, with the most harrowing of escapes. My personal favourite was when he'd lock himself in a glass cell full of water, while his arms and legs were bound in chains," he said, watching the girl's eyes light up. "But my Master is…" he hesitated to correct, "was the most powerful of us all. Yet he chose to live as a teacher. He was the one who taught me magic was more akin to an artist's brush than a hammer."

"Ammon," she guessed, turning apologetically to the spirit. "Charlie asked me not to say anything."

The magician nodded. "He was a gentle man, a saint. Everything I will never be," he said. Max had hurt many people, killed, much to his great shame. And he knew there were times when even he was wicked.

"There are men in this world who hate our kind to such a degree, they strive to be rid of us all, like the men hunting me now from the other side of that door. *They believe we are wicked things. But, Helena, magi are neither angel nor demon,"* he said. *"We are not guardians, nor slavers or heroes. Neither are we villains. We are just simply people with extraordinary gifts who live very ordinary lives."* His words were soft, reassuring. *"Our gifts, themselves, are not good or evil. Our intent makes them so. You used your gift to save my life. I used mine to save Charlie's soul. But that hardly makes us wicked."*

She sat in silence, allowing his words to sink in, but eventually nodded.

"And you will face these choices one day, as well. You will make mistakes."

"If I'm… angelic, am I even capable of bad things?"

"You're asking the wrong person, my dear," he mused. *"But you're also human. Folly is in our nature. So take my advice: surround yourself with great people, Helena,"* he said, looking at his brother. *"They'll keep you on the right path, even when you stray."*

"But you're trying to save him," she reaffirmed.

Max nodded. "When I find a way, his soul will finally cross over. But he has been trapped by my side for too long. The truth is… Charlie's spirit is dying."

"Dying?" she repeated, looking at the ghost.

It's true, I'm afraid, Charlie said, with a shrug.

"The longer he is trapped here, the more he loses his humanity," Max finished. "He is like a ship anchored in a storm. One day that chain will snap, and then…" but he caught himself, forgetting he promised himself he would spare Charlie the truth of what could come. But Max knew his brother's humanity was the only thing that kept him from becoming a shadowy wraith, a thing that gave men reason to fear the dark; a shadowy, abominable thing that preyed upon the living.

The magus would be tethered to something insufferably wicked. There would be no escape, no safe quarter. It would have been like being shackled to a rabid wolf that never tired, never stopped, and something that couldn't be put down. Max would have been consumed by his brother's spirit until there was nothing left but a husk.

But the girl was enthralled. "What happens then?" she asked.

The magus just shook his head. "Another time," he lied. His life was nothing but loss, and the last thing he wanted to think about was also losing his brother again. *Max returned to his feet, and gave himself a firm stretch. "I've been at this long enough," he said. "If Hexenhammer was to break through the door, they would have done so already with fire and brimstone, and we have s*even more hours to go until this horrid situation is behind us."

It could be worse, you know. Tomorrow, we could end up in Paris.

He didn't dare risk a laugh. "Charlie, don't try to cheer me up. Not today," he bemoaned. How he hated Paris.

The hallway expanded with his every step. The west ward contained his extensive library of every book on magic he had ever found, bought, or borrowed with absolutely no intention of returning. Max had an apothecary that housed bones, poisons, vials of blood, and hundreds of trinkets collected from every dark corner of the globe. And there were even wards Helena had yet to discover; even some that were forbidden to her.

I never understood the allure of this place, Charlie said, floating beside his brother. *You could have conned your way into any penthouse, any hotel suite around New York, around the world, for that matter. Yet you continue to cling onto this apartment.*

"I don't expect you to understand. This was never your home. Not really."

Charlie shook his head at the claim. *Thanks to your spell, I can never leave your side. I go where you go. I live where you live. We are tethered together, after all.*

Max found himself reminiscing about the early days, after the war, after Charlie's murder. He had returned home with only a single teal-coloured suitcase half-full of worn clothes, his solider uniform, and his Webley revolver to his name. He had a wallet plump with his jinxed American cash. Yes, he could have hustled himself into a finer place on the East Side overlooking the park, but he had chosen Alafair, the Romani ghetto, to honour his mother. It was a noble idea at the time, until the neighbourhood soured into something ugly. Even then, he refused to leave.

"You don't even remember, do you, Charlie? Breaking through?"

From the spirit realm? Charlie asked, shaking his head. It was like trying to remember the day he was born. *My memory is fragmented like cracked ice. I can recall certain events in my life, but hardly the details.*

"It was the first time I saw your spirit. You came to me disjointed and frightened, and argued vehemently you were still alive," he said, with a sorrowful smile. "You had forgotten all about India. I had to tell you again all about your life, and… your death." His smile faded away as he remembered how harrowing those days truly were. They were a frightening first few months, trapped together in his apartment. But the ordeal brought them closer than ever, and for the first time in their relationship, they had finally become friends.

That's the reason why you chose to stay? I never took you as a sentimentalist, Max. Charlie flashed his brother a warm smile. *I guess this place grew on me, too,* he admitted, *considering how it even served as our failed detective agency, for a time. How I miss those days. Look what a difference a little time makes.*

"Failed?" he repeated, genuinely hurt. But Max missed those days, too. They were simple, carefree; that was, until Uriel led them on their current, trying path.

Charlie observed his brother. It felt good to distract him from the actual terror of that day. Max had his secrets, he knew, but his brother was never a difficult man to figure out. Ammon's death had shattered a piece of Max, he saw it in his soft, grey eyes. But the rumblings of despair were only tremors. The true impact on his psyche had yet to come, the grief, the mourning, the anger. When that time came, Charlie felt he wouldn't know what to do. But, as his brother liked to say, one problem at a time. *So what now?*

"We hunker down and hope for the best until dawn," he said, plainly. "It's all we can do. This spell has cut us off from the world. We are floating in a void. The only way in and out is through the front door, and ultimately, through Hexenhammer, itself, and that is one battle I am not ready to fight."

Because of the girl?

"Absolutely," he returned. "They are a battalion of armed men. I just have trinkets and a young girl. I will not throw her into this fray," he vowed, turning to face his brother.

But that wasn't good enough for Charlie. *What about finding Crowley?*

"Crowley and the Golden Dawn went to ground." he stated. "Far from me, far from Hexenhammer. Gone," he stressed again, "To the space between spaces. And much like my front door, only a few traces of it remain here in the real world."

Well. if the skeleton key opens the door, how do you find the door? Do you even know where yours is?

"The door's location never changes," he said, vaguely.

But Charlie caught on. *You don't, do you?*

"I never thought I'd have to," he admitted. "But I can find out."

The magus turned a corner into a hallway fitted with russet wooden panels and forest green wallpaper. It was the first of his vaults. But this particular ward made Max apprehensive. He used it as a place for magical trinkets that had grown unstable. Other objects he found to be too controlling or corruptive were locked away for his own sake. But it wasn't the power that tempted him, it was the allure of simplifying his life. And Max was suspicious of all things that made his life easy.

Aesthetically, he had designed it after a grand ballroom of an Austrian baroness he once foolishly tried to court. It was a precious sight of golden wallpaper and rich tapestries. As he walked across the polished floor, a dozen candelabras magically flared to life in his presence, casting the entire room in a soft, fiery glow that accentuated the artefacts locked away behind small boxes of iron and silver. He felt the dark power emit from each item as he passed, as if they begged to be taken out once more.

Every inch of its four walls was nearly covered with lavish oil paintings of all sizes. Each one quivered as Max walked across the room, triggering their magic. Each contained a dark memory torn from the magician's past, trapped eternally in oil. Some had cracked over time, others utterly crumbled to pieces, depending on how corrosive the memory. They helped distance himself from the accountability for his past actions, the horrors of war, among other countless nightmares. The oil paintings were the only way he could continue living with the pain of being alive. One canvas was left blank. It had been reserved for the memory of Charlie's murder, but he had decided it was the only memory he never wanted to forget.

Yet there was one painting in the gallery unrelated to Max: a lifelike portrait of a young Aleister Crowley given to him after joining the Golden Dawn. It was the blight of his collection, even amongst his darkest of memories. It was a cursed gift given to all members of the Golden Dawn, once thought to be a symbol of Crowley's hubris: his reminder that he was always watching the magicians like a benevolent god. Instead, it served as a warning, a symbol of what awaited them all if they had ever betrayed the Order, for the portrait was a doorway to a very wayward place. It was a nexus between his world and another, a hellish domain crafted with the machinations of a self-righteous, deluded magus. It was Crowley's legacy: the Glassworld, a prison for magi.

He kept it as another grim reminder of his past.

This place makes my skin crawl, Max, figuratively speaking, of course.

"It feels a bit like climbing into one's own skull, this room."

And the answer lies somewhere from your past? Charlie asked, nodding towards the paintings.

"From my past? No," he said. "More like from within." At the epicentre of the room was a cursed object hidden beneath black velvet atop a stand of granite. The magus knew using any object in the room came with great risk, and could possibly even be fatal. It was the first piece he had ever locked away. It was what inspired the vault he now stood within, a magical item of ultimate convenience, which made it that much more dangerous.

Max shook his head as he gripped the black velvet tightly in his fist and yanked it away. Atop the stand was a jagged shard of mirrored black glass, which shone in the soft candlelight. He hesitated to pick up the shard, closed his eyes, but then reached forth. Max felt it grow hot to the touch, like metal heated by the summer sun. "Nostradamus once used this accursed glass to peer into the future. I will try and do the same."

Any port in a storm, Charlie mused.

Max ignored the comment. "This glass reflects the holder's innermost desire. In a way, much like how a djinn grants its master's wish. For Nostradamus, Ammon once told me he wanted a place in history, so that's what the glass revealed. When it fell into the hands of Grigori Rasputin, it showed him how to charm his way onto the laps of the Russian aristocracy."

And what did it show you?

Max hesitated to answer. "I used the black mirror a few times in my life," he admitted. "The last time was a year ago. I used it to find a way to save you."

And what did it show you then? The Devil? Was that the reasoning behind this mad quest of yours?

"No," Max whispered, shaking his head. He turned to Charlie, with eyes of stone, "I saw my dead body on the street, broken, exactly as it happened."

I don't understand.

"It was how things were just before Helena saved me… I know she is the key to all of this," he replied. "That's what the mirror showed me that day. The girl: she's part of this quest. You, me, and her: we're all connected. I just didn't understand it at the time." Max turned away from his brother. "For years, I thought I was lost—that everything happened because our bloodline was cursed, Charlie, that my every chance at happiness was thwarted by forces well beyond me. But, despite the darkness closing in, I believe I am still on the right path, and Helena was the last piece of the game."

Game? Charlie spat. *No, Max.* The spirit shook his head in disgust. *I don't believe that for a second. Are you saying no matter our choices, we're destined for one finality? That your friends had to die—Ammon had to die—just so it could lead you here, to this very point, trapped in your own home?*

Max placed the black shard back atop the stand. He couldn't stop his hand from trembling.

That, ultimately, you knew you were going to die? And you never told me.

"Yes," he confessed.

And your search for the Devil—that was for you, wasn't it?

Max shook his head, regretfully. "I sought the Devil to change my fate, Charlie. How could I possibly save you if I were a dead man?" he pleaded. "The mirror's prophecies come true— they always come true," he stressed. "But they're vague: they never tell you when or where. My death, it could have been that day, or years from then. Eventually, I stopped looking over my shoulder."

Charlie was beside himself, seething at the frustration of it all. *I can't tell where the lies with you end or begin anymore.*

"Do you believe, for a single moment that I would ever leave this world before I saved my baby brother?"

Save me? At what cost? he retorted. *Did you really think I'd want people to suffer in my name? Do you even know me at all?*

"I know you better than you know yourself," he said.

Charlie glided over to the other side of the room. *Are you even listening to yourself? The events of today have cracked that mind of yours. Your death, Ammon's, the attack on the funeral. You're drowning in madness, and you're taking us all under with you.*

"Madness?" Max choked.

You need time, Max. Time to heal, or you will be lost to me—lost to us all. And I hope, for your sake, peace finds you this day, and not Hexenhammer. With that said, he left his brother alone to his own business.

"Charlie," he called after him, but it was no use. Hexenhammer, Ammon's death, the public outing of magic. Was he right? Was the cost too high a price to pay to save his brother's soul? Had his selfish actions doomed everyone around him, including Helena? But he knew Charlie was wrong about one thing: he still had a chance to save them: to save his brother, Helena, his friends at the Golden Dawn, and even Crowley. And, maybe, his own soul as well, when his quest finally came to an end.

Max picked the glass up again, and glared into the shard of the black mirror, allowing himself to become lost in its opaque reflection. He felt adrift on an ocean of doubt and uncertainty. But the shard's heat grew in intensity. It burned Max's fingertips and the palm of his hand, but he endured. It was a simple sacrifice for knowing his true path. The heat meant his life force was fuelling it. That was the cost of the magic. After all, what difference would one less year make to life already lived too long?

He blocked the world out of his mind and focused. The truth was about to revealed. Max Thanatos saw into his heart.

"No," he gasped.

He gripped the shard so tightly in his hand, it sliced his tender skin. He didn't even notice the crimson band trickling down his wrist to his elbow. "You weak, feeble fool," he cursed himself, as he threw the shard with all of his might towards Crowley's portrait; the sick, foul, corrupted thing. "Damn you," he screamed. He felt sick, betrayed. How he hated himself so. Its magic was faulty. It had to be. He remained planted where he stood, panting with stress. He closed his eyes, blocked the visions out of his mind, and focused on his breathing for minutes, hours, he wasn't sure.

Then a meek voice spoke out to him from the doorway. "Mister Max," Helena said. "There's someone's banging on the door."

CHAPTER EIGHTEEN:
BACKS AGAINST OBLIVION

"What if it's not Hexenhammer?" Helena tried to reason with the frantic man, as Max paced in front of the door.

"It must be— it has to be," Max flustered. "I highly doubt there's another magus on the other side, giving us the all-clear." It was a preposterous notion. "It's them, I promise you," not that he wanted to be right. "Our enemies, like us, have been biding their time, and now they're finally making their move." Max was ready for a fight, or so he believed. His cane was strapped to his belt like a sheathed sabre, but it was hard to ignore the revolver trembling in his red right hand. The bogeymen were at his door. "Charlie," he shouted, "where are you? Now isn't the time for one of your fits."

"Can they get in?" she asked.

"My spells will hold," he returned, clenching his jaw.

"Then why do you sound so uncertain?"

There came six hard knocks, slowly in succession. They were being taunted, toyed with, like a cat torturing the mouse before the kill.

Max ran his hand over the door. His spells were firmly locked in place, but then he felt an almost minuscule murmur of frailty in the magic. The blood drained from his face. No, he thought, burying the terror away, he had to trust his craft. He had done all he could outside of barricading the entrance with his leather sofa.

He didn't even realize he had taken a step back away from the door. Subconsciously, he was already in retreat. He knew something was terribly wrong. Unlike New York, where his door remained anchored to reality, his apartment was now in Limbo, essentially cut off from all of Creation. Someone wasn't knocking on the girl's dormitory door. It was his. How could anyone have found it? Hexenhammer couldn't have detected his apartment beyond the door without magic, even if they tore the place down around it, and witch hunters were not in the business of employing witches into their ranks. Yet someone had impossibly breached through the threshold.

There came six more knocks.

"Mister Max?" Helena exhaled.

The urgency in her voice was plain. She was terrified. She had every right to be. His apartment was their last stand. But his home was also a construct of his making. It was Max's sanctum. He was far from helpless. Max could twist the corridors into an endless labyrinth, trapping his enemies inside until their last breath. The walls obeyed his commands, the rooms, the hallways. He could have collapsed them all, crushing their pursuers like a hand caught in a vice. If Hexenhammer were to indeed breach that door, God help them all.

Something heavy slammed the door again, this time like a battering ram, and Max felt the girl's hand slip into his. Now her hand was trembling. Whomever was on the other side of the door was no ally. They were prepared to break their way in. "My barriers," he said, "they're failing." He turned to the girl. "Helena, go. Get to the vault room. I will seal the way behind you."

"No," she said steadfastly.

"Do as I say, child," he snapped.

"I'm staying," she insisted. "I can… help."

The crash came again, followed by another strike. The door would not last.

Max didn't have the luxury of time to argue with a stubborn child. "Then so be it," he snapped. With a command, Helena was ported away to the gallery. It was an argument he knew he wasn't going to win. Hexenhammer were zealots, and they were soldiers. He would be outgunned and overtaken in a matter of moments if he didn't stop them at the door.

He reached into his vest, and pulled forth three pinkie-sized toy soldiers of the King's guard, with their iconic red uniforms and large black hats made of bear fur. They would only slow them down, he knew, as he tossed them at the door, and held his breath. A thunderous strike hit the door, nearly cracking it down the middle. Then another, and then came a third. Bam! Bam! Bam!

In that brief moment, in that one, infinite moment, when the door smashed into pieces, as splintery fragments of wood exploded across the foyer and death was all but assured, Max made his peace. Even after the stark realization Hell would soon claim him, no prayers came. He would die with his brother's name on his parched lips, "Charlie, if you can hear me, I'm sorry," he said, "for everything. You deserved a better brother."

Impossibly, the barrier between the university hostel for women and Max's apartment had been bridged. Max prepared himself to use magic after his bullets had found their marks, but no men charged over the threshold. The air rippled with anticipation of an attack, but he heard only the shuffling of metallic tins from the hall. It was a sound familiar, yet one he couldn't place until the first metal canister was lobbed into the apartment, quickly followed by another. They spun across the floor as the cans depressurized, spurting out a thick, fruity-smelling smoke.

"Tear gas!" Max spat, as the familiar odour of chlorine assailed his nostrils. It was a foul concoction left over from the war, engineered to make men suffer. The effects were almost immediate. He already felt his eyes water, his vision blurred. He tried to summon a gust of wind to disperse it back into the hall, but the spell would not heed his command. Again he tried, and again he failed. It was hard to breathe. The apartment was thick with it. Max panicked. The spell was second nature to him, rudimentary. Even his toy soldiers remained still at the door, instead of growing to blockade their path. Magic had abandoned him, as it had his Master.

The first of the men in crisp white suits came through the doorway, crunching the King's guards under his boots. Through the smoke, he stepped. A mask covered his head with its two wide lenses for eyes, and a small box respirator that hung from an accordion tube. Max fired his first shot, wide of the target. He was hardly a marksman, and that was without the brutality of the tear gas singeing his sensitive eyes. But his assailants did not return fire. They wanted him alive, he realized. But Max had no intention of returning the courtesy.

He was a terrible shot, but even he could hit a man at point-blank. As more men in gas masks poured into the apartment, Max felt the original intruder's firm hand grip his neck. It would be the man's last mistake. He should have reached for the revolver. Max shoved the barrel into the man's ribs and fired two rounds into his heart and lungs. As the body dropped, the magician tore the gas mask from the face, and struggled to fit it over his. He had to retreat to the vault, he knew. He had already lost the apartment.

A wild shot rang out in the room, hitting the wall.

"Hold your fire," came a muffled scream. "Remember your orders!"

Max recognized the voice. It was his Master's killer, hidden somewhere behind a mask. He could hardly make out their numbers in the smoke, but he saw too many silhouettes for comfort. He had to slow them down. But in the haze, Max witnessed little flickers of red lights ignite one after another around the room. His enemies had lit lanterns burning with a bright, crimson flame. And as the light drew nearer, Max felt a ripple of agony crackle its way through his body towards his heart. It nearly brought him down to a knee, but he stepped back, keeping himself just outside of the light's radiance. He threw his weight up against the wall to keep himself from falling over.

He removed a strand of ivy from a hidden pocket within his vest, used to entangle anyone caught in its path. But the vegetation simply hit the floor and lay there limply. Again, he reached into his vest, and unleashed a small arsenal of magical trinkets upon Hexenhammer, to no avail. The men did not falter in their advance, nor did anything delay them. He even heard them laugh. With their lanterns held out before them, they slowly approached the magician one step after another. He would have assailed them all with Smite, but his cane, he finally came to realize, was as useless as he was.

"Maximilian Thanatos," the man known as Mr. Dove began, "it's no use. We have been hunting down your kind for quite a long time. Your magic will do you no good now. The Lord's light will forever protect us against the darkness."

"You killed my Master," Max snarled.

"Aye, that is true. I slayed the beast. Drawn and quartered its giant body, cut out and burned the internal organs, and buried the parts in unmarked graves, with the head face down so it shall never witness the Lord again."

"You still have one chance to leave before it's too late for you," blustered Max, but he sounded unconvincing even to himself.

"I'm afraid I can't do that. You see, God gave you the gift of life, and you betrayed Him by consorting with the Devil. It would have been a simple matter, really, taking your life as I did your master's, but even I have a master I must obey. And I have been ordered to take you in alive to stand trial. And believe me when I say it'd be much easier to tell him I killed you in self-defence."

"Then let me help you along," Max replied, coughing from the gas. He emptied the remaining bullets into the room. The shots lit up the smoke like thunderheads during a lightning storm. The men scrambled for cover, he heard one fall hard. But it was not enough. They were experienced, well-trained. They must have known when Max fired his last shot. The men looked like beasts emerging from the fires of Hell. They were ghastly in their masks. Frightening. Max dropped his own mask in the chaos. He couldn't breathe, his eyes blistered with pain. The air was thick with gas. He lurched for the hallway, nearly toppling over his leather couch. He was defenceless without magic, without his trinkets. He was an old man, alone, against Hexenhammer.

So he ran. He held his ground for as long as he could. There was nothing left to gain. He had bought the girl precious time. That was enough. But his own lead was pitiful. He already heard the stomping of their heavy boots storm behind him. He ordered the hallways to close in his wake, but it was only a matter of screaming at a wall. Nothing obeyed him. In all of his years of studying the arcane arts, he had never heard of a light that could dispel magic. That was how they had killed Ammon. That was how they had broken into his apartment. And that was how he was going die.

But his constructs were still cast. His hallway didn't dissipate into nothingness, nor did he find himself floating in the limbo outside his magic. The floor was still solid beneath his feet. How? he wondered. Those lanterns must have had a weakness. Some limitation. There was something about the magic that remained impervious to the light. But what? What? he screamed in his head. If he only had more time to work it out, he might find a way to fight back, to survive. But his pursuers were relentless, and would not grant him that luxury.

He crashed into the room, and shoved the heavy door closed behind him, latching the bolt shut, as if that would have stopped them for long.

"Are we safe?" Helena asked, as she ran to him.

Max just shook his head. "No, my dear, far from it." He swept across the room, and took her by the hand. "I need you to trust me, Helena— do you trust me?" His voice was distraught, frantic. He could hardly contain his own panic.

Helena didn't quite understand, but nodded anyway.

He led her to Crowley's portrait, and stood her before it. Its magic rippled at their presence. "I'm sending you away."

"What, through there?" she balked.

"It's the safest place for you to be. It's a prison—"

"A prison," Helena choked, not letting him finish.

Max placed his hands on her shoulders, hoping she'd find reason. "Listen to me," he pleaded. "The place everyone sees on the other side of a mirror is a purgatory created to punish magi. It's called the Glassworld."

"I'm not going in there," she protested. "I'm staying here, with you."

Their pursers had already reached the door. "We're out of time. Aleister Crowley is the master of the Golden Dawn, a secret society of magi just like me, and he's the warden of the Glassworld. You won't belong there; he will sense your presence immediately you step inside. He will find you, and when he does, you must tell him everything that has transpired: Ammon, Hexenhammer, the skeleton keys. Do not spare a single detail."

The fear washed from her face as the realization came to light. "You're not coming with me?"

Max shook his head. "Charlie— he can't pass through. The magic won't let him, and if I'm separated from my brother, I'll die."

She collapsed into his arms, pounding his chest. No," she whispered. "We go together!"

"When it comes to my accursed life, my dear, every wonderful thing always begins at the end. I wish we had more time." He saw Helena's face assume stubborn lines. He knew she didn't understand his choice. He averted his eyes, finding it impossible to face her. The girl's compassion overwhelmed him. Max felt small in her presence. He then understood how Ammon must have felt as a teacher: conscious of how his students depended on him, cared about him. And he already missed her. Once she stepped into the painting, they would never see each other again. Crowley would ensure that.

"No. There must be another way."

"There's not," he said, and without warning he abruptly shoved the frail girl into the painting. It was the only way to save her. "He will find you," he called after her. It was as if she had fallen backwards into a pool of water. The canvas swallowed her completely. Once the oil stilled, he saw her image from the other side, he saw her tears, her mouth scream his name. He picked up the shard of black mirrored glass and tore and slashed the canvas into ribbons, severing their connection for good. "I'm sorry."

As tattered pieces of the portrait fluttered to the floor, the agents smashed the door from its hinges. A score of men in white tailored suits stormed unstoppably into the room with their lit lanterns held before them, brutalizing the old man with the light's power. One by the one, the candles dispersed the magic within the paintings. Like wisps of colourful smoke, they serpentined and twirled through the air, and once again found their place in their owner's mind, returning every single horrid memory he had purged long ago.

His legs betrayed him. Max dropped to his knees, howling from the pain, the misery. There was nowhere left to go, nowhere left to run. Hexenhammer was the sworn enemy of all magi. He doubted he would live to walk the streets of New York again, or to curse the name of Crowley, or even save his brother's soul. Nevertheless, as they toppled him to the ground, bound him in chains, and gagged his mouth, Max knew somewhere in the depths of him that, as long as his heart still beat, there remained a chance.

CHAPTER NINETEEN: OLD GHOSTS

Tillie Grey screamed for her boys, screamed for help, for God, for anyone, but her desperate words were lost—muffled, as the sounds of terror bled through the silk scarf shoved far into the back of her coarse throat. She wrestled against her restraints, her thin legs flailing wildly as dark-skinned men fought to bind them to the bed of Maximilian's birth.

"Do not let the creature break free," the gruff man commanded over the woman's noise. As he drew closer, she struggled even harder to escape the men's grasp. He turned and pointed to a corner of the master bedroom. "Maximilian, don't just stand there! Help us restrain your mother."

Unlike the dark-skinned men, he did not fear the brute. "No," the little boy defied. "She is just sick! She needs a doctor."

Little Max Thanatos received a backhand the size of a house for his insolence. The taste of copper was on his tongue.

"I *am* a doctor, and don't you dare challenge me again in front of the niggers," his father warned. He shoved his way past the three other men in the room, still struggling to contain the woman's legs. On the nightstand was a physician's black bag. He flipped open the brass latch, and rummaged inside. From it, he removed a vial of water, a series of scalpels that glinted in the soft light of the room, a bible, a purple stole—which he kissed and draped over his shoulders— and finally a revolver.

"Tillie, love, if you're in there, I want you to know I'm going to save your soul, no matter the cost," her husband promised. He picked up the largest scalpel from the nightstand, and slowly approached her, sending the woman into another frenzy. "You need to understand. I have to bleed the Devil out," he said, making the first incision. "Your blood, it's spoiled."

***

The soft rustle of chains over stone woke Max from his slumber. Nothing had changed. Thick manacles still bound his wrists and ankles with just enough slack to allow him to brace himself up on his bony knees. His wounded flesh around the metal had become septic; pus oozed from the sores. There was no escape from the pain. His jailers had locked his head in an iron cage nearly too heavy to lift under his own power, so he spent much of his time staring at a small drain in the floor. One he often pissed into.

That day, like the day before, and the day before that, the magus didn't know if it was morning or night. His cell of rock and dirt had no windows. Max felt like he had been asleep for a few minutes, but it could have been hours. Days, even. There was no way to tell. He struggled to keep track of time. When he was tired, he slept, or tried to. In the beginning, his jailers were habitual with their routines. Once a day, someone would slide a piece of mouldy sour-dough underneath the door. Some days, the plate would reach him, and he would fit small bits of the bread between the bars of his helmet cage. Most days, the plate stopped just out of reach.

Every other day, the same ragged, one-eared man would enter with a bucket of icy water, and splash him, washing away the shit and the food and the filth. Sometimes, he would even catch a mouthful of the foul water as it hit his face. That was a rare treat. After a while, he wouldn't see anyone at all for extended periods of time. Those were the times he feared the most, thinking he would be left to die.

He didn't know how long he had been imprisoned. But, by how skeletal his arms were, he knew he was starving. His thoughts drifted. Max imagined his apartment was on the other side of the world by then, lost to him forever. But he was too weak to mourn his loss. Smite was gone, his spectacles, and his numerous trinkets and vest were also gone. The only things he had to his name were the soiled tatters on his person. Even magic had abandoned him. His jailers were thorough. He looked up at the high ceiling to see a lantern burning the accursed red flame. Its terrible light just reached the magician's head if he sat up tall. And every time Max returned to his knees, the pain would bring him back down again.

Not that it mattered. He rarely stirred anymore. He hardly had any reason to move, to keep himself strong—to be ready to escape from his captors. Max didn't know where he was, or whether he was still in Edinburgh or even Great Britain. His new world consisted of filth and chains and white Portland limestone. He hardly even remembered what happened after being seized by Hexenhammer. He was drugged, and his world faded to black. Their brutality came in flashes. He remembered the screaming, how he tore his jailer's ear off with his teeth, which was why they locked his head inside a cage, he gathered. But given the opportunity again, he was too weak to take the other ear.

"Charlie," he lamented. He missed his brother, dearly. Max hadn't seen or heard from him since the day he was captured. He deduced this was due to the designs of that vile light that suppressed magic, somehow keeping one from the other. Even though he couldn't see him or hear him, he knew Charlie was there by his side, for Max was still alive. But even that small flicker of hope seemed fleeting. Was he alive, or was he back in Hell, drowning in the muck?

Despite starving to death in a pile of his own shit, he knew the worst days had yet to come. He was still to be tried for witchcraft. Max clenched his fists, and lashed forward in anger, hoping that this time, unlike the hundred times before it, his chains would finally snap. But they never gave way. Not that day, at least. Instead, Max sat up against the wall, closed his eyes, and allowed sleep to take him once more. It was the only way to pass the time. If he was really lucky, he would never wake.

***

Max had the dream again. It was the same he had every time he closed his eyes: one where he was back home in New York. Always in the winter. He would walk the streets, aimlessly, as it snowed, searching for his home in Alafair. He was lost in an unfamiliar world, yet he always knew his apartment was only just one block away. But he never could find it. The dream was comforting. It had the solace of being free.

***

"Young creature."

The softest imaginable voice jarred Max from his slumber, as if someone whispered directly into his ear.

"Do not be alarmed," the voice continued, "I am Ezekiel."

Max saw a figure floating before him, a woman of olive skin and white, flowing hair. Her robe swayed in a breeze that did not exist. Her face conveyed a tender pity, her eyes were gentle. Her body radiated such a loving warmth, the magus wanted to sink into it. "Am I dead?" he asked.

"I have felt your suffering, young creature, and have come to release you from your pain."

The cage was too heavy to look up properly. "You mean, you've come to kill me."

The figure shook her head. "No," she said, "to offer you salvation. If you so desire."

To Max, it was the same thing.

"I will ease the storm in your heart, quell the madness within," she purred. "I can end your pain. I can end your suffering."

"What do you want from me?" Max asked bluntly.

"The smallest of things, really. All you have to do is tell me where to find the abomination," she said.

There it was. The chains rattled as Max shifted again where he sat, and used what little strength he had to finally lift the iron cage enough to look the angel in her face. "Go to Hell," he managed in a firm voice.

He was beyond exhausted. The reality of the room bled into his dreams. He saw visions of men storming into his cell, he felt the pressure of water splash into his body again and again. In his dream, he was drowning. "Wake him," he heard a voice call out from the blackness. He was jostled awake by a clubbing blow against his cage. His bloodshot eyes opened to see the blurred image of his assailant come into focus. Mr. Dove stood over the magician with a cloved orange held under his nose to mask Max's stench. Other men gathered around him and gawked at the magician, as if he was a geek from a P.T. Barnum sideshow. He hadn't seen himself in an age. He imagined he resembled something akin to an undead thing in their eyes, skeletal thin and covered in unkempt hair.

"Where's my brother?" Max croaked, half-dazed by the impact.

"Seems like confinement has broken the beast," Mr. Dove mocked. "It's gone loony. Next, it'll probably be crying for its mummy." He shared in the laughter with the others. The men were not gentle as they unlocked the cage from his head, nearly taking it off along with the contraption. "Up to the tower with it. The Witchfinder General wants a word." As the men went to grab the magician, Mr. Dove interjected. "Not like that," he said, disgusted by the cretin kneeling before him. "Wash it, shave it, dress it: make it look human," he finished, inhaling the overpowering scent of the orange.

As Mr. Dove left the room, Max felt a dozen arms toss him around the cell like a child's doll. They tore the rags from his body, scalded him with blistering hot water, and took to his skin with iron wool brushes. And they scrubbed, and they ripped, and they tore. He felt himself being forced to his knees, as another man wrenched a thick arm around his neck to lock his head firmly in place. Another agent folded open a Genco cut-throat razor.

The first slash severed his extraordinarily long beard from his chin. "No," Max screamed. But he was only met with more resistance as the razor hacked its way ear to ear, removing the thick mass of hair from his face in patches. His skin stung from the countless little cuts all across his face and neck. His barber cared very little for a delicate touch.

"There," the man said, "you look almost human." He slapped Max's raw face.

That incited a rage within Max, one he hadn't felt in some time. It felt good. Oh, how he wanted them to pay. Max tried to lash at his assailant, but the arm around his neck squeezed tightly enough to make him almost black out.

"Looks like the beast still has a little bite."

"Then maybe it'd be best to lose its fangs," threatened the barber.

A dark-skinned agent of Hexenhammer appeared at the cell door holding a monk's habit of purple with a golden pentagram. "Mr. Dove wants to know why the beast isn't already on its way. The Witchfinder General is waiting." He tossed the habit towards the barber with blatant disrespect.

He snatched it in mid-air. "Looks like you'll get to keep your teeth after all," the man snarled, as he force-dressed his prisoner, and gagged the magician with one of his own fouled rags.

***

His head was covered by a sack that smelled like flour, but even that did little to dull the scent of incense that fluttered in his nostrils as his jailers marched him through what the echoes of their footsteps told him must be a spacious hall. With the habit he wore and the sour-dough they occasionally brought him, Max guessed he was imprisoned inside a cathedral, maybe a monastery. Given the religious zealots of Hexenhammer, it wasn't a difficult deduction. Max guessed he was still in Britain. He couldn't pinpoint where. Their dialects were from Scotland, Wales, even from the north and south of England.

None of the men walked close to Max. He couldn't feel their presence. But he was roped and guided by a long pole, a common practice for troublesome animals that had yet to be broken. They didn't speak once they left the cell. Instead, they chanted an unfamiliar hymn in Latin. He purposely stopped in place to infuriate his escort. By Max's count, there were seven men by their footsteps when they thrust on the pole and started their march anew. As they continued across the floor, others in the hall gradually joined in with the chant. A few, followed by a score, possibly even more. If they were all Hexenhammer, there could have been a hundred gathered in that hall. How could any magus fight an army of witch hunters?

Max reached a stairwell and began his ascent, often tumbling over, as his escort didn't have the patience to allow him to feel out each step. The stairwell was circular and narrow, built of stone. A warm wind howled as he went, and with it, a scent of lilac. His legs burned with every step. His lungs begged for air. It felt like he walked for an hour until he was forcefully stopped.

"By the Witchfinder General's divine mercy, it was He who ordered you to be taken alive, and only He. I don't know if you heathens believe in mercy, but pray that courtesy continues, for every other man around you wishes nothing more than to inflict grievous harm upon you," Mr. Dove warned. "In His presence, you will remain on your knees with your eyes to the floor. If you make eye contact with our master, I will kill you. If you speak out of turn, I will kill you." Mr. Dove gripped his prisoner by the robe. "And if you forget your station, I will personally throw you from this tower. Now nod if you understand."

Max found himself nodding. He was in no position to do otherwise.

He heard a heavy door strain to open, and the magus was immediately overwhelmed by the lovely scent of flowers. He smelled lavender, lilac, roses. It reminded him of his mother's perfume. Even with the sack restricting his vision, the brightness of daylight seeped through the fabric enough to sting his sensitive grey eyes. He hadn't seen it in an age. But Max did not turn away. The brilliance was the most cherished thing he had ever seen in his life, for Max had been certain, beyond all doubt, he never would see the sun again.

But the serene beauty of it all was short-lived as he was shoved into the room, and brought down hard to his knees to the stone floor.

"You are all His servants, not common hooligans," Max heard someone say from the other side of the room, a tone of anger washing his English voice. "Look at the state of him. You nearly let him rot in my absence."

"With all due respect, Great Witchfinder. It is not a 'him.' It is a thing. An agent of the Devil."

"Even Lucifer was once an angel, a servant of the Lord. No matter our path in the end, our Lord was our beginning. This man, like all men, can repent. He can be saved." The man's voice was confident, commanding, as if he had never known doubt. "Release his bindings, and leave us."

"I'm afraid I can't do that, Great Witchfinder. It is a menace. I haven't broken its will, not fully. Not yet."

"You will leave us, Mr. Dove," he repeated, "or I will condemn you to the same miseries you have offered unto him. Or have you already forgotten the teachings of our Lord? 'And as ye would that men should do to you, do ye also to them likewise?' Or, perhaps, should I address you as the brute you have become in my absence, by using simple terms even you can understand?"

Max could sense the man gritting his teeth in forced compliance. The magus could tell there was no love between these two, and he wondered if he could use it to some advantage. The ropes loosened as his hands were untied, the rope around his person went slack and was removed. The pole was gone, and he was finally free from all constraints. But Max remained on his knees, unsure if Mr. Dove's threat would still hold.

"You may stand, Mister Thanatos. They are gone."

Max hesitated to trust him.

"It's no trick, I assure you."

Max reached up, and he pulled the sack from his head. It took his eyes a moment to adjust to the unfiltered brightness of the room, but he found himself inside a tower of white marble, both pristine and inviting, a robust garden in the sky containing hundreds of bouquets of every spectrum of colour.

Cascaded by the angelic light of the midday sun breaking through the windows, an elderly man, dressed queerly in a white cassock with a black clerical collar, lovingly pruned the stems of his white roses. But it wasn't the man in the garden that caught his attention, it was the sight beyond him, beyond the flowers, beyond the large, rectangular windows.

"How long?" he heard himself croaking.

"Three months."

"Three months," he whispered, in disbelief. He pressed his palm against the clean, warm glass, leaving behind a greasy handprint, and stared out over London in the springtime. There was no other skyline like it in the world. From the tower, he had a clear view of the city. He was south of the river Thames. "I'm in James House, aren't I?" Max asked, but he already knew the answer. There was only one monastery in south London, and only one building with the tallest tower in the city.

The man nodded.

Max had often studied on the bank of the river, staring out at James House from across the Thames; he had no inkling Hexenhammer was hiding in plain sight. It was chilling to know Magi lived on the edge of annihilation for so long, and they didn't even know their enemies were at their doorstep. He just shook his head in dismay. It felt like the final humiliation. That final speck of hope Max had held onto in the deepest recesses of his mind was snuffed out like a candle.

And for three months? Max thought to himself, again. What of his friends? Were they all dead? Was he the last of his kind?

"You were never intended to be imprisoned for so long," the Witchfinder General admitted, "and certainly not in such wretched conditions. My mission in your country had become quite vexing, to say the least. It delayed all of my plans. I left Mr. Dove in charge in my stead. As you have unfortunately discovered, the man can be quite… fanatical. And given our reputation, that's saying something," he said, walking over to his desk buried beneath bouquets of sunflowers. "I'm quite sure you've worked out who we are by now, Mister Thanatos."

"Hexenhammer."

The man nodded. Behind several pots of plants was a collection of wine. "Come," he said, motioning for Max to join him at the desk. He poured two generous servings of red into glasses, placed one atop his desk, and then pulled out a chair for Max.

Max was reluctant to yield to the kindness at first, but ultimately sat down. Months of confinement had made him weak. The man perplexed him. Why would the Witchfinder General show hospitality to his kind? Was it a cruel tactic? Some level of compassionate interrogation designed to win his trust?

"Eat," the old man said, plopping a clay bowl of apples atop his desk. "Again, it's not a trick," he reassured, as he himself bit into a green apple. "I know you must be famished."

He was. The magus snatched an apple and sank his teeth into the waxy skin, breaking through. The sour juices were as sweet as sugar. It didn't take long for the apple to be consumed to its core. Max eyed the bowl again.

"Have as many as you want," his host invited. "He has blessed us with a plentiful orchard on our grounds, and the fruit from last season has stored well." After he watched the second apple disappear, he continued. "My name is William Hopkins. You probably never have heard of me, but your people would certainly know my ancestor, the first Witchfinder General, Matthew Hopkins."

Max nodded. "All magi know his name," he spat. "During the English Civil War, he murdered hundreds in your Lord's name: women, children, men. He was indiscriminate with his horrors— not all were witches."

William nodded. "You're absolutely right," he said. "Anyone my ancestor suspected was an agent of Lucifer was falsely tried and subsequently put to death, guilty or not, a tradition Hexenhammer honour even to this day."

Max gulped down the glass of wine. He had never gone so long without alcohol, and it tasted even sweeter than the apples. He eagerly poured himself a larger, second fill, nearly draining half the bottle. "Hexenhammer has slaughtered my kind practically to extinction."

"So you openly confess to being a witch?"

Max had nothing to hide anymore, as if his jailer didn't already know. "I am a magus," he declared.

"That's incredibly brave of you to say so in my company, or incredibly foolish. But I will still grant you the fairness of a trail."

"How kind," he snapped. "But I think I'd rather meet the executioner's axe, a noose, or a shot to the head this very moment than face your ludicrous trials of being crushed by stones or drowning. Was that how you murdered Harry Houdini?"

The man ignored the accusation and pressed, "But not being burned alive at the stake?" William asked, nodding to the clay bowl now half-full. "As I spoke before of our past, the apples you just gobbled up were grown from trees fertilized with the ashes of your kind."

Max stirred in his chair.

"Now, now, Mister Thanatos," he warned. "We're just having a conversation." William refilled his own glass. "Looks like we'll be needing another bottle, to soothe our nerves," he said, bringing over a second red wine over to the desk. "When my men found you in that apartment of yours, they told me you had a Webley revolver. A bit odd for an American. Did you fight in the war?"

The question caught Max off-guard. "Yes," he answered, eventually. "On the side of the British, before my country joined the fray."

"You fought for us?" he asked, leaning forward. "Why?"

"Because, at the time, I wanted to die."

"Yet, you survived."

"I was never very good at dying," Max returned.

William gestured if Max would like more wine, which the magus answered with a raised, empty glass. "I could think of easier ways to die. Like turning that Webley on yourself."

"I guess Hexenhammer will save me the trouble," he stated.

The elderly priest just shook his head at the notion. "There are two faces of Hexenhammer, Mister Thanatos. One is the stories your people tell amongst yourselves, the tall tales of bogeymen hiding in the shadows. That was my ancestor's way. That is the way of Mr. Dove and men like him. Killing in His name."

"But not yours?" Max asked.

William shook his head again. "Just the opposite," he said. "I served as a loyal servant in His service since I could walk, like all men in my family. I served the Lord, never questioned, never strayed from my given path. At my worst, I, too, was a fanatic," he lamented. "Mr. Dove learned from me, after all. And I hunted your kind down like the inescapable hand of God. It was my birth right.

But then the world went to war," he said. His expression darkened with gloom.

William continued, "I'm sure you faced your own demons on the battlefield, as did I. A million Englishmen died in the mud in the name of King and Country. My God died alongside them." He tipped the wine bottle over his glass, but not even a drop remained. "I thought my life's crusade was just, all done in His name. Yet, as millions upon millions of young men died in the war, where was He?"

"Why did we survive?" Max asked.

William nodded. "Why did we survive, indeed?" he sighed.

The two mortal enemies shared a brief moment of reflection.

"The war changed me, as it had my men. It twisted them into something wicked. For me, it showed me there was enough death in this world. There had to be another way."

"So, what, now you want to broker peace between our people? You may have seen the light a little too late. Your men still killed my Master. He was a good man— a teacher. He served no one. Not the Devil. Not the Lord. And he loved Great Britain, above all else. He made it his home. Yet your men still butchered him into pieces like livestock!" Max said bitterly.

"The war taught me there is no peace to be found in this world," William admitted, shaking his head. "Mankind wouldn't accept it; wouldn't trust it. If only two men were left alive, one would want to go to war. That's our nature."

"I agree," the magus said, fidgeting with the empty wine bottle.

"But Ammon Safar was a great loss," William admitted, uncharacteristically for a witch hunter.

It even surprised Max. "Don't you dare speak his name," Max found himself warning.

But the priest with the black collar cocked his head. "Why?" William asked. "I knew Ammon far longer than you. He would have been a trophy in my dungeon— he might have even been your cellmate."

Max didn't quite know how it happened. He heard the glass shatter against the desk, and the next thing he knew he was puncturing William's neck with the broken shards over and over again in a blind fury, each attack made a sickening slushy noise as the bottle turned flesh into pulp. The magus assaulted the body with maddened rage, pausing only to catch his breath.

But sanity returned abruptly, together with the realization of the horror of his action only after the fact. "No," he cried, letting the bottle shatter on the stone floor. The only agent of Hexenhammer who had shown him mercy was now dead by his hand, and there was nothing left to protect him from the fury of Mr. Dove waiting just outside the door.

But then the body stirred, ever so slightly, as if it tried to sit back up.

"Temper, temper, Maxi-boy," the body said. "You were always the loyal student, but also a slow learner. Didn't you know Ammon was my master, too?"

Max felt an invisible force sit him back down in the chair, holding him fast into place. "What's happening?" He rocked violently where he sat, but it was to no avail. William sat up in his chair, revealing the gaping hole where his neck used to be. Every time he spoke, the muscles quivered. "I had you conditioned, Max. The Hell Wax that hung in your cell? The one that suppresses your magic? You've lived with it for so long, you never even noticed its absence in here." The man gave out a light chuckle. "You had access to your magic the moment you stepped foot into this room, and you didn't even know it."

Max was beside himself with mortification.

"And you thought you were the only magus to use trinkets," William continued, still smiling. He reached into his jacket's inner pocket and removed a tuning fork. "A little insurance. I couldn't have you fighting back. Not yet."

Max felt his heart drop into his stomach. "Sexton Graves."

The man he had thought to be William Hopkins answered with a curt nod, nearly separating his head from his shoulders. "Oh, Max, I waited a long time to see you again. After you burned my beloved Nightshade back in New York, you have made my life a living hell."

"Nothing could have survived that fire."

He shrugged. "Not entirely. Your plan almost worked. The fire obliterated nearly all of my body, along with most of my power. My spirit was left to wander. I wasn't entirely free, mind you. Living on the run didn't quite suit me. But after I heard about Uriel's murder at Grand Central, well, it was time for me to return and rebuild, and all the while, I just wanted you to die. Problem was, I couldn't find you. But then, I had the most brilliant of ideas," he said. "I paid your little brother's grave a visit."

"What?" Max choked.

Sexton opened up a desk draw, and placed a human skull right in front of Max, with runes carved into the bone. "Don't you recognize your own brother?" he mused, flapping the skull's jaw with every word. "While you and the ghost ran around town like a couple of lunatics, I had a front row seat to it all. Everything Charlie heard, everything he saw— everywhere you went: mine to know, and you had no idea. The girl was warned not to trust Charlie, as a link to me." He laughed. "She should have listened."

"You betrayed your own kind!" Max shot back. "You nearly killed us all!"

"Almost," he crooned, smashing the skull against the wall. "But unlike your friends, you had the audacity to survive. There you were, on the front page of every New York rag in the city. And you even had a new friend: Helena, a girl who can bring back the dead."

Max struggled again in his chair, hoping something would give.

"Your boat-rocking sent waves around the world, Max, even the Witchfinder General came for you. And believe me, it took some rather tiresome manoeuvring to find him, and a lot of dead bodies, but I eventually climbed my way to the top, in a matter of speaking," he said, showing off to the tower around him.

Sexton smiled at the magus, still trying to break free from his spell. "I was the one who tipped Hexenhammer onto your old pal's funeral, and waited for you to die. I made sure everyone knew your name: the press, Hexenhammer, but when I heard you were in Scotland?" He wagged his finger at the magus. "You complicated my life yet again," he snapped. "The hardest part was the slow sail back to London in a rotting body. I had the Witchfinder General's body, but I could only slow the decay for so long. The flowers are here just to hide the smell of decomposition. I couldn't give up my prize just yet."

"And all of that nonsense about the Great War?"

"This body's memories, his past," he said, "A performance piece, nothing more. I wanted to put on a show. I just had to see the look on your face, Max, when all was revealed, and you did not disappoint," he grinned. "One benefit of possessing the dead is retaining all of their memories, their experiences. To this man's credit, William Hopkins really did desire peace between us and them. Can you believe that?" he laughed. "How scandalous."

"So that's why you wanted Ammon's body," Max spat. "For his memories?"

"More specifically, his knowledge. But, because of Mr. Dove's actions in Edinburgh, that's now off the table. His body had no more use. He will suffer for that, I promise."

"So I'm next on the list?"

"Oh, I wish. You have no idea how badly I want to return the favour of breaking a bottle over your head, and stabbing you to death with the shards. But I can't have you, Max," Sexton lamented. "Charlie already rented that room."

"Then what the hell do you want, Sexton?"

"The girl's going to restore my body."

"Good luck finding her. Even I don't know where she is."

"I know she's with the Golden Dawn."

"Good luck finding them. They're lost to us both."

"But thanks to Ammon, I have your skeleton key, Max."

"You have a key to a door you'll never find."

"Ah, but that's where you're wrong. You will help me. Of that, I am most certain."

"Sexton, over my dead body."

The necromancer shook his head. "No, not yours."

The room grew incredibly cold, cold enough to wilt the sunflowers on the desk. Max was just able to turn his head to the left enough to see the incorporeal image of Charlie manifest inside the room. He was panicked. He saw his brother try to speak, but being unable to. It looked like he was gripped by an invisible hand.

"I've had plenty of time to ponder how exactly I would pay you back for destroying my life," Sexton began. "I like to consider myself something of a creative person. I had so many wonderful ideas. But, back at my speakeasy, I saw how much you loved your little brother, so the answer was plain. You see, Max, since our last encounter, I've learned a few new tricks of my own."

William Hopkins's corpse collapsed face-first onto the desk.

Now, I can even possess spirits, Charlie spoke, but it was Sexton's voice.

"You son of a bitch," Max screamed. "Give me back my brother!"

It's very simple: give me Helena, and you'll get your precious Charlie. Until then, and only then, you and I are going to be as thick as thieves.

The door handle to the tower rattled violently. Mr. Dove screamed from the other side. Several fists pounded the wood nearly off the hinges.

Now, Sexton said, *what are you going to do about that door?*

CHAPTER TWENTY: THE COMPANY WE KEEP

There was a fleeting moment when Max thought his current nightmare was a delirium— that he still remained imprisoned deep within that dungeon, half asleep, half dead, waiting for the last flicker of his candle to burn itself out. That he had slipped so far beyond madness, he could no longer tell what was real and what was fantasy. He had lost too much: his brother, Helena, his friends, even his own life. A man only has so much sanity. The ghoulish hallucinations of a dying man were the only plausible explanation. In the tower of Hexenhammer, the sworn enemy of all magi, he was trapped with the necromancer, Sexton Graves, who had possessed the spirit of his dead brother. The reality he once knew— the stark, cruel reality of magic and witch hunters and ghosts—had finally perverted itself that much further into the surreal.

He had faced monsters and demons, war and himself, even trekked through the depths of Hell itself. To him, they were only complications. He had always found a way to fight back. The paramount quest to save Charlie's soul pushed him past the pain, past the agony and fear. But those days were no more. His brother was held hostage by a magus more powerful than he, and Max didn't even have the glimmer of an idea how to save him.

Now, what are you going to do about that door? Sexton teased again in Charlie's gentle voice.

Max couldn't have imagined a scenario leading to greater despair. The tower room was a dead-end. That one heavy door was its only exit, and jumping from the windows at that height would have been fatal without his trinkets. With Sexton to his front and the witch hunters at his back, he was trapped between the bull and its horns. "I'm in no shape to fight," Max whimpered to himself. And it was true. He had been starved for months, chained to a wall. He was skeletal. His mind was porridge. He was tipsy from the wine he had drunk. He struggled to even recall the simplest of spells.

Maxi-boy, you'd better get ready, Sexton warned. *I can taste their malcontent. They will kick open that door to find their beloved Witchfinder General quite dead at his desk, and they will have no one but you to blame. If they don't throw you from this tower, they most certainly will boil you alive in the blackest of pitch.*

He didn't need the necromancer to remind him of the menace. Max heard the commands to open the door from the other side, the pounding. Witch hunters had nearly rammed the wood frame off of its hinges.

My simple magic can only hold the door for so long, he mocked.

"Are you an imbecile?" Max retorted.

Excuse me? The indignation was like bile.

"If I die here, everything ends with me. You'll never unlock the door to the Golden Dawn. You'll never find Helena. They will all be lost to you forever."

I have forever, Sexton assured him.

"But do *they*?" he shot back. Max risked a smile, realizing he might just have gained the upper-hand. He had dealt with the necromancer before. As powerful as he was, Sexton was vain and selfish. He was no different to any other evil he had faced before. All he had to do was threaten to take his wants away, like a child. "They will all have died of old age long before you get your revenge. Without me, your plan would be all for naught. So, Sexton," he said, folding his arms across his chest, "what are *you* going to do about that door?"

It was a perverse mockery, watching Sexton twist his brother's face into something vile. *When this is all over, Max, I will torment your soul until the end of days.* The room's temperature dropped to below freezing. Icy crystals frosted over the windows, glowing like Edison bulbs as they caught the midday sun.

As the last of the beautiful bouquets wilted into death, Max was the only living thing left in that room. "What are you doing?"

Sexton focused on the door, ignoring the magician behind him. *Did you even realize for a second just how powerful your precious brother was?* he asked, rather impressed. *I can feel the spectral energy coursing through this being. He is unlike any spirit I have ever handled before. He's like an artillery shell in a canon just waiting to be fired. I never felt anything like it.*

"Power didn't matter to Charlie." Max returned. "He wasn't a madman like you, obsessed with it."

Sexton sneered. *It never mattered? Just fathom all of the trouble he would have spared you on your quest. If he knew about his wonderful power all along, and still chose to do nothing, ever consider that maybe he just enjoyed watching you suffer.*

"Enough," he warned.

The necromancer shrugged. *Let's be honest, Max. You ruined that poor man's world the moment you became a magus. It'd be only natural for him to hate you, as I do. And you think I'm the madman? I'm about to save your life,* he said, raising an arm at the door, *unlike how you failed to save Charlie's.*

The moment the door was finally kicked in, the men of Hexenhammer were already as good as dead. The mage never knew his brother could move so fast. Max saw the first agent turn dreadfully pale, as if his life force had been ripped from his body. His curly black hair turned snow white, his eyes burst, spurting flesh and fluid into the air. The next man in the stairwell fared even worse, as his entire body instantly turned black with frostbite. And that was just the two Max did see. The tortured screams of dying men chorused through the winding stairwell as Sexton continued his rampage down into the main hall below.

And Max followed.

He hated Sexton, but deep down in Max's soul, the magus was content with Sexton's wrath. The necromancer did what Max never had the courage to do— what his brethren never had the courage to do: take the fight to his enemies. In one day, Sexton was doing what other magi only whispered about for hundreds of years: he was destroying Hexenhammer. And based on the cries of anguish bubbling up from the stairwell, he was being wildly successful.

His bare feet went numb on the icy steps. Nearly each one presented a different dead body: he walked over one broken in half, others were obliterated into slimy bits. He saw a nose, an ear. He even saw a body melded into the wall, as if the stones had come alive and swallowed him up. The walls were slick with thick layers of blood. He took his index finger and smeared a streak from the wall, and painted an "x" in a circle on his forehead.

With a word, the blood on the stone steps and walls burned away into a crimson vapour, and Max inhaled the cloud deeply into his lungs. It smelled of coins and tasted metallic in the back of his throat. He felt the vitality return to his body; the fog, which hung heavy in his mind, burned away. Clarity was his once again. The chill was gone. His skin was warm to the touch. But there was nothing he could do about his frailty. He would just have to avoid another pummelling. He felt like a man reinvigorated, ready for the worst of Sexton Graves. Against the necromancer, he would need all his faculties.

The echoes continued as he descended. There was no mercy within those walls, and Max spared no compassion for the dead. He was in a house of murder. Hexenhammer had hunted down his kind since the discovery of magic. Not just hunted, but burned and drowned, and tortured without remorse. And that was their idea of fair trails. His generation was lucky. Despite their few numbers, they thrived as magicians, and lived full lives without having to hide in the shadows.

Those days were no more.

His Master was gone.

Houdini was gone.

The Golden Dawn?

He knew Sexton just wasn't going to stop with Hexenhammer. The Golden Dawn was on the verge of extinction, and Max was being forced to bring another enemy to their doorstep. He understood the sick irony of it all: with his final failure, he would be the instrument of their complete and utter annihilation.

Max, do join us. Charlie's voice sang blissfully through the stairwell. *There are so very few of them left.*

It was the siren's call, luring him deeper into the abyss. And he answered.

For the last few months, Max had drowned in his own sorrow. He was a lightning rod for catastrophe, nearly of his own doing. He had relived such wretched memories of his life in that dungeon, watched the events unfold like Edison's moving pictures again and again. He had barely survived a deal with the Fallen angel. Banished an old friend to some forsaken corner of the globe. He had spared Helena and others from the horrors of the Murder Society, only to bring Hexenhammer down upon them all. Sexton Graves had his brother. And then, there was the loss of Ammon.

No, Max thought, shaking his head. He had wallowed in despair for too long, borne the weight of the world on his shoulders. There, in the heart of his enemy's cathedral, he vowed before God to end that vicious cycle, along with Sexton's life. He would fail no more. He had hidden his miseries away in those paintings, but facing them again gave him the clarity he needed to remember who he was.

His name was Max Thanatos, a master of blood magic and the arcane arts. He wasn't as brilliant as Sexton, that he also knew, but he was resourceful, unpredictable, and creative. Ammon had believed in him. And despite what the necromancer said about his brother, so did Charlie. He had spent his childhood in New York. Max knew a thing or two about how to handle a bully. When pushed to the brink, you fight. After wading through the bodies in the stairwell, he finally reached the last step on the ground floor. His path was clear: he was going to exorcise Sexton's soul straight to hell.

***

The world felt normal, almost peaceful, as Max made his way across the black and white-tiled floor of the grand cathedral. The Saxon-built, Gothic James House was quiet like the grave. There were no screams, no echoes of fighting in its ancient halls of wood and stone. No blustering from Sexton, no curses from Hexenhammer reverberating from the crypts up to the spire. Just the soft sound of his shuffling feet as Max navigated through the wake of a battlefield.

The cathedral inside had been shattered, distorted, and stripped of its majestic beauty. Rows of pews were splintered and piled atop each other as if thrown across the room. Fixtures of gold and silver were bent and broken. Decorative chandeliers of bronze and crystal had crashed to the floor. And chunks of marble from the obliterated statues of saints were scattered everywhere, making it painful to walk as he felt little shards underneath his bare feet. There was no doubt in Max's mind: Sexton's reckoning was thorough.

Come, Max, claim your prize, Sexton's voice resonated from the building's west side.

Max saw what awaited him, what the trail of carnage had led him to. Beneath the intricate stained glass windows of Adam slaying the Serpent with a shining sword, the true horror of Sexton's vengeance was on full display.

A bit hastily constructed, I know, but do tell me what you think. I am not above criticism.

The architect presented to Max his monument of murder: a mound of broken bodies tossed onto a pile at the cathedral's altar. It was impossible to count the dead. All he saw were arms and legs sprouting out from the spaces like weeds. And the bodies were fresh and still bled. Crimson bands trickled down over the dead like rainwater over rocks, and pooled onto the floor. But the corpses served merely as a foundation to its grotesque centrepiece. The man he knew as Mr. Dove was nailed onto a wooden cross atop the pile like a witch about to be burned at the stake. He was alive, but far from well.

I was aiming for irony. What do you think? Sexton asked, looking over to Max.

Half of Dove's face had been flayed off. His right eye slashed. His crisp white suit was washed in blood. Max didn't flinch at the state of the man. Instead, his lips snarled into something of a smile. Mr. Dove was the one who had killed his Master in Edinburgh. Max had watched as the man butchered Ammon in the street for all to see, the kind man who had lived millennia as a teacher, who loved tea, and set Max on his path as a magician: put down like an animal. The very sight of the man drove Max to anger. No, Max understood anger. This was something else. What he felt was fury, and it surged through him like gasoline in an automobile.

He was so focused on the witch hunter that he barely felt the chill of Sexton, as the spirit floated besides him next to the pile. *I understand how you feel, Max,* he said, in a rare moment of compassion, *Ammon was my Master, too. I had to restrain myself from killing him in that tower. But I want us to do it, together. For closure,* he said, with a nod.

The sentiment felt poetic, and certainly alluring. Max couldn't deny he gave it some thought. But rage and fury, he knew, were only finite. It was like tensing a muscle, eventually it tired. Max felt those emotions wash away as he watched Mr. Dove struggle foolishly to free himself from the cross. Even though his master lived before Christ was born, and, to Ammon, their years together were like a drop in a bucket, Max believed he knew his Master better than anyone else. "Ammon wouldn't want this man to die," he said, adding, "and I am my Master's student. There has been enough killing today."

Charlie's body squirmed at the sickening loyalty of it all, and sneered with as much bile as he could muster. *You are a weak, weak man.*

But then a third voice boomed in the hall. "Where is my son?" Mr. Dove commanded. "Where is Howard?"

Oh, I'd imagine the brat is somewhere here, amongst the bodies, Sexton said, revealing himself to the agent. *With all those white suits, you all look alike to me.*

But the man remained steadfast. "Do you think this changes anything, Devilborn?" Mr. Dove yelled, as spittle dripped down his chin. The edge of death did little to ease the righteousness of the fanatic, it only served to empower him. "Kill one of us, or a kill a thousand. We are legion."

The blood of the dead pooled at Max's feet.

You are nothing! Sexton shot back. Mr. Dove screamed in agony, as the nails hammered below his wrist bones twisted tighter with a wave of the necromancer's hand. *For months, I was your precious Witchfinder General. You did my will. Mine! Not God's. I commanded you, I led you,* he screamed. *And now I know all of your secrets, your hidden locations around the world. The war in Europe left you scattered, weakened. And once I am done here, those who remain elsewhere will suffer the same fate as you.* Then a wicked smile stretched across Charlie's face. *No, not the same as you,* he corrected. *Not at all.*

Sexton stretched his arm out towards the agent of Hexenhammer. *I know what you want. I know the very spark that drives you all: you believe your work to be divine, and has earned you a seat at God's table.*

"I will join my brethren at His right hand in Heaven," he swore.

With his arm still stretched towards Mr. Dove, Sexton, instead, turned to look at Max. *Not without your heart.*

The magus heard the snapping of rib bones as Mr. Dove's chest burst open from the inside out, his heart torn from his body. Arteries straggled behind the muscle like loose thread. Then, in mid-air, an invisible hand crushed the organ into nothing. Sexton condemned the agent to hell without his heart, the very thing that contained the human soul. But it was more than a mere execution, more than damnation, it was a mockery of Charlie's death.

But Sexton underestimated the magician's resolve. "Did you think that would break my spirit?" Max bit. "I have lived with the horror of Charlie's death every day of my life since." He looked down at the black and white tile at his feet, drowning in blood. "And now I'm going to take my brother back," he said, planting his hands into the blood beneath him.

It was a bastardized variation of the spell that bound his brother's soul to his. A magical shockwave exploded outwards from the point of impact, causing the blood to ripple like wind flirting with the surface of a still pond. Sexton's spirit was jettisoned from his brother's incorporeal form.

"Charlie," Max shouted.

The ghost looked like he had been struck dumbfounded by a fist. He grabbed his head to shake away the confusion, but finally laid eyes on his brother. *Max,* he gasped. *What happened? Where am I? Max—*

It was over in an instant. The confusion upon the spirit's face switched back into something sinister. *That wasn't very nice,* Sexton's malevolence spewed from Charlie's mouth.

The magus felt himself flying backwards through the air. All Max saw was a blur until he came crashing down hard into the mound of pews a hundred feet away.

I have been kind, to a point, Max. My quarrel with you had nothing to do with your brother. He was just leverage. But that courtesy ends right now, he proclaimed, floating up to meet Max. *I do not just possess the bodies of the dead, I devour their very life. Every memory they've ever had becomes mine like a book to read. And now I know all there is to know about your brother, and the life you shared. Your adventures, your losses. Your filthy little secrets.*

Max was hardly moving atop the pews.

And if you only knew what this little sodomite really thought of you, he said. *There is so much anger where his heart used to be, it's almost inspiring. But as much as I want to turn you inside out, like you said up in the tower, I still need you. Charlie, on the other hand, I can torture forever,* he threatened with a smile. *I can't kill what's already dead, but I can lock his mind away inside a labyrinth of absolute anguish, like a nightmare he'll never wake from again, as I play his body like Geppetto.*

"Don't," Max exhaled through the pain, stirring from the rubble. "I'll do whatever you want, Sexton. Just let him be."

Are you willing to play nice, Max?

"Please," Max begged.

After a long moment, the spirit of the necromancer eventually nodded. *Alright, I believe you.*

The same magic that crashed the magus in the pews now tenderly lifted him from the pile, bringing him back to his feet. It was hard to look at this brother. Max was helpless to save him. Despite best efforts, sometimes the bullies win. He had nothing else. He had failed Charlie, probably for the last time. At the very least, Max could spare his brother from Sexton's promises of torture. It might be all he could do.

That's a good little puppet, he mocked. *But don't look so glum. You might be at the end of your rope, but not all is lost. Come.* He motioned for Max to follow.

Max was hesitant. Nothing Sexton ever said or did had good intentions.

Now.

It was dangerous to follow that man anywhere. But against Max's better judgement, they went past the main floor and into the crypts, realizing the irony of there being more corpses above ground than there were buried below.

When they found your apartment, I had them save what they could. That little portal spell of yours was quite inspired. It was a shame they couldn't secure more before it vanished. I heard you were quite the collector. Max trailed the spirit of his brother as they traversed a dark corridor that opened wider into a vast chamber of dusty bookcases and artefacts locked behind glass cases. Along the walls were racks of automatic rifles and revolvers, crates of ammunition and other munitions piled into corners, all of which were best fitted for war, not a cathedral.

The room was damp and musty. Black mould grew on the spine of several books, ruining them for good. Some tomes he recognized, all of which were about the history of magic and demons, and all things Devilborn. But there was a great wealth to be discovered. He wished there had been time to study them all. The room was alive with energy. He sensed power pulsating from the artefacts, from the books.

"Hexenhammer used magic to fight us?"

Sexton agreed. *Their hypocrisy knew no end. Like all zealots, they become the very thing they hate the most. I actually pitied their Witchfinder General. His ancestor started Hexenhammer back during the English Civil War,* he said, admiring a worn Bible hundreds of years old trapped within a glass case. *But the man I possessed was ashamed of his past. He actually planned to end Hexenhammer, in time. But he lacked the conviction to do it. I guess, in a way, he got what he wanted,* he smiled, proud of himself.

The spirit pointed to the other side of the room. *There,* he said. *If you're going to take me into London, I need you to, at least, dress the part. I know your door is in the city, but just no more than that.*

At the opposite end was an assortment of his personal items organized and catalogued on several shelves. The suit he wore when he was captured was draped over a tailor's mannequin. Considering he had spent months rotting away in his own filth, it was the most beautiful thing he had ever seen, and it included his custom vest with dozens of hidden pockets sown in.

I can see it on your face. No, I had them take those troublesome trinkets away. The last thing I want to contend with is a magician with a trick up his sleeve.

Max cursed the man under his breath. But there was nothing he could do. He loved his trinkets. The other novelties he cared little about. But he immediately snatched his spectacles from a shelf and plopped them onto his nose, with their lenses tinted fully black to shield his sensitive eyes. But one shelf above contained his greatest prize: his wolf's head cane. It wasn't lost after all. "You kept my things. Why?"

I wanted them as trophies, to be honest. And I plan to do the same for the rest of the Golden Dawn, after I kill them. I must admit, Max, the cane is a bit morbid. Even for me, he said, nodding towards it. *Not even your brother knows you've been carrying the instrument of his death with you for all these years, does he?*

Max held the cane in his hand, and appraised its every inch. "No," he said. He ran his fingers over the wolf carving, made from Indian ivory, which was also the pommel of the hidden sword within. "It only serves as a reminder of my greatest failure."

Was that why also you grew your beard to such a ridiculous length?

Max rubbed his smooth chin. "It was last thing Charlie said to me while he was alive," he said, trailing off in reflection. The memory was still raw, even after so long.

Sentimentality. I can respect that.

The thought of the man's approval turned his stomach. But moments later, he was dressed, and felt like his old self again. Inside his coat pocket, he felt something heavy bump up against his chest. He reached in and removed a long, crooked skeleton key dangling from a brass ring.

The time for pandering is over, Sexton growled, his patience finally run to its limits. *Ammon died protecting that key. Now, don't let his death be in vain. Take me to the door, and honour his death, as you did your brother's.*

How he wanted to strike the man, lash at him with a spectrum of his most painful magic. The necromancer wanted to stir him to anger, and he very nearly succeeded with every word he said from Charlie's mouth. There was no escape from him. It didn't matter if Max was in the belly of Hexenhammer's cathedral or walking along the Thames. His brother's shell housed a wicked thing, a man without remorse, without restraint. A dead thing far removed from the bonds of the living world, free to torment without repercussions. Sexton Graves, once a prominent member of the Golden Dawn, was now his oppressor. Max's greatest of fear of being chained to something insidiously evil had finally been realized, and he couldn't break free.

CHAPTER TWENTY-ONE:
THE FIRST BEAST

London was beautiful in the spring, angelic even, until the black industrial soot of midday soiled its delicate splendour. The city was hardly ever left unmolested for long. The capital was an engine of global industry, never ceasing progress. Its skyline was rife with smokestacks, spewing thick, dense clouds of ruinous smoke. It always smelled of sulphur. Machines pumped like a heartbeat, fuelling London with life, and the working-class toiled endlessly to keep them running. And, somewhere, within that maze of machinery was his door to the Golden Dawn.

Max flicked a cooling ember from a fold in his jacket. Behind him, James House was burning. The strong spring wind whipped the fire into a roar, carrying with it the scent of charred flesh. The dancing blaze flirted with the sky, yet the magical flames would not extinguish until all was burnt to ash. Both he and Sexton knew it was for the best. The evidence of their kind had to go up in flames, along with Hexenhammer.

They headed away from the Thames, deeper into south London. Max knew where he was going, more or less. The mirrored glass showed him his path. But he had no reason to rush towards his end. He knew Sexton wouldn't let him live once he had opened the door, and he needed time to think. He felt the weight of the key in his coat pocket bounce with every step. Every member had one, even Sexton, but the key wouldn't work without his body. Each one was unique to its owner, and each "door" was equally so. Only the owner knew the location, and only when he held the key could he unlock it.

Where are you taking me?

"East," he said.

If you think you can drag your feet as some pathetic ploy to delay my purpose, remember what I could do to your brother.

Sexton was certainly no fool. Max had to remember that. "The door was of Crowley's design," he said, "nothing is ever easy when it comes to that man." It was a half-truth, but true enough for Sexton to believe, as the spirit nodded. He was fortunate they both had history with that bastard, but next time, a half-truth might not be enough.

The necromancer was his own terrible challenge, but getting to the door was another. For respected members, it was just a matter of simply walking through. Max had been exiled from the Order long ago by Aleister Crowley; a man who hated the magician even more than Sexton. When Max was disgraced, the blowhard had warned him personally that he would add his own sinister touch to the door. Max never quite knew what that implied. He never had to a reason to find out. But it could have been a curse he had to break, or something far worse. What he did know was Crowley's sadism was enough even to give Sexton pause.

Max crossed through West Square Gardens, past a group of young women riveted by the sight of the smouldering building in the distance. The sunny midday gave way to a darkened overcast, chilling the warm spring day. No, it wasn't the building that had their interest, Max noticed. In the sky, the sun was being eclipsed by the moon. It was an unprecedented celestial event, and Max knew it was a terrible omen: when darkness vanquished the light, the Devil walked amongst them.

Is it true? Sexton asked, softening the perpetual scowl on Charlie's face since his possession.

"Is *what* true?" Max bit.

The rumours, of what you did in India, he said, *I've heard stories. Hearsay, really. Even your brother doesn't know, does he?*

Max refused to listen.

You often ride so tall on that moral high horse of yours, I just had to know if the stories of the 'Butcher of Bombay' were true. That, after Charlie's murder, you burned all those people to death, he said, sincerely curious. *To clarify, I said 'hearsay' because there was no one left alive to confirm what really happened.*

It was one memory Max could never forget.

But Sexton pressed on. *I'm not judging you, Maxi-boy. In fact, I might just be the only other person alive, in a manner of speaking, who would understand your position. Through the memories of Charlie's childhood, I saw the connection you had as his surrogate father. Your love for the man was plain. It wouldn't take a failed detective to guess what happened next: the heathens killed your brother, and you wanted them to pay. You wanted to make them all pay.*

Sexton floated around Max's body, settling at his side, as if they were walking together through the park. *Confession is good for the soul. From one killer to another, people should pay for their crimes. Did you know I was once married?* Sexton feigned shock with a theatrical wave of his hand as Max turned his way, *yes, it's true,* he said. *There was a time when even I knew love. She was a beautiful young thing, a dancer. Bella Ling. They called her the Yellow Rose of Chinatown.*

Every man desired her, chased her, but in the end, she chose me. Lord knows why. I was a mess back then, he added. *But things haven't changed much today. Hatred and bigotry were as alive then as they are now. Dating outside their race was considered a sin to their people, taboo. But marriage?* There was a break in his voice, a rare sorrow, but he continued. *While I was away by order of the Golden Dawn, her people dragged my wife from our bed in the middle of the night, boiled her face in cooking oil, and mutilated her womanhood. When I came home days later, I found her corpse outside our door. Her face had been plucked apart by the crows. The rats were nibbling at her fingers.*

I was younger then, my necromancy wasn't as refined. But her spirit begged for revenge. That, I knew.

Max looked at his enemy. For the briefest of moments, he felt conflicted. He wanted to somehow console the man; that would have been the normal human response, but then he saw the all too familiar expression of despair on Charlie's face, and remembered the monster hiding within. "What did you do?" he asked, instead, clenching his cane.

I sank that part of Chinatown into the ground, killing them all.

"The papers said it was a gas explosion," he blurted incredulously. "The Inverted Church. That was *your* doing?"

Sexton nodded. *Perhaps our paths were always destined to cross,* he said. *See, when it comes down to it, we're not so different, you and I.*

"We're nothing alike," Max bit.

Saying it aloud doesn't make it true. We avenge family. The Dawn's former master died before I had my chance for revenge. But Crowley will suffice.

The two men continued in silence for several blocks more. It was a welcomed reprieve for Max, given how gregarious the necromancer was. He wondered if the story about Bella Ling was true. The man was a sociopath. It could have been a lie he had told so many times that it became truth. But his gut told him otherwise. His enemy was haunted by his own memories. Sexton, despite all his maliciousness, was still once a man.

Now Max questioned Sexton, "Is it true about your deal with Heaven and Hell?"

Ah, Sexton said. *Did a little birdy tell you?*

"Do you think you're going to come out on top of this?" he asked. "Giving the girl to one side, failing to deliver on the other?"

He laughed. *Do you really expect me to just give away such a precious jewel? My deals are insurance, nothing more.*

"I think you overestimate your chances."

And I think you're not as clever as you believe, Sexton retorted, already tired of the game. *The way you continue to skirt us around this neighbourhood, drawing away when the key warms to the north. Lest you forget, I understand their properties, too. Charlie sees fields of warmth and cold like you see colour, and I can see through your pocket,* he revealed, more as a warning than a proclamation. *Perhaps the threat against your brother wasn't convincing enough.*

Max realized his folly. "Sexton, wait."

No, he said, *perhaps I will need to a new way to motivate you.*

The magus felt the air around him thicken with pressure. Charlie's spectral body just fell limp in mid-air, floating silently, but that wasn't what worried him. The solid concrete at his feet rippled like water. The people of Newington simply walked by, completely oblivious to the chromatic portal opening before them in broad daylight, for only those attuned to the spirit world could have experienced such an event: the merger of two planes of existence in juxtaposition to one another.

Spectral chains exploded from the chromatic portal. Charlie's visage stirred once again and dragged whatever was on the other end into the world of the living.

Entangled by heavy, wispy chains was the spirit of a woman with long, black hair, and a sad, but kind face. The magus felt his heart stop. "Mother," Max whimpered, as he lounged forward to free her, but was held fast by an invisible grip.

Max? The woman's voice trembled, barely recognizing her boy who had become a man. But when the realization finally hit her, a chain coiled around her neck, and wrenched her head back.

"You animal!" Max screamed with tears swelling in his eyes. It was the harshest blow ever dealt. His mother, the gentlest person he had ever known, a woman who had suffered beyond words in life, was now tortured in death.

Conjuring spirits is but a simple matter for me, Max, Sexton said. *All I need is a name, and I can drag anyone back from even the deepest fathoms of Hell.* He tightened the chains, and smiled as the spirit howled in pain. *Now do I have your attention?* he screamed.

"Let her go, Sexton, please," Max begged, beside himself.

Why should I? You have already lied to me once before, back at the cathedral. Do you think I'd be so foolish as to trust you again?

"The door—it's at Elephant and Castle, just a few blocks away. That's the truth—now, please," he trailed off, as he watched his mother's face twist in anguish.

Sexton tugged at the chains once more, relinquishing their hold on the ghost. In an instant, the portal dragged Max's mother back into the spirit world with a pop. He then set the magus free, and grinned as he watched him collapse to his knees, reaching for his mother.

Tillie Grey was her name. Your brother's mind may be fractured, like reading from a book with missing pages, but what child could ever forget his mother's name? We will go to Elephant and Castle. If the door is not there, I will summon her spirit again, but next time, I will condemn the woman to wander this plane forever. And you know what happens to spirits who cannot cross over, he finished, with another grin of utmost malice. *Now, to the Underground,* he commanded.

The last memory Max had of his mother was watching her pass away peacefully in her bed. Now, it was of her being tormented by the Sexton's gruesome display. He rose back to his trembling feet, matching the necromancer's smug look with his own quivering rage. He had been bested and cornered, and he could stall no longer. It was over.

***

Max had faced death before. For most people, it happened once in their lives: at the end. For Max, it was a recurrence. It often ignited his most colourful of emotions: stark bravery, bitterness, despair. However, this time, as the warmth of the key led him down deeper into the dimly lit tunnels, beneath the district of Elephant and Castle and leading from the station of that name, the magician retreated into quiet reflection. Everything had come full circle, he realized. The long winding path that had led him on his journey began with a girl in New York, as he worked a case that originally led him to Sexton Graves. Now, that same journey was to end in the London Underground with the very same man months later.

How he hated being below ground, being confined to narrow passages, the feeling of being buried alive. Charlie would have had soft words of comfort, but not that day. He knew the architect of his woe. Like any great agitator, Crowley took immense pleasure in exploiting his phobia. It was why the bald bastard personally crafted his door to be found in the underbelly of London, far from sight of a sky he might never see again. Even removed from life, the blowhard continued to antagonize him.

On he went. The tunnel was cold and dry, and smelled of grease and metal. The darkness was unyielding. Max summoned an orb of light to guide their way down the linear path. He saw nothing extraordinary. His spectacles, warded to expose hidden magic, revealed nothing in the darkness. The only telling thing was just how plain it all was. "Do you see anything, Sexton," he reluctantly asked, the man's name was like ash on his tongue. Charlie was adept at seeing things far beyond mortal eyes, so it sickened him to have to ask the necromancer for help.

Ley lines converge further down the tracks, he replied. *Nothing more,* he added reluctantly. The closer they drew to the door, the more it agitated the spirit. Sexton didn't even bother to conceal his anticipation. His quest was nearly over.

They followed the tracks into another tunnel that split into a fork, and the left path took them into a derelict tube junction once used to house inactive cars. Now, it was just abandoned with a single car left at the centre of the vast chamber. With a word, Max expanded the orb of light for a better look, driving scurrying creatures back further into the shadows.

The room was damp, the ground mucky. Foul water dripped down from the tall ceiling in several spots. Max had noted their direction since they first entered the tunnels, and guessed they were well under the Thames. He knew that not every portal to the Golden Dawn was an actual door. He felt the key's heat through his clothes. What they sought was near, just within reach, and he wondered if the subway car was the source. But the chamber was also supernaturally frigid, a sign of evil. Some*thing* lurked about.

"Sexton, there's a presence here. I need your eyes."

I care little for what you need, he raged. *Where is the god-damn door?*

"Enough of your nonsense," he responded testily. Max was tired of the endless bickering. "Tell me what you see," he demanded. His body crackled with uneasiness. Something else stirred in the chamber. "Crowley laid a trap for me, if I ever were to return. It may have already been sprung."

God help your loved ones if this is another one of your tricks. There is nothing here. Not even a wandering soul, he spat.

Max split the orb apart into four smaller spheres, and sent them out into the far reaches of the hall. Three revealed nothing, but one orb simply dissipated away into darkness. There was something there that even his light couldn't touch. "Still think this is a trick?"

No, Sexton replied, *but I do believe you should run.*

The darkness in that sector of the chamber was quivering into a globulous form, twisting and folding into itself like a baker kneading dough. The mass's growth quickly spiralled into the shape of something beyond natural, something beyond monstrous. Its body was serpentine, scaled, and the thing continued to grow until it reached the size of the subway car. The creature's neck was as long as its barbed tail, and its face looked reptilian, with its beady eyes. Its girth crushed the ground beneath its four legs. The abomination let out a roar that rattled the stone walls, showing its maw of spiny teeth.

"That bastard summoned a dragon."

Crowley must really hate you.

There was no disputing that. The serpent was the strongest of all beasts. The First Beast, as he knew it. A creature born from hatred and strife, bred to maim and wreak havoc upon the world of men. It was a devourer of armies, destroyer of kingdoms. And Max watched as the greatest of horrors turned to cast its red eyes upon him.

The magus paid no heed to the necromancer's continued warning to run. Instead, he stepped forward, squaring himself firmly in the beast's path, as its heavy steps quickened their pace. "There's a reason why all evil knows my name, Sexton. Just like the First Beast, I, too, sit at the top of animal kingdom."

The snarling dragon was in full stride, making great gains across the chamber. It would be upon the magus in mere moments.

"But there's only room for one of us at the summit." Max did not cringe at its imposing sight, nor did he step back. He held his ground, like an ancient tree rooted deeply in place. He held forth his wolf's head cane before him, horizontally like a sheath. "Great Beast," he beckoned. "Cease your attack, or face oblivion."

The creature ignored the warning, and continued at Max at full speed, crashing down its legs upon the ground with each step.

"Then so be it," he whispered.

The serpent lashed out its head to cleave the magician in two with its incredible mouth. But it only bit air. With a dexterity he rarely unleashed, Max stepped to the right, twisting the wolf's head, carved from Indian ivory, and unsheathed the blood-stained blade within; which shone red with immense power. In one wide slash, the magical blade cleaved the dragon's head cleanly from its long neck, denying it even its final death wail. Both body and head collapsed to the ground, as Max stood victorious with his sword held forth, stained with the serpent's golden ichor and Charlie's blood from so long ago.

'One, two! One, two! And through and through the vorpal blade went snicker-snack! He left it dead, and with its head he went galumphing back.' Sexton quoted from *'Jabberwocky'*, and beamed, genuinely impressed. *Well done; I always pegged you as a bit of a Nancy, like your brother, but looks like you had some moxie after all. I can't wait to see Crowley's face when I tell him you felled his beast.*

Max just shook his head. "I have endured your prattling and madness for long enough, Sexton. I stood by your side and watched helplessly as you plagued Charlie, and tortured my mother. My mother!" he screamed. "You are a far greater monster than that thing lying dead at my feet. For the sake of all things good left in this world, you need to be put down."

Careful, Max, I don't think I like your tone. We still have a door to open, or must I teach you another lesson?

"No," Max said, stepping forward into the serpent's ichor that was saturating into the ground.

No?

"You've been so obsessed with the girl's power, you never even considered the source was the ichor in her veins," he said, nodding towards his feet. "Now, the world's most powerful blood mage is standing in a pool of it."

But before Sexton could register the danger, Max knelt down to the ground, and slapped his hand into the ichor of the serpent with a splat. His spell from before was strong, but it hadn't been enough to keep Sexton away for good. Now, it was fuelled by the monster's ichor. The explosion of energy expelled the necromancer from Charlie's form like a bullet from a gun.

And then chamber fell deathly still.

Max, Charlie said, in the soft voice Max had cherished throughout the years.

"Charlie?" he asked, uncertain of his victory.

The spirit slowly nodded, but more to shake the memories away, as if waking from a terrible dream. *I saw everything,* he hushed. *I saw everything, and couldn't do anything to stop it. That man— he made me watch—*

watch, as he hurt our mother. His words were scattered. His thoughts frayed.

Max didn't know what to say. He hadn't believed he could save his brother from Sexton. He didn't even expect him to still be alive. "I'm sorry," he said, eventually. "He was too strong. I couldn't do anything to help you until now. But I stopped him, Charlie. I stopped Sexton."

No, his brother screamed, *Sexton's still here.*

Before Max could register the implications, an unseen power forced him to drive the sword into his own chest.

I don't need Charlie's body anymore, came Sexton's voice from the darkness. The visage of the real necromancer materialized before Max. The scrawny dark-skinned man, nearly skeletal, grinned a toothy smile as he watched the magus drop to his knees. *I only used him to make you suffer. But everything I need is here together: your body, the key, and the door. I just have to wait until you die, and then twist your corpse around this chamber like a rag-doll with your key in-hand.*

Max tried to speak, but phlegmy blood spat out from his mouth. It was a miracle he was still alive; the blade had nicked his heart by the breadth of a hair. The pain was insurmountable as he slowly slid the weapon from his chest. But the wound was grave. That he knew. He was alone in the dark, far from any means to reach the surface. He didn't want to expire underground. But he knew he'd bleed out long before he managed to crawl his way back to the station.

Your mother's spirit, he began, *I want you to die knowing full well that she will never rest peacefully again. It's the least I could do for all of the irritation you have caused me. But, as for you, Max…* He paused to relish the prospects, *no, Hell would be too good for you. Once this is all over, I will tear your soul from the Devil's teeth, himself, and unleash you upon the world as the very thing you hate the most: a monster.*

But then Sexton felt a queer sensation, one hadn't felt since he was alive. It was the feeling of someone gripping his wrist.

My brother was right about me being a pacifist, Charlie said. *Even when people threatened those I loved, I still fought to find some kind of amicable solution to it all, because that was just my nature. But,* Charlie said, wrapping his other hand around Sexton's neck, *but that was before you brought our mother into this.*

Sexton smiled. *Oh, how dramatic. You can't kill what's already dead, stupid boy.*

You're right, Charlie said, looking past Sexton, *but my brother can.* The stalling tactic was desperate, but it did the trick. It gave Max just enough time to use the dragon's ichor to paint a crude pentagram onto the filthy ground.

The magus breathed through the pain, as he rose back to his feet. "I've spent the last year exhaustively studying the Devil, which led me down the path of all things demonic, including how to summon things from Hell. I never went deep enough to stare into the abyss, as you did, but I did learn that that gate swings both ways." The pentagram pulsated with power. The ground at Sexton's feet shifted into a black pit. Tendrils slithered up from the bottomless darkness, and lashed about like gnarly, thick snakes searching for prey. "I promised myself that I would send you to Hell, Sexton, and a man is only as good as his word."

No, Sexton screamed. For the first time in his life, he was afraid. His spirit tried to flee, but he was held fast in place by the spell. *Max Thanatos!*

The tendrils lashed around the necromancer's visage, his incorporeal legs, torso, and then his neck. The Brothers Thanatos watched with bittersweet catharsis as the necromancer was dragged down inexorably into the black pit, damned to freeze in the coldest depths of Hell for eternity, and with the name of his enemy on his lips.

The pit evaporated into nothing, like pieces of ash caught in the wind. The chamber remained still. The orbs of light flickered out the last bit of their magic, sending the junction back into darkness. Max reignited the light. Sexton Graves was no more. It was over. "That was for our mother," he affirmed, nodding towards Charlie, who stretched a weary smile in return.

CHAPTER TWENTY-TWO:
END OF THE LINE

"Are you alright, Charlie?" Max asked.

Me? Charlie balked at responding, nodding towards his brother's stab wound. *How bad is it?*

"Bad," he assured him. Max sheathed the sword back into the cane's shaft, and, for the first time, used it to walk. He clenched his jaw with every step. He tried to breathe through the agony, his heart felt like it was on fire, but he had to keep going. As long as Charlie was fine, he would endure the pain.

And there's nothing you could do? No spell?

Max just shook his head. "Not even the ichor," he said, taking another painful step. "My blood magic can do much, but it cannot undo what has been done. The sword's damage is absolute, as I designed it to be so many years ago." How damning it was to know the blade that killed one Thanatos brother would soon take the other. He gripped the car's railing, and hoisted himself up the exterior steps to the car's back entrance, nearly passing out from the pain. He felt the concerned look from his brother, but dismissed it with a gesture of his hand. "Only Helena can save me now."

Helena? Charlie recoiled. *You don't even know where she is.*

"Sexton said she's with Crowley, and Crowley will be with the Golden Dawn."

You're risking your life on that man's word?

Max didn't disagree. "It's my only option, Charlie," he said, tenderly. "I'm dying."

He slid the subway car door open, and made his way within. Unlike the septic chamber he had left behind, the interior was remarkably pristine. The mahogany benches shone with polish, the brass-lined fixtures and poles caught his reflection as he passed, as if they had never once been touched by the grime of human hands. The entire car looked like it had just come off an assembly line, except for the droplets of blood left in his wake as he crossed towards the conductor's console. In his hand, the skeleton key glowed orange like heated metal ready for the anvil, but it did not burn. Instead, it transmuted into a modern key no larger than his thumb, revealing its true form before the door.

What's happening here, Max? I thought you were looking for a door.

"And I've found it," he said, relieved, as he placed the key into the ignition. "Not every door is a door." With a twist, the subway car rumbled to life. Geometric buttons lit up on the console, dials came to life. He had awoken the steel beast from its slumber.

I don't think I'll ever fully understand magic, Charlie confessed.

"Believe me, brother, neither will I," Max winced.

Beneath the subway car, the massive platform sputtered to life. The mechanism rotated the car nearly a full circle before aligning it to face the thick chamber wall.

Max. The urgency in Charlie's voice was clear.

But the magician just focused through the pain. He gripped the lever on the console, and pressed it as forward as far as it would allow. The cabin jolted. The brakes were released. The car dislodged itself from its spot and rolled forward. There was no electrical wire powering it from above. The thing was fuelled by the magic of the Golden Dawn, and it immediately accelerated towards the wall at full-speed.

Max, Charlie repeated. This time, fearing for his brother's life.

Even the magus didn't quite know what to expect.

But there was no fatal impact. Like a spirit, it passed through the masonry wall of the chamber undamaged. Light shone in feebly through the windows. Max peered through the glass to see a queer world around him. Nothing was familiar. It was desolate, alien. It was both night and day, but there was no sun or moon in the sky. No star constellations Max could recognize. They rode through a valley atop magical tracks that formed as they went and vanished just as quickly behind them. The magus saw rounded mountains in the far distance, or so he thought. But as they drew closer, he saw that they were gigantic monoliths of stone figures, human-like, but not. And he could have sworn one of them moved.

Where are we?

"My guess is we are in the space between spaces. A world just outside the reality of men."

You mean, where rabbits go right before you pull them from hats? Charlie half-joked.

The excitement was causing his damaged heart to thunder, and he collapsed into a seat bench. The pain was too much to bear, and he had a feeling their journey still had some distance—if one could call it that—to go. He ignored the cries of his brother, and instead focused on his breathing. He had to slow his heart. "No more jokes, Charlie," he said, his tone softening. "I don't know how much time I have left… I have to tell you something, in case I don't make it."

Charlie hated to hear his brother even allude to his end, but he let him speak.

"Sexton told me confession was good for the soul. I thought it was just more of the man's nonsense, but there was truth to his words," he said, shifting uncomfortably on the bench to relieve the pain. "Do you still remember much of your time in India? In Bombay?" he asked, watching the world outside roll by.

The ghost habitually rubbed his chin when lost in recollection. *Few memories are vivid,* he began, *but most are like remnants of a dream. I can recall images, faces, but hardly details anymore. But I remember our last brunch together. You came all that way for my wedding—* he said, trailing off in thought. *My wedding,* he repeated.

I don't even remember my fiancée's name, he admitted, peppered with shame. *But I treated you with such disdain that day.* Charlie's voice was heavy with regret. *I was always a boorish brother to you, no matter how much you sacrificed for my sake. For that, Max, I am so truly sorry.*

The magus shook his head. "I loved you no matter how 'boorish' you were, Charlie. You were, and will forever be, my brother. Know that. No matter what happens," he urged, "but this is my confession," he said, with a beguiled smile. "Do you remember a man named Mahesh?"

Charlie rubbed his chin again, but eventually nodded.

"And what he meant to you?" Max stressed. He had to be certain.

Yes, he lamented.

It wasn't a wound he wanted to open so near the end of his life, but it was a secret he refused to carry over to the other side. "The night you were murdered, at that port, I… lost control," he said. "The spell I cast to bind you to me, also took the life of the man you loved. I murdered him. I murdered Mahesh." Max bowed his head. He had finally confessed it out loud. He just sat and waited for his brother's judgement. His wrath.

I know, Max, Charlie revealed. *I've… always known.* There were no sharp recriminations, and no animosity sounded in his voice. Just a gentle declaration, as if it was a confession of his own.

But Max hardly believed it. "All these years?" was all Max could muster.

Charlie nodded. *Don't' forget, for a time, we were both detectives. It took a few years, but I eventually pieced it together. But, when my memory was stronger.*

"Then do you forgive me, Charlie?" he breathed. If Max had the strength to kneel, he would have dropped to his knees that very moment. "Please, forgive me."

Charlie hovered his hand just above Max's shoulder. *I never blamed you,* he said. *You have been burdened by so much in your life, it would have been cruel to do so.*

Max felt the subway car slow, but it could have been time, itself, doing so. He had carried that secret with him like shrapnel. Since that day in Bombay, every time he had looked upon his brother's kind face, the secret broke his heart that much more.

I know this might sound ironic coming from me, but I think we should let the ghosts of our pasts rest in peace and move on. If Ammon was right about Crowley, you may need your strength for what lies ahead, and it seems like our journey is coming to an end.

"So you *did* eavesdrop on us?" Max wanted to laugh when his brother coyly shrugged, but it hurt too much. His brief reprieve of happiness faded when Helena entered his thoughts. Was she really at the end of the line? Having sent her away into the Glassworld was foolish, reckless. It wasn't a prison of cages. It was a plane of nothingness that trapped people inside their own head, freezing them in a moment in time like purgatory. It was designed for turmoil. And damning her to that place, even briefly? Max wouldn't have wished that end for anyone, but it was a rash gamble to save her life.

And the only way out was through Crowley.

The man was volatile and cantankerous, and a master manipulator. If he had Helena, he would have won her to his side with promises and security. Max knew their short time together had hardly been a pleasant experience. It began with his death and ended with Hexenhammer. The blowhard was a survivor and a provider: everything Max, who had failed Uriel, and failed the girl, was not. Deep within that strange world, Max finally came to realize Helena would be better left with Crowley.

The brakes squealed as the subway car slowly lurched to a complete stop. Max had finally reached the Golden Dawn. He sat upright for a better view, and immediately regretted it. The pain surged through his body like hot needles. He had lost a lot of blood, nearly too much. He fought just to stay conscious. When Crowley hid away the Palace of the Golden Dawn, Max never would have guessed it would have been taken so far into another realm.

He edged his way outside, leaving behind bloody handprints with every touch. His body couldn't stop shivering. "Charlie, I'm nearly done," he said.

You fought too hard just to give up now.

"I can feel it."

We've been in this spot before. You're too damned stubborn to die.

"Maybe not this time," he sighed, as he hobbled onto the platform. "After all, death is our namesake."

The portal's spell had been spent, thrusting Max into a magical construct of a London Underground station, his backdoor to the Golden Dawn. Nothing scurried. Nothing stirred. The place just reeked of magic, dark and chilling, reminiscent of hell. He flopped his bloodied hand against the white tiles, cocking his head as the Edison bulbs flickered above, barely illuminating the path down the station's only exit, ushering him forward.

Is this it? Charlie asked, hardly believing it.

"It has to be," Max hoped. "We are well beyond turning back." And so he marched, mustering whatever strength he had left to just to move forward. He strapped the wolf's head cane to his belt, for it no longer held up his weight. He was at his limit. He continued, step after step, pushing past his own Herculean threshold of pain, an endurance beyond the tolerance of any normal man. He wasn't even sure how he was still conscious. He just kept pushing forward as if by instinct, through muscle memory, using the wall as he went.

Max followed the light to the end of the passage. Voices perforated the air. He tried to call out, but his voice denied him. His world faded to black. The magician's next step wobbled under his weight, and he slumped to the ground.

Death was upon him, but yet he urged himself on. He reached out with a shaky arm, and clawed his way closer to the light. Again and again, dragging himself inch by inch.

But the light dimmed, as did the pain. A moment later, he didn't hurt at all. He no longer heard Charlie's voice. The passage ceased to be. Even the hard floor melted away as he found himself floating aimlessly in a vast, black lake. Max called out for his brother, but he couldn't hear his own voice.

Then a voice sounded across the darkness, seemingly from everywhere and nowhere at once. It was a snarky, sinister tone, one he never expected to hear again. "Oh, Maxi-boy," it said. "When will you ever learn?"

The black lake rippled at its every word.

"Did you really believe Hell would keep me, after I made a deal?" it taunted. "That your little stunt in Elephant and Castle would be enough to rid me from your life?"

The water began to boil.

"Wallowing in the black pits, I bided my time. Waited for you to lead me right to the girl, and to the Golden Dawn. And you did not disappoint."

Max's body sank into the abyss, deeper into the gloom. But the voice still broke through. "I'm going to keep you where you are, Max: not alive, not quite dead. I want you conscious enough to hear the girl scream for you— to revel in your final failure until I am ready to release you from one Hell and send you into the next."

The magician couldn't even flail in panic as he felt the boiling water fill his lungs.

"I want you to hear me toast your name as I split Helena into two, and drink her soul like a fine wine of ichor," the voice spat.

Max drifted aimlessly in the cold, darkness of it all. As his words had failed him, so did his body. All he had was Sexton Graves taunting him from beyond, and the revelation of the black mirrored glass, which prophesied for the last time that he wouldn't live to see the end.

***

Charlie had already seen his brother die once before; he couldn't let it happen again. Max was one man with two souls. They were linked together through magic and by blood. The sword's wound was absolute. That he was told. There'd be no coming back without Helena's power. Yet there was one risk Charlie had left to take, one he never would have considered unless all was lost.

It took tremendous energy for him to cross over into the realm of the living, but when he did, it was at the grave cost of his humanity. He saw Max's body writhe on the ground, but Charlie sensed the man's soul was adrift and held by one of Sexton's accursed magic spells; one that kept Max from crossing over as the necromancer abandoned him to search for the girl.

He hovered above his brother's cooling body, and slowly slid his spectral hand through Max's chest. Charlie didn't exactly understand how it worked, but because their souls were tethered, he could feed him bits of his own energy, like through an umbilical cord. It would stem his wounds for a short time, but would not save him from death. It'd only be a short reprieve, the pain would soon return, and Charlie wouldn't have the energy to save him again, or he, too, would be lost.

And so, Charlie fed him. And gone were more memories from his life: the name of his father, of his childhood home in Louisiana. Gone were the wonderful memories of the days he had spent at Coney Island with his brother, of his first years in London, and of a man named Mahesh.

Gone.

***

Max, he heard his brother say through bleak maw of nothingness, *get up and fight.*

The darkness around Max was burned away by the light, and he was thrust back into the world of the living once more. He found himself lying in the middle of an audience theatre of rows of plump, cushy pillows. It was where Houdini once perfected his tricks for the Dawn before taking them on the road.

"What happened?" Max asked, feeling woozy.

I don't know. Perhaps some residual magic of Helena's was still in your system? he lied. Charlie knew Max would have never allowed him to feed him his life force. His stubborn brother would have chosen death, instead.

But I'm afraid Sexton Graves beat us here. Somehow.

"Hell seeped its way in," Max knew. "And Sexton along with it." He took a step, and felt a stake of pain run up his spine. "The threshold weakened just enough for Hell to slip through when I opened the door." He already felt the residual magic wearing off, "Charlie, I can't fight Sexton in this state."

You may not even get the chance, he said, pointing behind Max.

The room was washed in a brilliance as Ezekiel and three other angels manifested inside the audience theatre, their white robes flowing in a non-existent breeze. "Young Creature," the olive-skinned figure boomed, with the full authority of Heaven. "Take us to the abomination."

***

Sexton walked again. His body had been magically reconstructed by Hellish power, gifted by the three demons who now marched behind him. He was over a century old, but his youth had been returned. His mind was sharper than ever. He had Hell on his side, power in his veins, and the girl at his fingertips. He walked taller than ever, confident, like a man who even death refused. He was only a custodian of his new body until the girl was delivered, but he had no intention of ever handing over his prize.

The demons could not see the Nephilim, but they were like bloodhounds, closing in on the ichor flowing within her. Crowley had not made it easy. The Palace was a web of its maker's design, and changed at his whims. In essence, it was part of him, it *was* him. There was no doubt the man knew it had been breached, and breached by the worst adversaries. But there was nowhere left to go. Taking the Palace in-between realities had cornered the survivors, and Sexton was nearly upon them.

The necromancer heard the thoughts of Theo Hardeen and Lynn Lin well before they launched their pathetic ambush. Theo struck first, from the shadows like a coward. But his incantation became a gurgle as Sexton crushed his throat with a thought. Lynn Lin didn't fare any better, but Sexton had a particular hatred for the Chinese, and snapped her spine just enough to sever her ability to breathe. He knew she'd be dead in only a matter of moments, so Sexton paused long enough to squat over the body and smile as he watched the woman suffocate to death. "I always liked you the least."

Sexton tapped the side of his head. Crowley may have been adept at hiding his thoughts, but the girl was still just a girl. He could hear her prayers, her promises to God. He turned east towards the audience chamber, laughing to himself as he suddenly realized that Crowley would naturally be sitting on his throne, like a prideful king waiting to be conquered.

"You pompous prat!" Crowley cursed at Sexton from across the chamber. "How dare you come here with those *dogs*— to my home!" In the gilded throne room of the Golden Dawn, the sweaty, cherry-faced Crowley sat dressed for battle in the polished, glinting armour of a pharaoh, undeterred by his enemy.

Sexton just shook his head. "Knowing your hubris, Crowley, I imagine the girl is close by, cloaked by a spell. But that is neither here nor there. I hear her, and my 'dogs' *will* sniff her out," he promised.

"No," Crowley returned. "The Nephilim will remain with me. You shall not have her. I have prophesied about this moment since I wrote *Moonchild*, and this girl, born of an ethereal being, will bring about a new dawn to this world, one you have already poxed with your ugliness."

"Sorry, Crowley, I don't read fiction," he sneered, twisting the man's head a full rotation with a thought. But the ludicrous scene was only beginning to unfold as a hundred Crowleys marched into the chamber, all dressed like clowns, dancing and twirling around the lavish throne room like court jesters parading for a king. Their faces twisted in mockery, laughing at the necromancer as they surrounded him. For every one Sexton and the demons decimated, another took its place, never faltering in their performance.

Each projection of Crowley had their own thoughts, own curses to spew at Sexton, it was impossible to find the real one. Even the demons began to seethe with frustration as they smashed, bit, and clawed. But Sexton Graves saw past the petty, childish nonsense of his former leader. He wasn't looking for Crowley, instead, he searched for the girl, whose thoughts screamed for it all to end only a few feet away. So he obliged, as he snatched the girl's frail wrist, breaking the illusion that kept her shielded from view. "The little brat is mine."

"No," she screamed.

But Sexton looked down to see the girl had already broken free from his grasp. No, he noticed, she had not broken free, it was his wrist that had been severed completely from his arm. The necromancer turned just fast enough to see the glint of a red sword swing for his neck, removing his head.

Sorry we're late, Charlie said to Helena.

"And you thought my place was big," Max said, smiling at the girl, before collapsing at her feet.

"Mister Max," she panicked, flowing her power through his body, saving his life for a second time. It was a bittersweet reunion, one she had never expected to have.

He looked down at his chest, and saw the wound had complete healed, thinking back to the black mirror. "The vision…?" he said to himself in bewilderment, touching the spot where the wound used to be. Nothing made sense. Another vague prophecy? Or another step along his path? But as soon as he was able, Max shielded the girl behind him, for they were caught between the angels glaring imperiously at the demons, and the demons snarling at the 'Doves'.

"Give us the abomination," Ezekiel said.

"No, the girl is ours!" the demons howled.

"I don't think so," the real Crowley barked as he entered the audience chamber, dismissing his projections into smoke. "No one is going anywhere with the girl, for I've called both parties here to work out a deal."

"You did what?" Max yelled.

"The girl told me everything," he sneered at his rival. "Throwing her into the Glassworld. I should have you shot."

Crowley walked past the angels, ignoring them with his chest puffed out, as if they were common guests. "It was hardly a difficult feat. I am Aleister Crowley, after all. *Everyone* sees me," he said, straightening his polka dot bowtie.

"I have business of my own," Max said, addressing the shadows. "Sexton," he bellowed out, "I know you're still here, waiting for your opportunity to strike again, but I had a little confessional with the angels on my way here. They know all about your planned double-cross," he said, with a smile, "and now, so do your demons," he finished, nodding towards the beasts which were beginning to seethe with rage. "You should have stayed in Hell. It would have been a mercy."

You've meddled in my affairs for the last time! Sexton screamed from the darkness.

"Hiding will do you no good, not from them."

With divine speed, the angels grabbed the spirit's arms. "You have sinned and sinned again, young creature, having cursed the name of our Father, and disturbed the sanctity of the dead. For that, you will never see salvation," Ezekiel proclaimed.

But the demons would not forgive such a betrayal, and pulled at Sexton's legs, in an attempt to rob the 'Doves' of their victim. "The hu-man broke his word, *lied* to us, and we take breach of contracts very seriously."

"Yes, very seriously indeed," snorted another. "He is to be our plaything."

Both groups of entities fought to claim the spirit for their own, and yanked and pulled and tore at the screaming spirit of Sexton Graves like animals fighting over a carcass until the necromancer was torn in two, damning his soul into the farthest, deepest recessions of purgatory; a place so far removed from Creation, nothing would ever hear him curse the name of Max Thanatos again.

"Good riddance to bad rubbish," Crowley spat, wiping his hands of it all, having been saved the trouble. "Now," he said, addressing the demons, then turning to the angels. "The deal is—"

"—the girl stays here at the Golden Dawn with Crowley," Max interrupted, "never to return to the mortal world again. The balance so you desperately seek between good and evil will remain as it is: no side will be the victor or loser. He will be the girl's guardian, he will raise her, protect her, and grant her sanctuary within these walls."

Crowley glared at the magician. "Never speak for me again," he warned, but then cleared this throat, "but…

what he said," he agreed. "It's a deal worth taking, if you ask me, and you practically did, without saying as much," he prattled on, rippling his chubby cheeks into a smile. "Now, do we have an accord?"

"No!" the tallest of the demons roared, pouncing for the girl, but the creature was swiftly struck down by the imposing might of an angel, as if the hefty creature weighed naught but a feather. The other demons latched onto the bony back of Ezekiel like lions, digging in deep with their claws, tearing and slashing. The angel was brought to her knees, allowing the tall demon a chance to break away towards Helena.

But right before the girl was torn asunder into fleshy strips, the demon was ripped in half, spilling black, fleshy bits across the marble floor. The remaining demons burned to ash before Max's eyes, in such a shocking display of brutality it even gave the angels pause.

But they fared no better, for, in a moment, their seemingly impervious bodies contorted well beyond their limits, as if a force crumpled them all like paper balls. Even Ezekiel, the beautiful, composed creature of Heaven, cried a final, horrid scream of agony before slumping to the ground.

Thinking he was next, Crowley shielded himself behind his throne. Max threw himself in front of Helena, while knowing with despair that he could do little protect her from whatever nightmare had just slaughtered both angels and demons alike.

A voice resonated within the room, bestial, almost primal. "There is no deal. There never was," it said from everywhere. "The girl is of my blood, and therefore belongs to me."

"Uriel?" Max called out, but to no reply. Instead, there was an ungodly chill in the air, something far colder than anything he had ever experienced before, as if Hell had opened its maw inside the throne room. As he looked around, he saw Charlie frozen in mid-air, Crowley in mid-retreat. Even Helena remained in place. Time had stopped. Only he could move.

"Show yourself," Max demanded.

"I am not Uriel," the voice said. "His loss was insignificant, like a dove who flew too close to the sun. You have been searching for me, yet I've been by your side all along," a figure said, appearing within the room as if it had been there the whole time.

It was a strange sensation, looking upon the being. Max's eyes saw the shape of a person, he saw a face, but nothing made sense, visually, as if his mind couldn't process what he saw before him. But its presence, he knew, was beyond anything he had experienced before. It felt primordial.

"The truth was I wanted to meet you. To challenge you. To test your mettle as a man, and as a brother."

"Test me?" he shot back. Its body radiated such unrelenting cold, he had to step back just to keep himself from freezing. It felt like the creature below Chinatown, but exponentially more powerful. Max had an idea, but it was too abstract to grasp fully. He felt like he was trapped within a wakeful slumber.

"Uriel thought Helena was his, but she is my daughter, and you, Maximilian, are my son," the figured proclaimed.

"You are not my father," he spat, disgusted by it all.

"No," it said, with a smile, stepping closer. "Tillie Grey is your mother. Jack Thanatos is your father. But *all* magi are my children."

The revelation nearly swept him off of his feet. "I am Devilborn," he whispered. "No," he said, taking another step back.

It gave a curt nod. "I influenced your path, Max. Nothing more. Uriel's murder, the warning at the train station. My work. I was there when you were struck by the bus. I saw her bring you back. When your Master died, I was there, too, in the street, watching. Waiting," it said. "But the events that led you here… they were of your own doing: Hexenhammer, Sexton Graves. I merely course-corrected, bit by bit. It's amazing you lived to see this day," it admitted. "I would almost say it was the Devil's luck."

Max balled his fists. He felt so small. So insignificant. Most of all, he felt ashamed to have been manipulated. The Devil: the creature before him, was beyond all things he knew. It was the creator of beasts. The father of sin. To say he had been tested? Max couldn't process it. "Why?" slipped from his lips. "Why me?" It was all he could say. And it was the most poignant question of all.

"Long ago, I committed the first sin. I took the guise of Adam and seduced the girl in the Garden. She birthed my children, Cain and Abel— I'm sure you know the story. They were the first Nephilim," he revealed. "Magic was born from my offspring. But then Cain killed his brother, and my bloodline was diluted after thousands of years of breeding," it proclaimed. "Nephilim blood courses through your veins, Max, but that's not why you were special to me. You killed Charlie, indirectly," it added. "But killed nonetheless."

Max choked on a denial. He couldn't refute the accusation.

"The pattern had repeated itself once again. A son who rebelled against his Father, a brother who killed his brother. I just had to meet you, to understand you. I thought you would grow up cruel, monstrous, even. But I was wrong."

Max shook his head at it all.

"What is the one question that haunts you?"

Max was certainly a haunted man. It wasn't just one question, it was a constant barrage of self-doubt. He had spent a lifetime trying to fix his mistakes. But he looked upon the Devil, as if he was conversing with another man, not the Great Beast. He knew the very question that it spoke of. It kept him up at night, haunted his dreams, it was always by his side like a dreadful companion. "After all of the things that I've done," he lamented, "the sins, the killings; all of the lies and the years fighting to save my brother's soul at any cost, I must know... am I a wicked person?"

The world around him felt eerily still.

"Your way of thinking is black and white. Is a mother wicked for killing to protect her child? The stories say I am the personification of evil, but evil existed before I did. After all, I am merely a creation, much like you. But I was created to bear that burden. Does that make me a 'wicked' person? Nothing happens in Creation, not even magic, without God's permission. Does that make Him 'wicked'?"

The figure drew closer. "You actions say one thing, Max. I know the lives you took. Most of their souls belong to me. But your heart, Max. No matter what adversary you'd faced, no matter the consequences that threatened your own self-being, you risked everything to save Charlie's soul. So, Max, from the one who understands it best, you are far from wicked. You are... remarkable."

Max shook his head. "But I saw myself in Hell."

"You saw your own Hell," it returned. "Hell is what you make of it. Take it from me: most people are quite adept at punishing themselves. That is what happens when souls cross over still burdened by life. Now, Heaven is sparse. You could wander for a thousand lifetimes before you meet another soul. It was once my home. Dreadful place."

The magus just shook his head. It felt impossibly good to be absolved by the sole creator of sin. In a way, it was like being touched by the hand of God. But he was far from done. "Where are my friends? Where are the others? Theo and Lynn?"

"Dead, but I will have the girl bring them back."

"What about Crowley?" he asked. "Will you allow him to raise the girl?"

The Devil laughed. "He will be punished for his Glassworld. No man should hold dominion over another. That is my purpose."

Max nodded, and left it at that. "You wanted to meet me, and now you did," the magus said. "If you already know why I've fought so hard to find you, let's get down to brass tacks: I want you to save Charlie's soul from damnation. He has suffered enough. Let him rest in peace."

"No," it said plainly.

"What?" Max shot back, flabbergasted. "What do you mean, no?"

"I am not a djinn. I do not grant wishes. Everyone knows you make deals with the Devil. That is what I do. Despite my fascination with you, Max, you are no different."

"Fine. If that's what it'll take. What do you want?" Max asked, without even caring about the repercussions.

The Devil smiled. "It's not that simple, Max. You agree upfront, no questions asked. I will save Charlie's soul from Hell, and then you will find out what I want. That is the deal everyone gets."

Max looked at Charlie, who had been unfrozen for some time, and was simply observing quietly, mostly out of absolute terror of the creature in their company. But even dreadfully afraid, the spirit still shook his head.

"Is it a deal or not, Mister Thanatos?"

"Done," he said, without thinking.

"Done," the Devil agreed, waving his hand. "I have released the curse upon your brother. You don't have long, so make your peace before Charlie is gone for good."

You fool, Charlie was finally able to scream. *He can make you do anything. Anything! I wasn't worth it. Why would you agree to that, Max? Why?*

"Because I love you, Charlie," he said, and it was the greatest truth ever told.

But the spirit just shook his head. *You've fought so hard for me, Max. But the cost was too high. How can I ever rest in peace knowing that?*

"If it's any comfort," the Devil said, "know that you won't be alone. I said Heaven was sparsely occupied, but Sexton was wrong about your mother. Her soul is not in my domain. What he cast for you in the street was an illusion. She will be with you."

Mother, Charlie whispered with longing.

It was a beautiful thing to know. "Tell her about our adventures, Charlie," Max said, proudly. "She always loved to hear our stories."

Even the bad ones, Charlie laughed.

"Even the bad ones."

"It's time," the Devil said.

The Brothers Thanatos wished they had longer. But they also understood that their time had been borrowed from the very beginning. Both Max and Charlie had something so blessed, so utterly unique, and so desired by anyone who has ever lost a loved one before; for in the end, the Brothers Thanatos still had each other.

Thank you, Max, he said. *For everything.*

And with that, Charlie was gone. Forever.

Max did not cry. He had fought besides his brother, laughed, and faced hardships together with him for so long. Their relationship was never solid, that he knew, but death had brought them closer than ever. He was happy for Charlie. Proud that he had kept his promise, no matter what. But he had spent so much of his life living only for him, Max had no idea what to do now Charlie was gone.

"So what now? What do you want from me?" the magician finally asked, without turning to face the Devil.

"Despite my reputation, Max, I am not a monster. You, Helena, and I are going to take a trip," the Devil said, taking the girl's hand into his own, and smiling down upon her. "The world is full of undiscovered magi, well beyond you, beyond Crowley, and the others. Now that I have crossed over into your realm, I am bound to walk amongst you for a hundred years. We are going to find my children, all of them, and then rebuild the Golden Dawn stronger than it has ever been before," it said. "And you, Max Thanatos, will be the one who ushers this world into a glorious new age of magic."

Max shrugged. It wasn't the worst of prospects. "So," he said, gripping his wolf's head cane, "when do we start?"

THE END